W9-ASX-094

10¢

Stephen Sohmer————

THE WAY IT WAS

SIMON AND SCHUSTER · NEW YORK

ALL RIGHTS RESERVED
INCLUDING THE RIGHT OF REPRODUCTION
IN WHOLE OR IN PART IN ANY FORM
COPYRIGHT © 1966 BY STEPHEN SOHMER
PUBLISHED BY SIMON AND SCHUSTER
ROCKEFELLER CENTER, 630 FIFTH AVENUE
NEW YORK, NEW YORK 10020

FIRST PRINTING

"Entropy" first appeared in Modern Occasions, *edited by Philip
Rahv and published by Farrar, Straus and Giroux. "Nine-Five"
first appeared in* The Southern Review.

LIBRARY OF CONGRESS CATALOG CARD NUMBER: 66–21827
DESIGNED BY EVE METZ
MANUFACTURED IN THE UNITED STATES OF AMERICA
BY H. WOLFF BOOK MFG., NEW YORK

FOR STANLEY KUNITZ

Contents

In all natural processes the organized motion of molecules has a tendency to become disorganized or random. All processes go in the direction . . . of entropy.

—GEORGE GAMOW, *Biography of Physics*

He sat in the window thinking. Man has a tropism for order. Keys in one pocket, change in another. Mandolins are tuned G D A E. The physical world has a tropism for disorder, entropy. Man against Nature—the battle of the centuries. Keys yearn to mix with change. Mandolins strive to get out of tune. Every order has within it the germ of destruction.

—NATHANAEL WEST, *Miss Lonelyhearts*

HOW THE GRABBIES WERE

THE WHISPER OF JULIE'S BREATHING hung in the attic like a veil. They lay submerged in the jumble of corrugated cartons, and through the skylight that floated overhead Richard Conrad could see that the high summer sky was dappled with flying clouds. A gull turned soundlessly against the spotty cover two hundred feet from earth; its wings were stone-white, then sand-white, tilting to silver, gone black and the gull was gone and the flying clouds were drifting away.

There was a ring on the fourth finger of Julie's right hand. She wore plaid sneakers and cotton socks to mid-calf and her blue denim skirt was pressed, even in sleep, into the crease of her thighs. Her black hair fanned across his sweat shirt.

Conrad knew the attic door was closed; no breeze came up from below. Like a colloid, the heat of the attic held a fine dust suspended throughout the trellis of beams beneath the roof of the summer cottage. The dust was motionless; the huge spiral cobweb in the angle of timbers under the skylight might have been wire or glass. No echo of an underlife rose around them and Conrad knew that the downstairs was empty.

He knew the doors of the summer cottage were locked. He knew the television set stood mute and blind in the sitting room. He knew that the pilot light in the propane stove had flickered and gone out, and that the ironwork of the stove was cold. He knew that the kitchen curtains had ceased to flutter and balloon; that the red circle had appeared between the hands of the electric clock over the dinette table; that the linoleum had ceased to crawl and curl in the corners of his parents' bedroom. He knew that a hundred yards from the cottage the Atlantic Ocean had ceased to roll and had come, somehow, to stand still.

Beneath the curve of Julie's arm, his left hand stirred. The expansion band of his wristwatch snagged in the folds of her linen blouse and then came free. Conrad crossed his legs. The corner of a carton had him under the shoulder blade and her weight screwed him to it. He saw his fingertips against her side; he saw that the span of his hand would cover the rise of her breast under the linen.

Her ankles were touching, and at the hem of the denim skirt, her knees touched, closed like a bud. The silence of the wedge-shaped attic room drove him against the carton's point. His fingertips touched linen, pressed. The linen settled down.

He didn't know the feel of silk from that of nylon. His fingertips had been prepared for lace in concentric circles. Instead, the linen slid with the movement of his hand across the unfurrowed walls of a perfect cone.

In his dreams, Julie always slapped him. Or else she walked away, as she had done a Saturday night before, from their driftwood fire. She had risen from their blanket between the dunes with the sand coming off her palms and shoulders like smoke and blowing back at him. On the far side of the fire she had bent for her terry jacket, and the halter of her bathing suit leaned away from her bosom. There had been white beneath the pleated ribbing of her halter, and her cleaving breasts had startled him. She had marched beyond the play of the fire without speaking. She had left him. And the picture of her sudden ferocity and the glimpse of her breasts had aroused Conrad even more than his clumsy handful of the bathing suit with the nettles of sand in its folds.

Conrad closed his eyes; he felt a need for the anonymity of darkness. Julie's flesh bulged at the periphery of the brassiere's cupping and tunneled to a nub end. He wasn't at all aroused; not the way he had expected he would be. Instead he reasoned that the areola must be like a pink poker chip with the nipple at its bull's-eye. He reasoned that her breasts must tumble down without the brassiere as though deflated; like the thin leather flaps of aborigine women in his social studies texts.

Julie shifted her arm as if to help him. Conrad's eyes opened. The measure of her breathing rolled on; the frilled fringes of her lashes remained meshed. The skylight showed a remote, empty blue. Then she hadn't moved. She was really asleep. He was having thoughts.

It wasn't at all like holding a pigeon. Under the swells were creases which were probably damp with perspiration. Her breasts probably got in her way when she tried to lace her sneakers. Or when she pulled on her panties. Unless she put her brassiere on first. The way his mother did. Or did his mother put hers on first? His mother probably put her eyeglasses on first. How did Julie read in bed? Did she have to lean back to read the dial on the bathroom scale? Or did she weigh herself naked with her breasts sagging out of the way? Sometimes nursing mothers fell asleep and the suckling baby suffocated. Did his mother have breasts or had they shrunk and was her brassiere padded up with cotton?

In any case, Julie's breasts probably didn't sag. Probably she looked like one of the girls in *Dude* or *Nugget*. Probably she wore panties with cutouts at the hips. Probably her navel was as tiny as a smile. Wrong. One time she'd worn a two-piece swimsuit; her navel was like a bullet hole. When she stood before him with her legs together he could see a wedge of ocean through the space where her thighs met and the bathing suit curved under. That was an odd emptiness, as though something were missing. His mother's bathing suits had a little skirt, like a baton twirler's. His mother's panties looked like pillow cases in the laundry hamper; Julie's were probably no more than tissue, wispy, the size of a leaf.

Conrad's palms felt slick. He wanted to pinch the point of Julie's breast until it popped like a node of seaweed. He stared at her face. When he went to college at the end of summer she was coming to see him weekends. He'd put her up at some motel or something like that. Probably there would be a dance. They'd drink beer or whiskey sours. He'd take her back to the motel. Send the taxicab away. Then they'd be standing at the motel room door on the second-floor balcony. There'd be a railing. She'd lean back against it, bend back against it like the grasses on the beach. He'd open the door and she'd bend forward away from the rail, drifting past him like blown sand. And in the motel bed together, alone, naked, the night around them would draw down until its four corners touched the four corners of the room with warm, perfect black.

Julie hadn't moved. Conrad was certain of that; he was certain she was sleeping and he wouldn't be slapped. Still, he drew his hand away. His back ached; the front of his sweat shirt was soaked through. He heard the screen door at the front of the cottage slam closed, footfalls and voices. He sat up, buoying Julie with him.

"Rick?" She was looking at him and not blinking.

"They're home."

"Who? Your—"

"The trunk," he said. He dug his elbows into the cartons alongside him. He rose halfway; the cartons slipped aside. He fell and the back of his head rapped on the fir planking.

"Rick, did you—"

He pulled the cartons over in his hurry; yellow books with tattered dust jackets spilled. Dust came up all around him. "That trunk," he said. "Go on, Julie." He pushed up with his hands. His shoulder hit the old bentwood hat rack. It rotated slowly on its base. Conrad caught at it, missed. The antlers of the rack heeled over. Conrad kicked at a book, clutching. The rack fell at Julie. Easily, smiling at him, she caught it. Then the door up from the downstairs opened.

"Richard, are you . . . what are you doing up there?"

His mother was squinting through her eyeglasses from the bottom of the stairway. Her squat body filled the lower two-thirds of the lighted rectangle; there were sharp Irish angles at her jaws.

"I'm right here, Mother." He was inching away from Julie.

"I know where you are. The whole house is shaking. What . . . ?" She began the stairs, pulling herself along the banister.

"Just thought I'd have a look at Uncle Peter's trunk," Conrad said. "I thought there might be—"

"Well, stop it right now. Whatever. I don't care what—" Her face emerged above the topmost step of the stairs. "Julie, I didn't know you were here."

"Hello, Mrs. Conrad."

"I didn't know you were up here, Julie." Conrad's mother stood at the head of the stairs, her bosom heaving.

"We were looking at this—"

"I thought there might be some stuff in it," Conrad said. "For school. Banners. For the walls of my room. For when I go—"

"Liz, what the hell is he up to now?"

His mother turned back toward the door below. "Who knows? He's wrecked the attic."

Conrad went to the railing. "I thought there might be some things I could use in Uncle Peter's trunk. I was looking—"

"With Julie," his mother said.

"Julie?" His father's round, bald face thrust into the doorway. The light domed his head with gold. "What do you want with Uncle Peter's trunk, son?"

"I thought there might be—"

"He wants some junk to put on his walls at school, Philip," his mother said. "Tell him to let it alone."

"I don't think there's anything you'd want, Richie. Where's Julie? Hi, girlie-girl. How are your folks?"

Julie leaned in beside Conrad. "They're fine."

"Tell him to let the trunk alone, Philip."

Conrad felt his mother glance at him. He didn't care what was in the trunk. He didn't even know why he'd thought of the trunk. "There ought to be something in—"

"There's nothing in it," his mother said at him.

Conrad didn't look at her. "I figured there might be a banner or some old pictures I could use for—"

"There's nothing you can use. Go on downstairs. Go ahead, Julie."

"Son, I doubt if anything in Uncle Peter's trunk would be of interest to you," his father said.

Conrad's mother had hold of his arm. "Go on downstairs. We're having dinner in a minute. Julie, do you want dinner?"

"Well, I'll have to call, Mrs. Conrad."

"You go on down and call, Julie. Say you're staying for dinner. Mr. Conrad will drive you home after." His mother wiped her forehead with a handkerchief from the pocket of her baggy shorts.

"Rick can walk me, Mrs. Conrad. It isn't—"

"Nonsense. Mr. Conrad has to take me shopping in the village anyhow. We'll drop you off."

"What about the trunk?" Conrad said.

"Let the trunk alone," his mother said, and started back down.

He wasn't going to. He simply wasn't going to let it be her way. "I want to look, Dad. At least you can let me look."

His father shrugged. "Richie, I don't see what good—"

"Well, for Christ's sake, I'm eighteen and you can let me do something around here when I want to do it without having to apologize to the whole world."

His mother said, "Richard, don't you dare raise your voice."

Conrad moved; he bumped into Julie. "Well, it's true. You—"

"Julie, maybe you'd better go home for dinner," his mother said.

"No," Conrad said.

"Look, stop it up there, all of you," his father said. "Liz, let them look through the trunk, would you, please?"

"Philip, they've torn this whole attic apart," his mother said.

"Well, we'll clean it up," Conrad said.

"I won't have them making this place a bedlam which they will, and besides, Philip, you know—"

"Dad, we'll clean the whole place up. No kidding." Conrad

17

felt himself grinning. He couldn't stop grinning. "Come on, Dad. Uncle Peter went to Yale. There must be some banners or stuff that—"

"Philip, I don't want him in that trunk."

"Liz, let him do what he wants. How much can he mess up an attic?"

"But everything's probably rotted. Bugs. You don't know what. The trunk's so old," his mother said.

"You don't have to tell me how old it is, Liz," Conrad's father said. "Come down and put dinner on, Liz. Liz?"

Conrad watched his mother descend, the heavy white flesh in her legs shaking at every step, her shoulders hunched, her bosom sagging under the front of the red blouse overprinted in blue with maps of France.

Julie had gone into the farthest corner of the attic. She had bent down. "Rick, how do you open this?"

"To hell with it," Conrad said. He swept up an armful of books; they were his: *The Pied Piper of Hamelin, An Introduction to Solid Geometry and Calculus.* Julie came over and began to help him. He had a solid kernel of headache above his left eye; he remembered his head hitting the attic floor. "What the hell are you smiling about?" he said.

She didn't look at him. "Don't talk that way to me, Rick."

He threw the books into the nearest carton. He went over to the skylight, swung it up, and propped it with the hat rack. The land breeze had begun; by scent alone he could distinguish it from the wind that rose off the sea in the morning. Below, at the side of the house, Conrad saw the row of gaping ash cans. A clothesline tethered the scrub pines to the cottage; curlicues of dry paint flaked from the picket fence.

"You don't want to look in the trunk at all," she said behind him. She laid a hand on his shoulder; he shrugged it off.

"What are you talking about?"

"I know why you did it, Ricky," she said.

He felt Julie lean against him. He felt the twin thrusts; one in the spot where the carton's edge had made his muscles tender, one against his spine. He said, "Listen, cut it out, will you?" She never realized when they were touching like that. Sometimes she would stand right against him, beside him, and put her weight against him. He would feel her breasts on either side of his arm, the back of his hand would be pressed against the base of her abdomen. He'd have a ridiculous sense of shame; his whole consciousness would focus on his knuckles. She wouldn't realize that they were touching. She'd go on talking about sailing on the weekend or whatever. The whole side of his body would congeal. He wouldn't be able to answer. Then she'd laugh at him because he couldn't talk and something would catch her attention and she'd move away. She'd be oblivious to it all.

"The trunk," he said; and when she turned away from behind him, he felt himself falling into the vacuum.

"I didn't know brass rusted," she said. "None of the fittings on our Pacemaker ever rust."

"It's plated or painted or something," Conrad said. He spread a newspaper; they knelt together. He opened the two toggle latches on the ends of the trunk. The hasp was closed and locked.

"Don't you have the key?"

"My mother had it but she lost it."

"Well, I don't—"

He had a knife—with red plastic inlays and the crest of Switzerland and ten blades. One of the blades was a screwdriver. He wedged the blade between the hasp and the wall of the trunk. The trunk was pasted with railroad stickers; their colors had all faded into brown and the paper chipped like the paint off the picket fence in the yard. Conrad held the knife with both hands and pulled it toward him.

Often at night when he had only a sheet over him and the only sound was the rumble of the ocean turning over, Conrad thought of Julie's smile. All the teeth she showed were white as gulls' wings, and they were straight and fit neatly. He thought about the way her mouth curved far back into her cheeks when she smiled, and how her lips formed a meticulous bow. He thought of the details of her: how her fingernails were always impeccable; the points of her sneakers; the way her legs were always smooth.

Once he had wondered whether she shaved her legs. He had known she shaved her underarms; for a long time he didn't see how she could do that without nicking herself with the razor. His mother didn't shave her underarms. For a long time he had thought that there were some women who had to shave and some women who just didn't have to. Where the roof had leaked in a corner of his bedroom there was a varicose pattern running down the wallpaper to the floor. At night that made Conrad think of the backs of his mother's legs. He never heard a sound from his parents' room after they had put their lamp out. Occasionally, he lay awake until long after midnight, but he never heard a sound.

The hasp sprang free; fragments of the lock mechanism, rusted, came off in his hands. Julie took a sheet of newspaper and wiped black circles in the dust on the trunk's lid until the circles were all cotangent and the lid was a shiny, split and puckered black. Inside, she lifted a sheet of checkered oilcloth.

There were white buckskin shoes in a paper bag on top of the stacks of clothing. The toes of the shoes had curled back almost to fists and the buckskin had parted from the soles in several places.

"Don't you think your uncle will mind?" Julie said. She showed the long smile again. "Maybe he has secrets in here."

"He's dead," Conrad said. He held up a pair of tennis shorts; their white had aged to the color of the nicotine stains between his mother's fingers. He tossed the shorts to Julie.

She said, "I'm sorry," and folded them on the outspread oil-cloth.

There was a navy-blue sweater. Conrad turned it over; the chest of the sweater bore a faded white Y. "How about that?" Conrad said. He hadn't expected to find anything of value. Actually, he had expected junk.

"Turn around," Julie said. She pinned the sweater to his collarbones with her thumbs. She set her head to one side and her hair poured. "Won't you look fine, Rick," she said softly.

Conrad extended the wool over himself. "Does it fit, Julie?"

She shook her head. "Too small."

"Maybe we could stretch it."

She shook her head again.

"Well, the hell with it," Conrad said, and flung the sweater aside. There were Argyle socks, a pair of wing-tip cordovans with leather as hard as slate, five shiny ties with broad stripes, yellow handkerchiefs, dress shirts with starched wide collars and outsized cuffs. And there was a roll of blue felt that opened up three feet long with a white border and the word YALE in letters eight inches high.

Conrad laughed. "Look," he said, and held the banner out to her.

"That's so old," she said. She ran her hand over the felt.

"Won't it look great? Over a fireplace or somewhere?" Conrad held it against an imaginary wall. "Won't that be the end though?"

"Yes."

Conrad stared at her. Her mouth was pursed; her hands were folded in her lap. "What's with you, Julie?"

"Nothing."

"Come on. Don't you like the—"

"You're looking forward to school, college, aren't you, Rick?"

"Sure."

She didn't say anything.

"Listen, Julie, will you—"

"I was just thinking—"

"What?"

"You know."

"I don't know." Conrad blew a breath away. "Listen, Julie, how am I supposed to guess what—"

"Just that you'll be—" She broke off there. "I was thinking about your uncle," she said.

"What about him?"

She shrugged her shoulders and the movement under her blouse caught Conrad's eye. "How did your uncle die?"

"How he died." Conrad couldn't turn his face. He had a headache. He had the feel of linen in his hands and something glossy underneath.

"Was he sick?"

Conrad looked at the banner; he began to fold it. "He drowned. I didn't know him. That was when my father was a boy. A thousand years ago. Right out front. In the ocean."

She was standing, and then she was walking away from him, toward the skylight, blowing dust from the sill, putting her elbows on the sill and cupping her face in her hands and looking toward the sea. "Right out there?"

"When my father's parents died my mother wanted to sell this place."

"I would have sold it," she said. "I would have sold it right away."

Her voice sounded strange. Conrad dug into the clothes in the trunk up to his wrists.

"What for?" he said.

"Because I wouldn't be able to stand this house ever again."

"Julie, you're dumb." He pushed the clothes back and forth, feeling for the trunk's bottom. "My father wouldn't do it anyhow. The place is paid for." The dream of straps and seamless cups came back to him. "Julie, when you come for the weekend in New Haven . . . do you think your folks will let you stay in a motel?" He coughed into his fist; that made the headache fill his eyes. "I mean, my grandparents live in New Haven. You could stay with them, I guess. What do you think?"

"I thought you said your father's parents died."

He didn't dare see if she were looking at him. Her voice sounded pinched, uneasy as his own. He thought of how she would crack him across the face if she knew that he had touched her. "The Kellys. My mother's folks. They've always lived there." He had to make conversation. "My father met my mother while he was at Yale."

"You all went to Yale," she said, dimly, distantly.

"That's right. Every one."

"You, too, Ricky," she said. "Soon."

"Sure." He pivoted toward her, leaning on the arm sunk through the clothing. "Well—" He had to risk it. "I mean, what do you think?"

"About what, Rick?"

He blinked. Her eyes were damp; her lashes glistened. "I mean . . . a motel. Julie, do you feel okay?"

"What?"

"Are you crying?"

"I'm not crying." She passed the backs of her wrists against her eyes.

"Sure you are." She was crying; and he knew it was because she understood that he was thinking about her and a New Haven motel.

"Honestly, Rick." She touched the skylight's sill. "It's just the wind. It makes my eyes teary, that's all." She came back to the trunk. "Is there anything else in there?"

"Well." His headache came on. "I don't . . . what's this?" From the bottom of the trunk he brought up a leather-bound book with NOTES printed across the cover in gold leaf. She squatted beside him. The leather was dry, but well preserved and had a deep grain. The pages were ruled in pale blue and had gold edging. A fine pen had written on the overleaf:

Notebook
Peter Ellis Conrad
September 23, 1920

Julie said, "It's a diary."

"No, it's not." Conrad thumbed into the book. "It's just some kind of notes." He read, " 'The wind drives her hair like horses. Simile. The wind has its horses in her hair. Metaphor.' "

"That sounds like maybe it's his notes from an English course," she said.

"Could be." Conrad leafed on through the pages. "Sure. That's what it is. 'Matthew Arnold. "Dover Beach." *But now I only hear/ Its melancholy, long, withdrawing roar,/ Retreating to the breath/ Of the night-wind down the vast edges drear/ And naked shingles of the world.*' Class notes," Conrad said.

From the bottom of the stairs he heard the door open and his mother's voice call, "Dinner."

"Bring it," Julie said.

His father met them in the sitting room. Through the door to the kitchen Conrad could see his mother stirring a black pot with a long wooden spoon. "Julie, you'll want to wash," his father said. "You know your way."

When she was gone Conrad said, "We found this banner and a book—"

"Before you go in to dinner . . ." his father said, and took him across the room. "Your mother hasn't been feeling well. I'd appreciate it if you'd control yourself."

"Dad, I was only . . . listen, I didn't—"

"I know." His father scratched at the cleft in his chin. "But we all have to make allowances. I have to live here, too."

"Well, Jesus." He knew what his father was going to say. About her mysterious infection and the pains and all the things he spoke of with such infuriating delicacy. He always felt his father was being a fool when he spoke in that confidential tone.

"Your mother's infection," his father said. "She may have to go through some little operation, but you know how nervous women are. Just go softly and we'll all live happily ever after, son." His father slapped him on the shoulders and went toward the kitchen.

Conrad weighed the book and banner in his hands. His father sidled when he walked, was Bible-backed. His father was fifty years old and he guessed that his mother was past her sex and he understood the silence in his parents' bedroom every night. He felt sorrow for his father. His mother's legs were veined and ugly. Her walk was plodding, awkward. Her throat was full of swollen nodes.

He heard the water flush and Julie came into the living room, narrow, supple. He had a slob of a mother and a doddering father.

"Did you show them?" she said.

"To hell with them," Conrad said. He wanted to heave the book through the front window and the banner after it. He wanted to rush into the kitchen, take the pot of stew and fling it at his mother, kick the dinette table over, smash the chairs and throw the plates and glasses in every direction. He wanted to beat his fists into the thin walls of the cottage until they collapsed on everything inside them.

"Come on, Ricky. Show them." Julie had his wrist. "Let's sit down."

"And is the attic completely wrecked?" his mother said, and thrust half of a honeydew melon in front of him.

Conrad glared at Julie; she smiled back. "We'll straighten up right after dinner, Mrs. Conrad," she said. "Rick found some things."

His father's cheeks were bulging with melon. "What you found, son?"

Conrad handed the folded banner along; his father unfurled it like a scroll and swabbed his mouth with a napkin. "Say, that's nice. What do you think, Liz? Peter must have prized it."

His mother put a green serving bowl filled with lamb stew in the center of the table and sat opposite his father. "It's filthy," she said. "Take it away from the table, Philip."

"Now, Elizabeth, don't be cranky," his father said. He held the banner aloft above his head and began to sing, "Boola-boola, boola-boola—"

"Philip."

His father lowered the banner. Under the table Conrad's hands were fists. His father put the banner on the floor beside his chair. "What else did you find, son?"

"That's all," Conrad said, and dug his spoon through the moist green flesh of the melon.

"We found his lecture notes from English," Julie said.

"Is that so? Where are they, Richie?"

"I ate them."

"Richard, you be respectful to your father," his mother said.

"That's all right, Liz. Let me see the notes, please, son."

Conrad threw the book on the table. His mother reached for it, but his father's hand was quicker.

"Let me have my glasses, would you, Liz?" his father said.

"You're not going to read that, are you?" his mother said.

"There isn't much else you can do with a book but read it, Liz."

"Don't read that, Philip," his mother said.

"Well, now, why shouldn't I?"

"You know why," his mother said. "It's wrong."

Conrad watched his father. If his father backed down, he was surely going to kick the table over and punch the walls down.

"I don't see anything wrong with reading it, Liz."

"Peter's dead, Philip. You can't do anything about it after almost forty years. Won't you believe that? It's wrong and it's crazy."

Conrad saw his father's brow deepen and the slick skin pull across his skull. Conrad had his hands pressed against the underside of the table. When it went over he would catch the tureen and crown his mother with it. Then he would stamp the dishes into smithereens.

"It isn't wrong to love the dead, Liz," his father said.

"Yes, it is for you," his mother said. "It's so wrong. When I'm dead—"

His father laughed aloud. "Don't pick fights just to be cranky," his father said. "Please get me my glasses like a good girl, Liz."

27

"I don't know where they are. Get your own glasses."

Conrad's father held the book out to him. "You read it, son. And you just relax, Liz. This isn't going to hurt much."

Conrad couldn't stop grinning. He took all three of them in with a glance: his sterile, flabby mother with her fat arms folded.

"There's a part in here about horses in her hair," Conrad said. He flipped the pages. There were clumsy drawings and designs in the corners of most of the pages. "Here's a poem." The sense in Conrad was glory. He read:

We live across the street from one another.
We meet, we smile, and go—
Hearts heavy—on.
We love, and yet we cannot hold each other.
There is much more between us than
The rain.

"That sounds like it could be original," his father said.

His mother said, "What a stupid poem."

"Well, I don't think it's too bad, Liz. Considering."

"Considering what?"

His father lowered his glance. "You read something else, son."

"I'd like to find—"

"Find the part about the horses," Julie said.

"That's what I'm looking for." On one of the pages, amid a tangle of sketches of stars, was the word *Grabbies,* circled again and again with a few sentences under it. "Here's something called 'Grabbies,'" Conrad said.

"Hold it there," his father said, and laughed. "I think we can skip that passage, son. Peter," he said, and laughed again.

"What's wrong with grabbies?" Conrad said.

"Let's just skip it, shall we, son?"

Conrad knew that delicate tone. "Well, I'll just read a little of it, Dad."

"I don't think that's a good idea, son," his father said. "Not with ladies present, if you understand me."

"Well, we're all grown-ups, aren't we?" Conrad said. The feel of the weapon in his hands was keen, needle-sharp.

"Yes, we are, son. But you see—"

"What?"

"I don't want to hear about it, Philip," his mother said. "This is a dinner table."

"Liz, it's not as bad as all that," his father said.

"The dinner table is no place for profanity, Philip."

"I know that, Liz. Don't you think I—"

"Just drop it, Philip."

"Wait a second, Liz." The way his father said that brought silence. "It so happens that *grabbies* isn't obscene or anything anyone at this table can't hear about. It just means that when a fellow takes a sweetheart out and they smooch a little, well, you know . . . men are supposed to brag. It's expected. So when a fellow came back to his room at school after a date, his pals would say, How were the grabbies? And you were supposed to grin. So it's just harmless smooching." His father gave them all smiles. "Nothing so sinister. Nothing to be frightened of. Nothing important. Was that so terrible, Liz? You and I still do it ourselves, you know."

His mother's thick, unpretty mouth curled almost imperceptibly; she turned her eyes down to the melon on the plate before her. Conrad's father was looking straight at him; then he looked at Julie.

"I wouldn't think our dear Julie less a lady if she permitted our son to kiss her," his father said. "Would you, Liz?"

29

His mother didn't answer, didn't look up. Conrad looked at Julie, at his mother, and back to Julie again. She had her chin against her chest and her eyes seemed to be closed just as they had been closed earlier in the attic, when he thought she had fallen asleep in his arms. Conrad raised a spoonful of the green honeydew to his mouth and closed his teeth hard on the stainless steel.

NINE-FIVE

─────────────────────────────

Wʜᴇɴ Cᴏɴʀᴀᴅ's ᴇʏᴇs became accustomed to the dark he could make out Greenberg's form in the bed beside his own. The motel room's sole illumination was a blade of light from between the door and doorframe. Conrad listened; Greenberg snored heavily. Softly, carefully, he slid aside his blankets and swung his legs over the side of the bed. A dull cold came up through the shallow straw rug from the concrete floor. He turned the spread back from the foot of the bed and found his shirt and the black chino pants. He buttoned down from collar to waist; Greenberg snored on amiably. A car passed on the Wilbur Cross Parkway, heading for the West Rock Tunnel and Hartford. The headlights threw the matrix of the windowpanes against the far wall and highlighted Greenberg. His face was turned away and his enormous body lay like an iceberg beneath the sheets.

Conrad found his socks in his sneakers before the car's lights drifted away. After that he had only the glimmer from the door and the heatless glow of the alarm clock to guide him. The clock showed 2:15. Outside in the parking lot, Julie would be waiting in her car.

Conrad stood, pulled the chinos up and buckled his belt. He bent, tied his sneakers, and picked the black crew-neck sweater from the arms of the chair under the windows. He went to the door and held his breath and listened. Silence out there. He touched the latch. Greenberg's voice said, "Wait, Connie."

Instinctively, Conrad began to duck; then he turned around. "Go back to sleep, Greens. Forget it. Go back to sleep."

"Where the hell are you going at this hour? Jesus." Greenberg sat up in bed. A car came on. Greenberg's body was whiter than the sheets and huge in the glare of the headlights. His chest was a pelt. Muscles swelled and fell in his arms and shoulders. "It's —Jesus, well, it's after two or didn't you know that or care? Hey?"

"I know. Look, shut up and keep your voice down." Conrad went toward his bed. He was between Greenberg and the light from the door. The room was in darkness.

"I get it," Greenberg said. "Where's Julie? Outside?"

"In the parking lot."

"You're crazy. But you know that."

"Look, you go to hell your way, I'll go mine." Conrad touched the door latch again.

Greenberg said, "Morissey's got a team manager stationed at both ends of the hall."

"Crap."

"Or so you prefer to think." Greenberg put the night-light on. He slept nude and he wasn't pretty.

"Kill that."

"Don't worry."

"Kill it, Greens."

"At both ends of the hall."

"That's nonsense. This isn't prison."

"Or so you think."

"Greenberg, put the goddam light out."

He did. "Both ends of the hall. Morissey told them bring a physics textbook, boys. Dry reading keeps the mind alert. He gave them a six-pack of Coke and a pack of butts and told them watch the door for signs of disloyal athletes. We've got Childress to the south and Babcock to the northmost. You lose, 'Melican flier."

"Not yet." Conrad moved across the room, feeling his way between the foot of Greenberg's bed and the dresser.

"Forget the windows," Greenberg said.

"Why?" Conrad parted the curtains. In the parking lot below he saw the gleam of the dome light within Julie's Chevrolet. He pressed the window up and hung his head beyond the sill. Thirty feet straight down the asphalt of the parking lot spread.

"Elephants don't fly," Greenberg said.

"Shut up," Conrad said. He put his back against the wall beside the window and slid to sitting.

"I'll tell you what if you really want to know," Greenberg said. "Why don't you just put her up in the motel? You could work it. Her room adjoins ours, let's say. Then you could zip back and forth like Ping-Pong when the spirit hit you. I'd never tell."

"It isn't like that with us, Greens," Conrad said. "You know it. Don't just shoot your lip off."

"Pardon my crudery," Greenberg said. "Hey, let me put the light up. I feel like I'm talking to the wall."

"You're talking to the wall."

"That's what I'm doing."

"Cut it." Conrad laid his head back. He didn't like the idea of her being alone outside. He knew he simply wanted to be with her—nothing fresh or rude. His head was full of Morissey's speeches on doing the impossible. The high tune on the muscles of his legs hurt him. He had a blister on his left heel that was chafing in its dressing. He wanted to take Julie to the top of West Rock, around the winding road to the top where the street-lamps ended, to the guardrail edge of the lookout. He wasn't thinking about petting her.

"What about nine-five?" Greenberg said.

The gun went off. He came out on the gun. Not just on the gun. Just a fraction late. A breath late. Spikes were flying. His knees were in his chest. He was face up, chest up, arms up, knees high, reaching out and kicking. The wind was in his shift and rattling his shorts across his thighs. The wind was up against his chest and blowing. The wind was in his face and fighting him. Up from Long Island Sound, over New Haven, the downtowns and the university, up climbing West Rock at the gallop, through the damp pine forest to the lookout where he stood with Julie's waist within his arm. Wind. A heartbeat late. The crack of tape parting.

Conrad covered his face with his hands.

"What about nine-five?" Greenberg said again. "If you're going to sleep, try the bed, Connie."

"I'm going out," he said, and stood up.

"You'll break your neck."

"Then help me."

"What? How?"

"Let me down."

"With what?"

Conrad tore his spread and blankets aside. "The sheets."

"Oh, come on. You've been watching too many oldies but goodies, Connie," Greenberg said. "Get serious."

"Listen, it can be done." He was tying the ends of the sheets together.

"Hey, hold on," Greenberg said. "I could always go out and strangle Childress and that bastard Babcock. They wouldn't be missed."

Conrad threw Greenberg's covers away. "Take the end of this. Come on, unass that bed." Greenberg rose, towering over him. Conrad pressed the knotted sheet end in his hands. "You stand by the door. I'll let myself over the sill. Then you just walk forward real slow."

"You don't want much, do you?" Greenberg said as he backed off.

"Just don't trip over your big feet."

"I want to see the university psychiatrist," Greenberg said.

"I'm going over now." Conrad tried the sheet; it went slack. "Wake up, dummy."

"Suresure. Let me hear that old Gee-ron-ee-mo."

Conrad threw a leg up on the sill. He ducked under the open sash. "Ready? Greens?"

"Go, will you? Stop making Niagara Falls out of it."

Conrad wound the sheets about his wrists. He slid off the sill. The fibers of the cloth went taut, crackling, and held. He heard Greenberg say, "So far, so good," and then he felt himself beginning to descend.

He remembered the way Greenberg looked in his shift and shorts with the number on his back and the shot cupped in his hand as lightly as an orange. He remembered the great pump in Greenberg's knees, the way he pivoted on his left foot as cleverly as a dancer, the way his eyes rolled up, and the way he roared when he cut the shot loose from gravity.

Somehow, that had always seemed a weak gesture to Conrad; the shot took a flat arc and went down heavily fifty-odd feet away. Somehow, that small distance made all of Greenberg's effort seem feeble. The sheet that held him swung like a pendulum; his heels and elbows grazed the brick facing of the motel wall. Conrad could drive his own hundred-and-ninety-pound body one hundred yards without a breath in the time it took to light a cigarette. The pendulum of sheets swung. The parking lot beneath him rolled and yawed. *Tick*. The parking lot pitched back. The electric timer sprang alive. His eyes came up. The impulse hit his ankles and his fingertips. Milliseconds ran like water. *Tick*. He scraped the serrated facing of brick with his knees and knuckles. The starter's gun's report depressed the malleus-incus-stapes of his ear; they tingled. Milliseconds charged. He came on, came up. The stopwatch clacked like a typewriter. His toes were leaving divots in the cinders. *Tick*. Electrons poured down the wiring of the timer in thimblefuls and bucketloads. Glucose and ADP blazed in his tendons. The parking lot whirled. His heels hit asphalt. *Tick*.

"Incredible," Greenberg said from the window above.

"Close that. I'll throw up some pebbles."

"Incredible," Greenberg said again, and brought the casement down.

"I saw you," Julie said. Tiptoe, she kissed him. "You're a maniac."

He pressed the ignition key clockwise; the Chevrolet trembled and began.

"I checked in at the Taft Hotel," she said. "The room is rotten."

"I'm sorry about that," he said. "You can't stay out here. Morissey knows you. There'd be trouble."

"I don't care."

"Well, I do."

"No, I don't mean that, Rick. I mean about the Taft."

"Oh." He concentrated on the back streets that turned toward West Rock. They were in and out of the glare of streetlamps. The night was humid, fat. There wasn't any moon. He felt damp behind his knees and under his arms.

"I saw your folks on Wednesday," she was saying. "They send regards. They wanted to come for tomorrow, but your father couldn't get away."

He wanted to tell her that she didn't lie well; that he knew all about his mother's operation and the biopsy report. "I told them not to come," he said. "Look, you tell them that when I want them to come up here, I'll let them know. All right?"

"All right, Ricky," she said. "Whatever you want."

"You tell them." He knew he didn't lie well either.

"All right. I will. Rick?"

"What do you want?" The streetlamps had ended and the blue cast from the dashboard glazed her face so that all her small features flowed together.

"No. Nothing," she said, and leaned back into the seat, away from him.

The road turned between trees. The flat snout of the Chevrolet bent with it. The road climbed. Pines closed in. There weren't any houses. There were stars above the trees where the road swept left. A sign that read WEST ROCK STATE PARK CLOSES 11 P.M. went by in the night, through the headlights and out of them. Conrad changed to low gear. The road climbed higher, turned. There were strayed rocks on the macadam, and a spidery retaining fence ran parallel to the car. Soon the trees came right to the edge of the macadam and the fence was gone. And then the trees closed in overhead and the stars were gone and the headlights of the Chevrolet burrowed forward and upward until there were no more trees but only stars, like dust and by the billions.

He kicked the parking brake down and got out; she was close behind him. Only her perfume identified her in the darkness against the hovering presence of green. He put all his weight on the wires of the guardrail. They hardly gave at all, were cold and dewy. He hadn't realized how suffocated he had felt in the motel room.

"How's school?" he said. "Did you go for your interview at Connecticut College?"

"On Thursday."

"Did it go okay?"

"I guess so. Are you in with Greenberg? Was that him I saw at the window?"

"Yes."

"He looks like a bear."

Conrad touched the throat of his shirt. Greenberg's hairy arms and chest. His own smooth body. Julie put her face against his arm.

"I'm glad you aren't like that, Rick," she said. "I'd hate that."

"You would, huh?"

"Greenberg's nice, but he makes me itchy."

New Haven blinked on and off below him. He knew the lights of the Taft Hotel and the university. The Connecticut Turnpike dotted its way south along the edge of Long Island Sound. Beyond the lights of the turnpike was an emptiness that reached to the stars at the beginning of the sky. There were small incisions like stars where the malignant node had been removed from his mother's neck. The warmth of Julie's cheek through his sweater. The dimples in his mother's face that weren't dimples. Of course it was curable, possible.

"I like Greenberg, Ricky," she said.

"I like him, too." Almost as a reflex, Conrad put his arm

38

around her. He was on the periphery of the sky. Both of them were on the verge of the sky.

"Won't it be great," she said. "I mean, when I'm at Conn College. I can skip down here for afternoons. Or you can drive up."

They were on top of West Rock, and West Rock was breaking away from the city of New Haven and the university and the Yale Bowl and the athletic fields and the stands and motels and eateries and parking lots and puppy dogs and eagles.

"I won't even have to ask my parents, Rick," she said. "When I want to see you, why, I just will."

They were standing on West Rock, and West Rock was beginning to spin. He was holding onto the guardrail and he had a grip on her. The lookout point was saucer-shaped and spinning like a merry-go-round, rising into the sky with the stars going past and the trees falling away and the lights of the city dimming down until they were aloft and all of North America spread below them going west into the Rockies.

"Won't it be fine, Rick?" she was saying. "Next year?"

She clung to him and they whirled. His mother went by them, jet-propelled, waving, leaving four vapor trails like a B-58, hell-bent for the pearly gates. He reached out, caught the trailing end of her shroud. His mother wagged her finger at him. He wouldn't let go. The ledge of West Rock fell away and they were flying on his mother's winding sheet. Lightning bolts flashed by. His mother spun like a barber pole; the winding sheet came free and she was naked, sailing off from him with her legs akimbo and her breasts flapping like wings. And they were slowing down, coming to the apogee, going over the crest, riding down, falling like a shot. With the winding sheet streaming after them like a parachute that has roman-candled and cannot possibly open;

39

falling back into the sticky night enveloping West Rock; falling earthward. *Tick*.

"Rick?"

He coughed against the back of his hand. "I'm sorry, Julie. What did you say?"

She pushed between him and the guardrail, facing him. Through the flying ends of her hair New Haven glittered. "You're awful sometimes, Rick."

"I'm sorry." He turned his face down. There were the shadows of pebbles near his feet; he kicked them over the lookout's edge.

"Sometimes I'm here and you don't even know I'm here," Julie said. She wasn't looking at him; she had her forehead against the center of his chest. "That's awful, Rick. You don't have to be that way with me."

"I know it. Listen, stop." He went away from her, hopped up and sat on the hood of the Chevrolet. The skin of the car was still warm with the heat of the engine. That made the breeze blow colder about his ears and neck. He pulled his knees up, rested his hands on them. She came along and put her hand on the bulge of muscle in his calf, caressing.

"Rick?"

"What?"

"You're going to try to run nine-five tomorrow, aren't you?"

The starter's gun; in his brain a synapse slammed shut on that sound. The muscles in his calves snatched closed. His eyes were closed and his fists were closed. His epiglottis closed his lungs. The electric timer's needle moved. His ankles hadn't moved. Milliseconds rattled like machine-gun bullets. His body turned, his weight was on his right foot. The muscles in his thigh had swelled to bursting. Milliseconds came like rain. Still he hadn't moved. And then a blade of gravel moved. A flake of gravel moved and his spikes were coming up like daggers. Head up, knees against his chest, head up, eyes up, arms up. On his front two spikes at fifteen feet, up on his front two spikes and kicking. Milliseconds flew like popcorn. The electric timer spewed them out like a calliope. Gears whirled and little bells rang. Circuits closed. The electric timer went mad, began to bounce around. The arteries in his throat were bulging. His toes were punching through the gravel. The wind raked him, blinded him. His legs were reaching out and kicking at forty yards and fifty. Reaching out and kicking at seventy-five. The timer bounced off the officials' table, hopped out on the track and clanked after him, cutting a swath through the cinders. The cinders caught fire. Glucose blazed in his chest and shoulders; blazed in the rhythms of runrunrun at eighty-five and ninety. Ninety-five. The timer blew itself to shrapnel with a roar like crowds cheering. Then the cheering stopped and he was a heartbeat late. Just before he hit the tape he realized that the tape was made of bricks.

"Aren't you going to try?" Julie said. She shook him with a handful of sweater. "Rick?" Then she let the sweater go. "I'll drop you off, Rick," she said, and went around to the driver's door of the Chevrolet. "Come on."

Coming down the steps of the bus behind Greenberg, Conrad could see only the great mass of shoulders before him. When Greenberg hit ground and turned, he could see the field house, the crust of ivy clinging to the low walls of the Yale Bowl. "Hold this, will you, Connie?" Greenberg said. He passed along a small canvas bag. The bag contained a sixteen-pound shot; it pulled Conrad's hand to knee level. "Look smart," Greenberg said. "That's my lunch."

They went up the brick stoop of the field house, through the screen doors. The floors of the building were green rubber tile and all its walls were painted green. Knots of young men moved every way at once through the corridors and on the stairways. Most of them wore gray sweat suits. The halls burned with sweat and antiseptic soap.

"It's the visiting firemen," Greenberg said. He took the metal stairs to the second floor two steps at a time without seeming to lengthen his stride. A gang of sweat suits overprinted with crimson lettering charged them from above.

"Hey, Harvard," Greenberg said. He stopped a narrow blond boy. "What do you do around here?"

"Lay off, Greens," Conrad said.

"You vault," Greenberg said. "You know, you look like you vault."

A voice below them called up, "Get the lead out, Eddie."

Then the blond boy said, "You're Richard Conrad, aren't you?"

"Yes."

"My name's DiMita. Hank." The boy stuck out his hand and Conrad took it.

"A sprinter?" Greenberg said. He laughed and clapped the Harvard on the back. "Where's your roller skates?"

"I'll see you in the hundred, Conrad," the boy said. "Good luck."

"Sure. You too."

The boy's spikes chattered down the stairs and around the corner at the bottom.

"A celebrity," Greenberg said, and started climbing. "Conrad runs nine-seven once in his life and he's world-renowned."

"You're a horse's ass, Greens." They went through a swinging door at the top of the stairs.

"On meet day I don't love my fellow man," Greenberg said. They went among the ranks of lockers; the perspiration was thick as fog. Half-dressed boys exchanged hellos and nods with them. The tin slam of locker doors. The rattle of spikes on concrete.

"I don't get you, Greens," Conrad said.

"Well, so what should I care?" Greenberg swung the canvas shot bag as though it were a purse. "You can't beat them if you love them too much," Greenberg said. "When I cut this pill loose I think about all the lousy things that guys have done to me. That's if you play to win." He smiled at Conrad. "If you play for records, well, I wouldn't know. Here we be."

Of the two lockers at the end of that row, the farthest had the word GREENBERG stenciled on in yellow. On the door of the other, 9.5 was painted in red.

Conrad said, "What the hell is that?"

"Surprise, surprise."

"Now look, Greens—"

"Morissey's orders," Greenberg said. He put his face down near his combination lock, and then swung back his locker's door. "Paint the number on, he said. Keep Conrad thinking nine-five. Greenberg, you paint it on. Use your lipstick. That's Morissey for you." Greenberg kicked his loafers off and dropped them into the bottom of the locker. "Don't you like it?"

"No." The number 9 was swollen like a pregnant woman; the number 5 was clumsy, seemed to be keeling over. The decimal point was the shape of a tear.

"Have a hot time with Julie?" Greenberg said. "Or ain't you talking?"

"I'm not talking."

"Hey, you got to stop being so polite with that girl," Greenberg said, and sat down on the bench in the aisle. "You know what you need, Connie? You need a full-bore piece of ass to straighten you out. That's what you need."

43

Conrad hadn't heard him. He stood where he was, holding his kit bag. 9.5 leered at him from the face of the locker.

Greenberg had taken off his socks and was inspecting the cracks between his toes. "It'd take all-the-way action to get me through a motel window," he said. "You've got less brains than balls and I've got dermatophytosis. That's athlete's foot to you." He pulled a pair of cotton socks from the locker. "See, I lead the pious life, Connie. No broads, no booze, no cigareens. And I get athlete's foot, and Harvards ask you for your autograph. There isn't any justice."

"No, there isn't," Conrad said. He let his kit bag drop and caught his combination lock.

"I take it that you like our artwork, Mr. Conrad," Morissey said behind him. The coach wore a blue serge suit and pencil mustache, was a tiny pearl of a man. An official's pass hung from a string looped over one of his jacket buttons.

"He thinks I missed my calling, coach," Greenberg said. "He says I ought to do landscapes instead of track."

"You ought to be my fairy godmother, Greenberg," Morissey said. He slapped him in the gut. "What did you do? Eat the bus?"

"Connie and me are going to have puppies," Greenberg said.

"See you a minute, Conrad?" Morissey said, and went around the row of lockers. They sat down together on an empty bench. "Your dad called me this morning, Richie. To say he'd promised to be up here and then couldn't make it. Just business and like that. He said you were expecting them and that you were disappointed."

Conrad shrugged. "You couldn't say I was really expecting them." His mother probably wouldn't be entirely recovered for a while yet. Probably she wouldn't be able to make the drive to

44

New Haven for a while yet. It would probably be some time before she would be able to make the trip.

"I see," Morissey said. He put his head to one side, watching Conrad's face.

Conrad yawned. These days, everything was curable.

Morissey seemed to be at the point of saying something else, but instead he got up. "Get us nine-five this afternoon, Conrad," he said, and went off down the aisle of lockers.

The three tiers of stands that faced the soccer field had been moved near the cinder track. From the back porch of the field house, Conrad could see that the pole-vaulting pit had been set up in the infield. Officials in white caps were smoothing the sand in the broad-jump landing. The stands were half filled. He saw girls in shorts. He saw blazers and skimmers. The noon sky was more bright than warm. Greenberg said, "There's Julie."

She was leaning back against one of the hemlocks that followed the path to the stands; she straightened up and waved.

"Hello, Greens."

"Hey, Julie. What's the saturation?"

"Ricky, don't you say hello?"

"Yeah."

"Well," Greenberg said. He flipped the cannon ball from hand to hand. "I've got to get this weighed in. See you."

Julie watched him go, and then said, "Don't you look fine." She ran her hand over the letters YALE on the front of his sweat shirt.

"Thanks." Conrad dug his spikes into the asphalt of the path.

"You don't want to talk?" she said.

"Not really." He sat down with his back resting against the hemlock. She stood over him.

45

"Do you want me to let you alone, Ricky?"

"No. That's all right. Look, sit down."

"I can't." She touched the white corduroy skirt. "It'll stain."

"The hell with the stain."

"Don't be silly, Rick. It won't come out."

He sighed, pulled his back away from the tree and rolled over, stretching full length. He locked his fingers behind his head. He began to do sit-ups. She crouched near him on her toes, leaning against the tree for balance. He was counting.

"I saw Mr. Morissey before," Julie said.

"Six. What did he have to say? Seven."

"He said hello "

"Eight. Hooray."

"He asked me how you were. Don't you feel well, Rick?"

"Nine. I feel great. Ten." The pull of muscles was sweet in his belly and legs. He felt the sweat begin beneath his arms, in the hollow of his back.

"I don't like him, Rick," she said.

"Who?"

"Mr. Morissey."

"What's this crap?" He sat erect.

She touched her tongue into the corners of her mouth.

Conrad said, "Well, what's this nonsense?"

"You haven't been right this weekend, Rick," she said. "It's not that I mind. Really. But you—"

"I'm fine," Conrad said. He let his shoulders fall away. "Eleven."

"I don't like Mr. Morissey," Julie said. "He's got you worked up. There are some things that aren't meant to be."

"Twelve. You don't know anything about it. Thirteen." Conrad pulled faster, harder. He hit his elbows to his knees. "Fourteen."

"He gave me this for you, Rick." She took a white canvas square from her straw pocketbook. "To pin on your shirt. Sit up a minute and I'll do it."

He stopped, brought his sweat shirt up, bending forward. The musky smell of perspiration enveloped him. He loved that smell. Better than any other that he knew. The smell of pure effort. Mindless joy. Julie circled behind him, the canvas square flapping. The number on the square was 95. Conrad caught it away from her. He got up.

"Listen, which way did Morissey go?"

"Toward the stands. I think so. Ricky, don't you want me to—"

"I'll see you later, Julie. Okay, Julie? Julie?" He trotted on down the path.

In the shadows behind the stands a crowd of boys in blue sweat shirts sprawled. Morissey stood over them. Orange peels littered the ground. Morissey looked at Conrad. Greenberg threw Conrad an orange. "Have some glucose," Greenberg said.

"Glad you could join us, Mr. Conrad," Morissey said. "I wouldn't want your athletics to interfere with your social life."

Conrad didn't say anything; there was some small laughter.

"I see you have your number, Mr. Conrad," Morissey said. "Hold your number up, won't you?" Heads turned. "Mr. Conrad has decided he can break the Ivy League record for the hundred-yard dash," Morissey said.

Greenberg put his mouth against the back of his hand and made a kissing noise.

"For that you can be camp mother and pin Conrad's number on him, Greenberg," Morissey said. "Haul ass."

Greenberg rose heavily and stood behind Conrad, drawing up his sweat shirt.

47

THE WAY IT WAS

Under his breath Conrad said, "What the hell is Morissey up to?"

Greenberg handled him ungently. "Psychological warfare. He's making you a hero. You're going to be a great man, don't you know."

Morissey was saying, "This is my one yearly quote sermon unquote. There isn't anything better than sportsmanship. Those of you who believe that probably believe that there's nothing as good as winning except losing." He put his hands in the pockets of his pants. "That's all. Get lost." The movement started.

Conrad broke away from Greenberg. "Can I talk to you, coach?"

Morissey took a step or two with Conrad after him. "Talk."

"I don't want to wear this number."

"That's too bad," Morissey said. He sat down on one of the raw-oak cross members that supported the stands. Behind him Conrad saw rows of shoes, the tails of skirts, the backs of slim calves. Candy wrappers flaked down. Someone dropped an empty beer can.

"I want another number," Conrad said.

"Or what?" Morissey said.

"Or nothing. I just want another number."

"There aren't any other numbers." Morissey touched his mustache.

Conrad shuffled his feet. "I don't like this business, coach."

"Can I tell you something, Conrad?"

Conrad didn't answer.

"If you don't like it, that's too bad about you. What do you think this is, Sunday school?"

"Look, I don't—"

"When you run for me, you run, boy."

Conrad shrugged. "Forget it," he said.

Morissey stood up, brushing the seat of his pants. "Now think on this, Richie," he said, and threw his arm up over Conrad's shoulders. "From now on I want you to eat nine-five and breathe nine-five and sleep nine-five. I want you to put nine-five on the wall of your room. I want you to stencil it on all your T-shirts. You're going to have your own little religion, Richie, and that religion is going to be nine-five." Morissey walked him around the side of the stands. "You want to know why, I suppose."

Conrad couldn't think of anything to say. Morissey's arm was light as a breath, his voice was smooth and easy. He felt the warmth of Morissey through the sweat shirt and he smelled the scent of pipe tobacco on his skin and in the fibers of his suit.

"You're studying to be an engineer and you should understand that you never know what's possible until you do it. It's mostly in the mind," Morissey said. "Things engineers do today . . . ten years ago nobody believed in them. So you think nine-five, Richie. And see what happens."

Conrad had a sudden fear that he was going to slip and put his spikes through the tops of Morissey's shoes. He felt ungainly, as though he couldn't coordinate his body. "But I keep thinking even nine-seven was a fluke," he said.

"It wasn't, Richie. You'll do that again and better," Morissey said.

Conrad's eyes were dimming; they didn't focus well. The faces in the stands were fuzzy, undefined. He felt dizzy, as if he were about to faint. His breath was shortening. He felt sweat forming at his temples, sweat forming on the soles of his feet. He felt remote. His hands began to tremble; he pressed them against his sides.

"Think nine-five," Morissey said. "Nobody knows for sure. Think nine-five."

49

Conrad had a dream. He saw the nervework of the starter's mind laid out before him. Lights were flashing; a steel ball was rolling between rubber bumpers, colliding with lights, clicking them on and off with its impact.

"Think nine-five until you can hit it on the button," Morissey said. "Not on the gun, but with the gun. Until you know when that gun is going to fire and you're moving in the instant just before it does. Until you hear that shot before anyone else in the world."

The steel ball rolled back and forth. Lights flashed, contact points closed. Then the ball turned left, began to fall. At bottom the FIRE light sat cold and dark. The ball fell toward it. The ball accelerated, sped. 981 cm/sec^2. Conrad was in the blocks, his muscles drawn like bow strings, cocked. The ball fell, homing on the FIRE light. Conrad turned an ampere loose in his brain; it sang into his spinal cord, out through the wiring of his legs and shoulders, wrists and ankles, arms. His feet began to move, a cinder's worth, a flake's worth. The timer's needle hadn't moved. But he was moving just that fraction, just enough. Then the gun fired.

"That makes all the difference," Morissey said. "You can beat the machine. You just keep thinking nine-five, Richie, and you can do it."

The pressure of Morissey's arm was gone; there was an emptiness about his shoulders where the arm had lain. Conrad's legs were moving. He was crossing the cinder track to the infield. He saw Greenberg's great round face, his body inflated with muscle, the way his shift stretched across his back. Conrad held his arms straight up; his hands described an arc toward his toes and caught the grass and held. He came erect, chewed some of the grass.

Greenberg was bouncing the shot on his palm, balancing it.

Then he held the shot to the nape of his neck, leaning out of the wooden circle with his left toe behind him touching dead center. Conrad saw the pump in Greenberg's right leg, the pump again, and then the leg went rigid and Greenberg wheeled, roaring, and his hand went up like a javelin and the shot became a falcon. High over his head and over Greenberg's head. Somehow become a bird. And drifting downward lightly as a leaf to the sound of shouting.

Sweat ran into Conrad's eyes; his mouth was dry. He yanked the sweat shirt off and kicked the pants away. His ears had popped. The membranes in his nose and throat were dry. His arms were tingling; the hairs on his arms were standing up. He saw Julie's face; he thought he saw her face pitying him from among the crowd filling the grandstands and he knew that she was wrong. Someone with a white cap was showing him his lane. A blond boy smiled at him. Conrad shook himself loose. He went down on one knee and the cinders cut him. He fitted his spiked shoes back into the blocks. Pain was beating under his sternum. He touched the cinders with his hands. The crowd noise stopped. A voice said, "Take your mark."

He looked down at the cinders; he couldn't catch his breath. A steel ball teetered in his brain, became dislodged, began to plummet. He stared at the cinders; his mouth was hanging open and he couldn't catch his breath. Sweat was pouring into the sockets of his eyes. A voice said, "Set." Then the FIRE light went on and the cinders turned to ashes under his hands and his right foot moved infinitesimally. And his mother went by him like a missile, high on her front spikes, high up on her front spikes, spikes up, head up, eyes up, reaching out and kicking away from him.

The starter's gun fired, but he didn't hear it. He didn't hear the cheering. He had no sense that the other sprinters had left him and he didn't hear Morissey shouting at him. He went down on both knees behind the starting line and the canvas number on his back spread until it wrapped him in black sackcloth. By the time Greenberg had begun to pull him to his feet, he had already smeared his face and his arms with ashes.

WHAT I DID ON MY SUMMER VACATION

──

I

How long since he had ridden an elevated subway? Conrad couldn't remember. The sunlight through the soot-grained window lay like a comforter over his lap and he had to close his eyes momentarily. The beginning of summer, and the laminated straw seat was sweated to his trousers. Long ago, an age before college began, he had been a daily commuter. Winter days his family lived at 85th Street near Madison and he was out before sunrise walking toward Lexington Avenue. Then it was down into the subway at 86th, the blackened bronze tokens that rang dull, the wooden sweeps of the turnstiles splintered and polished with generations of rough use. The express had yawed and pitched through the miles of tunnel beneath Manhattan, and in unison with laborers and bellhops and porters Conrad had swung from his strap, dreaming of basketball and movie balconies and so many things that had run dry over the years, coming up at last on 14th Street at First Avenue, a block from Stuyvesant High School, in the winter sun.

A strong July sun, and the rusted windows of the elevated subway open at the top for the breeze. The fans hung from the ceiling at either end of the car rotated slowly and beat the dust on the floor into the corners between the seats. A policeman was standing with his face close to the small plate-glass windows of the car's middle doors. The policeman kept his knees slightly bowed; that way the circulation in his legs went on unimpaired while he stayed erect for hours. There was perspiration gleaming above the collar of the policeman's blue shirt and perspiration shining on the backs of his hands. The elevated subway began to rise up the Manhattan side of the Williamsburg Bridge, and under his feet Conrad felt the honing of the wheels against the switch track, as though the steel crust were being sheared from the underbelly of the car. The policeman closed his fingers about the throat of a white enamel post and held. The darkly Spanish woman opposite Conrad looked up from the rosary beads twined like a garter snake among her fingers. The screeching wore on: from the first cars of the train through their own car, backward, away from them toward the cars trailing behind. A lace of peppered gray hair shone about the woman's forehead, at the hem of her black shawl. Her skin was dry and sandy, seemed brittle like layered mica.

The Spanish woman was staring at Conrad from the L of seats opposite his own. The corpus of Lord Jesus dangled from the onyx beads among her arid, desiccated fingers. The elevated subway car heaved and lurched; around went Jesus Christ on winged arms, like the monotonous fan above them, like the vanes of a turnstile.

Downward, experiencing a mildly sinking feeling, Conrad was riding away from his father's promise of a comfortable summer

on Atlantic Beach; riding into Brooklyn, toward his Ultima
Thule.

Then the elevated subway train stopped. Motionless heat of
the station platform with the breeze of the train grinding off behind him. The concrete beneath his feet trembled. He had always been frightened by elevated stations. He hurried down the
steel stairs. He caught the rungs of the EXIT door and brushed
them aside; down the stairs to the street. Overhead a westbound
express thundered by. Into the shadows between the elevated
railroad's legs.

He paused to look at the scrawled directions the interviewer
at the employment agency had given him, and then went up
Meredith Street. There was a corner bar with shingle siding and
faded red curtains behind the neon signs in its small windows.
Two Negro girls played hopscotch with a doll's arm for their
marker. They were barefoot, wore flimsy pinafores, and strings of
colored ribbon dangled from their fisted curls. Conrad turned his
face away. On the stoop behind the girls a pretty tan woman
held a gasping baby on her lap. The white of the infant's diaper
was dazzling against its dusky skin. The woman held her hand
between the sun and the baby's moist face.

Conrad turned right, crossed the street. Vandals had gutted
an old blue Packard convertible. The windows were crushed and
glass shimmered on the hot asphalt. The hood gaped and beneath it the picked vitals of the engine were coated with a fur of
dried oil. Stripped of its tires and wheels and canvas top, the car
hunched to the pavement like a chicken's peeled carcass.

Brooklyn. Everything he had ever thought about Brooklyn,
everything he had ever dreamed about Brooklyn. Coney Island
and beyond Coney Island, a jungle. A Negro girl of eighteen or
nineteen was walking his way. Tiers of decaying buildings like
an abandoned brickyard. The hot stink of asphalt and the smell

of overripe grease. Beneath the girl's flowered shift her hips danced, her uncupped breasts pecked the front of the cloth. Flat, yellow sky and mud brick. A community of brown. The girl was going to speak to him; he was sure of that. The natty pin through his collar and the blazer's shining brass buttons. Her salacious, wiggling steps.

Greenberg had told him how, in New Haven one night, he had climbed behind a flowered shift and bright black calves to a fourth-floor room with a mattress indecently naked on the painted floor; a single bulb hung from a lanyard of wire. Stripping nude, the girl had inspected Greenberg's penis, cleansed it with a coarse cloth and cold water from a basin nailed to the wall. She wouldn't let him touch her vulva; her breasts were empty, drooped like bay leaves. Greenberg said that her skin had the texture of oiled teak; he said that when he touched her the sensation was, frankly, stunning.

The girl walked by.

A man said, "You want something, pal?"

"Is the boss in?" Conrad looked at the name on the envelope from his breast pocket and then put it away. "Mr. Bodek."

"Bardek. I'm him." The man wiped his hands against the chest of his sweat-stiffened coveralls. He was bigger than Conrad, far over six feet. He had long blond hair, a chalky face. "You looking for work?"

"That's right." Conrad smiled and blinked his eyes.

"Come on inside," Bardek said.

The building had been a firehouse; the whole front of it swept open with weathered oak doors. Inside, the walls and ceiling and floor were the same glossy yellow brick. Cases of soda, cases of beer, lined the sides of the driveway head-high. Two black men worked on the back of a flatbed truck in the rear, swinging cases of soda, crashing them into place under a battery of fluorescent lights.

Bardek hooked his thumbs under the straps of his coveralls. "You a college man or something?"

The stackers on the truck wore denim pants, their arms and necks bulged white polo shirts. "Well, yes," Conrad said.

"Summer job or something like that, huh?"

He couldn't keep his eyes off the workers; they swung the cases of soda away from the walls, landed them, each in place, with a chatter of bottles. The sweet smell of syrup was thick in the old firehouse. "A summer job," he said.

"Yeah," Bardek said.

"I really need the money," Conrad said. The noise of breaking glass turned his head.

"No folks?" Bardek said. "Don't they take care of you?"

"Sure. But I figured I wouldn't sponge off my father in the summer too," Conrad said. He couldn't keep his mind on Bardek. A single bottle had fallen somehow, but the two black men paid it no attention. They went on in the rhythm of sweeping the cases aloft, crunching them into place.

"Good spirit," Bardek said.

The glass had shattered in thousands of slivers where the bottle had fallen. The pieces spread around Conrad's feet, clawed the yellow brick under his shoes. The purple soda welled before him on the tile, and the bottle's green wrapper floated slowly downstream toward him.

"Something worrying you, pal?" Bardek said.

"No. I'm sorry."

"You think you're up to that kind of work?" He jerked his thumb back across his shoulder. "You in shape to keep up with that?"

57

Above him on the flatbed, the Negroes stood staring, their white polo shirts gray, sweated to their chests, coursing with the roll of muscle.

"I don't know," Conrad said. In the pocket of his trousers, his hand became a fist. His toes were curling back and there was moisture on his upper lip. His jaws were tightening and he could feel the pressure high in his cheekbones.

"You, I don't think you're up to it, pal," Bardek said.

"Sure I am. Really. I'm a sprinter. I was."

"No, I don't think so," Bardek said, and started toward the wooden lean-to office that clung to the far wall.

Then Conrad remembered his father's apartment on 85th Street and how it could be his for the summer, providing he paid half the rent each month. He remembered how much he wanted that apartment, away from Atlantic Beach and his father and Julie. He couldn't understand how that could have slipped his mind.

"Wait," Conrad said. "Look, I need the work. I have to make some money."

Bardek smiled back at him and shook his head.

"You could give me a try," Conrad said. He had a vision of those two black men and the vision wouldn't let him alone. Their slick arms rippled against the weight of the cases and the nettles of glass ground between the wood and the heels of their hands and the dark acid soda was biting the yellow floor. "You could just—"

Bardek let him come inside the hut, and then closed the sagging pine door behind them. "I could give you a try," he said.

"Sure," Conrad said. "I just need a chance."

Bardek sat down on a bentwood chair. His desk was an old bridge table, and it listed heavily as he laid his elbow on it. Paper coffee cups littered the table and cigarette butts floated in the dregs. "Don't you see what I got out there?" he said. "What's your name?"

"Conrad."

"That your first or last?"

"Richard Conrad."

"Okay, Richie, let me give you a tip." He snapped two cigarettes to the mouth of his pack of Camels. "Go on. Take one. And get yourself a job in downtown somewhere. One of those fancy offices." He put a hissing wooden match to Conrad's cigarette and then his own. "Delivering the mail or whatever they have kids doing."

Conrad leaned against the side of the bridge table. It rocked wildly; he stepped away. He was tired with walking the streets all morning and afternoon, tired with the applications and the interviews, tired of the heat and employment agencies and the shakes of the head and Brooklyn. "It's not so easy. With everybody here for the summer. And they only pay fifty—"

"Who told you it was supposed to be easy?" Bardek said. He looked at the ceiling.

"Well, I didn't mean it to sound like that."

"Whatever."

"I didn't think it was supposed to be easy," Conrad said. "I don't want it to be easy. I don't want some soft job where they give—"

"All right. Anyhow." Bardek took a long drag. Conrad could see that there were streaks of gray in his blond hair. He hadn't noticed that before. "You take my advice, pal. You listening?"

Through the pine planking Conrad could hear the cases of soda colliding, slamming down on the truck, making the tiny room about him vibrate, tingle.

"This ain't work," Bardek was saying. "It's punishment. Just for dumb niggers and spics and guys." He dropped his cigarette

59

into one of the coffee containers and it hit bottom with a noise like spitting. "I'm forty-six and I know this kind of work. It's not for guys with a future."

There was the sound of a heavy engine starting and the sound of gears and then the walls of the room shook and the truck idled to the street and stopped. Bardek got up and swung the door open. One of the Negroes looked down from the cab of the truck and the other sat like a black emperor atop the stacks of cases and glittering glass faces of the bottles.

"Okay, Jesse," Bardek shouted. Then he turned back to Conrad. "You want me to sign the paper that I seen you?"

Conrad touched his jacket pocket. His eyes were on the black man astride the soda truck with his chunky arms folded majestically before his chest. "No, that isn't necessary."

"So just take some good advice and I'll see you around."

The truck bumped away over the low curb with a chorus of reverberating glass like a cymbal stroke and Conrad walked after it until it turned the corner of Meredith Street away from the direction in which he was going.

Above Brooklyn a while after, thinking about the terrible cheerful house on Atlantic Beach and supper with his father, he clung against his vertigo to the rail of the elevated station and tore the envelope and the paper it contained into shreds.

II

A LONG twilight through the kitchen windows of the house in Atlantic Beach. His father had prepared veal scallops à la provençale and salad with a clam-and-garlic sauce. The gray shreds of clam, the money-green folds of lettuce. His father poured Conrad a glass of Bolla Valpolicella. From time to time his father passed a comment on the tenderness of the veal or the richness of the wine. When they had finished eating, his father lit a cigar and asked if Conrad was going out and Conrad said he was. Conrad's father said that he was going out himself and couldn't spare the car. Conrad said that was all right. His father asked him if he wanted a lift anywhere, but Conrad said that he was going to walk.

"It may not be my place, son," his father said, and pushed his plate away with his napkin folded over it. "I'm just curious as to why I haven't seen very much of Julie this summer."

"Oh, we're dating," Conrad said.

"I ran into Harold Dixon this morning at the club. I told him I thought he must have sold his place down the beach. I hadn't seen his daughter."

Conrad didn't say anything. He fussed with the folds of his salad, put his fork down on the green oilcloth, touched the stem of his wine glass.

"Hal thought we'd done the same. Not having seen you, Richie. We had a good laugh over that. Son?"

Conrad moved his chair back from the table. "I guess I'll catch a movie and—"

"So I assume it's up between you and Julie," his father said, and rolled his cigar between his lips.

"I see her off and on," Conrad said. "I do."

"That's a pity," his father said, and picked a curl of tobacco off the tip of his tongue. "I liked your Julie."

Conrad looked at his wristwatch. "I'd better get—"

"That has to do with the note Julie sent me, unless I'm a long way off base," his father said. He drank what wine remained in the bottom of his glass. "This makes a nice change from Ruffino, don't you think?"

"It's okay," Conrad said.

"Hal Dixon recommended it. The man has taste."

Conrad didn't say anything.

"And his wife's every bit a lady you could want. You know she has a master's in anthropology from Cornell?"

"I didn't know that," Conrad said. Halfway turned from the table, he put his palms down over his bare knees.

"You'll freeze in those shorts," his father said.

"I'm taking my jacket." The butter-yellow-and-clover wall-paper of the kitchen. The moths raiding the yellow bulb beyond the porch screen door. The yellow firehouse brick. "I see Julie all the time," Conrad said.

"Oh, yes?" his father said.

"I just haven't been around her house."

"I see," his father said.

"It doesn't have—" Conrad stopped there.

His father rose from the table and began to scrape the plates into the white enamel pail under the sink. Conrad drank some of the red Valpolicella.

"I think maybe Julie and I are going sailing tomorrow," Conrad said.

His father looked back from the sink, nodding and smiling, the cigar stuck in the side of his face, the light gleaming on his high forehead.

"Swell," Conrad said.

His father turned the water off and stood back, drying his hands on a faded yellow towel.

"I thought you were rushing for a movie," his father said.

"Well, it doesn't start for a while yet."

His father sat back down at the table. "I seem to forget how long you've been friends with Julie," he said.

"I don't know," Conrad said.

"It would be about a year and a half."

"Sure, I guess so." He was going to miss the beginning of the movie. But that didn't matter. Because he had already seen that movie and he wasn't going to sit through it again.

"More nearly two years," his father said. "It was during the winter at one of those parties you went to with—what was that skinny fellow's name? Wittenstein?"

"Wittendorf. But I didn't really know her then."

"Not until the summer."

"Well, yes," Conrad said. He looked at his father; his father was wearing an apron but Conrad had gotten used to that now and didn't really notice. The apron had been his mother's, was printed with blue and red and yellow parasols. His father's arms were tanned to the color of rust under a mild fluff of white hairs. His father's biceps were limp; no pectoral muscles drove the front of the apron.

"You know, Richie, a man has certain responsibilities toward a lady. When you're involved—" His father broke off there and looked at Conrad and then tapped the ash of his cigar into the halved nautilus shell on the table between them. "No, that isn't what I'm getting at," his father said.

Conrad didn't know what his father meant.

"I know you always treated Julie as a lady should be treated," his father said.

Conrad blinked. "Dad, I—"

"Overlook that, son."

"Well, I never did any—"

"Of course not, son." His father patted his fingertips on the oilcloth for a while. "When you have a son your age you'll understand why a father can be apprehensive. But I know how you've been brought up. Still," his father said, "sometimes I think of how reckless I was myself at nineteen. You find that humorous?"

Conrad shrugged and turned his face away.

"Yes, I know," his father said. "I'm the old man to you, I suppose. But not that old." He took a card out of the hip pocket of his white linen trousers and spread it before Conrad. "I had an eighty-seven today and there's Hal Dixon's attest to prove it."

Obligingly, Conrad picked up the scorecard.

"Oh, I missed a putt on the sixth, I don't know. A fifty-footer. By this much."

His father's square, professional numbers; the engineer's respect for numbers. Harold Dixon's curled, feline script. Had he seen that long, hooked blade of an *x* in Julie's letters? How long since he had put his own *x* into the address on an envelope? Since semester's end he hadn't seen that last name in writing. Now, in dulled pencil, it trembled on the card in his hands.

"But we've all grown older since your mother left us," Conrad heard his father say. "How about— Look out, son. I want to save that scorecard."

Conrad put it down.

"What do you say we finish off the *vino*, Richie?"

"Bring it on," Conrad said.

The tight kitchen with the black showing through the chipped oven door of the Tappan range. The refrigerator hurriedly painted white, with the shadow of grease on the linoleum floor between its knees. The scent of veal basted with white wine that had replaced the smell of allspice sweated into cabbage and corned beef. Cool beach night. Cool Valpolicella in the old, prized goblets with the bouquets etched into the glass.

"Here's to our pleasant summer of ease and relaxation," his father said, and touched the rim of his goblet to Conrad's.

"Okay," Conrad said, but he barely moistened his lips.

"I've been meaning to ask you, Richie—wait. Why don't we

adjourn to the porch? That is, if you still have time."

Under the tent of screen. Moths spinning about the lamp and the land breeze running strong. The inland smell. His father's rocker grinding its mahogany staves against the concrete floor. In the soft plastic lap of the reclining chair. Lights in the houses down the beach, twinkling through the tight web of screens.

"You know Larry Simons, don't you, Richie?"

"Critter?"

"Is that what you call him?" his father said, and laughed aloud.

"Everybody calls him Critter."

"For goodness' sake, why?"

"I don't know," Conrad said. "Because he's such a little—"

"Well, in any event," his father said, "I can't seem to recall when it was that his father passed away."

"Oh, he isn't . . . hasn't passed away," Conrad said.

His father took a sip of wine, and laid his head back against the padded top of the rocker. "Neither one of us seems to be able to use that horrible word," he said.

Conrad poured some of the wine for himself. He looked at his father.

"I simply assumed," his father said. "In that I've never met the gentleman."

"They're divorced," Conrad said. "Since Critter was . . . I don't think Critter even remembers him."

"Yes, well," his father said. "We were having a little straight talk about responsibilities, weren't we?"

Conrad said, "I guess we were."

"Then all I really wanted to say to you was that it isn't quite proper simply to stop calling on a young lady without giving some sort of explanation."

"But I still—"

"I consider us to be friends of the Dixons and I think Julie's parents are entitled to some indication. You don't think so, I take it?"

"They never—"

"Not that they would think of meddling. You know what sort of people they are."

"Dad, I still take Julie out sometimes."

"But when a man and his wife entrust the reputation of their daughter to you for two years . . . I think they were very understanding about letting Julie spend weekends in New Haven," his father said. "I don't think you'd want to disagree with that."

"No," Conrad said, and settled into the reclining chair.

"And they've certainly made you feel welcome in their home. I would say that was quite true. Son?"

"You didn't have to show me that letter," Conrad said.

"You'll have to speak up, Richie."

"Her letter. You didn't have to show it to me."

His father raised his chin. "Frankly, I thought you would be proud to know how courageous a girl your Julie was."

Conrad looked down at the shredding toes of his tennis sneakers.

"It seems that I've overestimated your maturity," his father said. "And exposed someone with an honest interest in you to a good deal of unpleasantness." His father crushed out the end of his cigar. "Or do you think that your behavior was entirely normal?"

Conrad looked up at the whirling moths, the yellow bulb. "I told you I tripped," he said.

"So that your friend Greenberg had to half carry you to the lockers?"

Conrad put his hands against his eyebrows.

"Now, I'm not trying to shame you, son."

66

"Just let me alone," Conrad said.

"I want you to rest up this summer and get hold of yourself again. So that you can go right back to the track team next fall and—"

"Stop it," Conrad said.

"Son, I want you to go back to that track team and run nine-five every—"

Conrad took hold of his temples. "Will you shut up?"

The dim grating of his father's chair against the concrete floor continued easy, unbroken. "I don't see the necessity for that tone of voice," his father said. "And I think it's about time that the word 'dead' became a part of your vocabulary again."

Conrad uncovered his eyes.

"As when you didn't care to admit that Mr. Simons was dead." His father patted the arms of his chair. "You're running away from Julie because she wants to help you. And I can assume from your silence that Mr. Simons is, in fact, long dead."

"No," Conrad said.

"The man is dead, Richie. Mrs. Simons told me that herself yesterday afternoon."

"Not dead," Conrad said. "They're div—"

His father came forward in the rocking chair, folding his hands. "Listen to me a moment, son. There isn't anything more bitter in life than having to face the death of our parents. All the people we love. Someday they have to die."

Conrad's throat had closed up; his teeth ached from the pressure of his jaws. Somehow he couldn't remember what it was that Critter had told him about his parents. He couldn't even remember the last time he had spoken to Critter on friendly terms.

"When my father and mother died . . ." his father said. "But in the end, I'll tell you, I loved your mother enough to get

67

down on my knees and pray her suffering would end. And you should have thanked God."

How they had stood in the green light through the bedroom curtains. The round, small Jewish doctor with sweaty eyes. His grandfather Kelly sitting blank and gaunt in a corner with the shawleen over his vague shoulders. His mother's high, hoarse wheezing and the doctor's stethoscope pressed to her wrist. Her starved gray face. His grandfather squeezing the ancient, tattered Bible. And then the wheezing had stopped.

"When my brother Peter drowned, it was quiet, I mean quite another matter," his father was saying. "When it isn't in one's time there's—" His father stopped speaking and cocked his head toward the inside of the house. His father's eyes narrowed down. "Was that the phone?" his father said. But Conrad knew he was listening for some sound that neither one of them would ever hear again.

III

ON PARK AVENUE, watching the taillights of the Pontiac disappearing toward Lido Beach. Leaning against the tall stem of a parking meter, watching the flux of neon blue and darkness across the marquee of the movie house. Bright summer colors under the canned light. Atlantic Beach and its sunburned, casual population. Conrad had no intention whatsoever of crossing the street to the movie theater.

He went through the aluminum screen door into Delany's and elbowed his way to the bar. The women in toreador pants with bleach-demolished hair. Dark faces that he didn't know. Dark, sandy Löwenbräu. The walls pasted with gaudy travel posters from places he had never been. The gigantic Schlitz pocket watch dangling from the low stucco ceiling, revolving slowly as the fans in the elevated subway had revolved. Without socks, through the rubber soles of his tennis sneakers, the sand and splinter grain of the floor.

"Hey, Connie. What's this? Yale?"

Who had hold of the front of his jacket? Who but Greenberg called him Connie? Who had he ever known with red hair cut close like bud grass and a girl's pretty nose?

"Man, you really made it in spades. Hey, it's Losch. Remember? The American Legion ball club last—"

"Sure. Frank. Right?"

"Yeah."

"Well, how've you been?"

"Okay, but not. Man, you're really the Ivy League with tuned exhausts, ain't you?" Losch brushed the felt lettering on his jacket.

"So what do you know from the old crowd?" Losch said. He was gangling, like a reed; he held a tumbler of colorless liquid that floated ice and a wedge of lime.

"I've been a little out of touch," Conrad said.

"This joint is coming down," Losch said, and waved his thumb. "Man, it used to swing like sixty-five."

"I guess they're getting older people now," Conrad said.

"And what the hell was her name? Julie? That dark one. You kept up with her?" Losch lit a cigarette. "Use these?"

"Thanks," Conrad said. The sweet taste of tobacco. Married people, people of his father's age. Shorts and sneakers like his own. "Where is everybody?" Conrad said.

Losch scratched under the collar of his black crew-neck. "Probably over to Sally Warner's. What you doing this summer?" Losch said.

Conrad wiped the foam away from his mouth with the knit

cuff of his Yale jacket. "I guess I'll get a job in the city."

"I'm working around Midway Esso in the afternoons," Losch said. "Get to use their tools on my rod that way. Man, I'll bet you say Yale and they swing the goddam doors wide open."

Conrad wondered where his father was; if his father was sitting in some bar like this one. He wondered if Julie would be at Sally Warner's party. Delany's had become a cocktail lounge. All the people playing teen-ager.

"Hey, I'm gonna bomb out," Losch said. "Maybe make Sally's place and then maybe cut out for Coney with a couple of the chicks. What about it, Connie?"

"I don't know, Frank." Cigarettes still made him a little giddy. His Löwenbräu had grown warm; the inside of Delany's bar was too warm. He didn't give a good goddam if Julie were at Sally Warner's party and he couldn't care less who she had gone with.

Losch dropped the butt of his cigarette into his glass. "You coming, Connie?"

"Sureokayfine."

On the hip of Losch's black Chevrolet convertible the word SUDDENLY was painted in metallic red. Thin pinstripes curled back from the headlights along the doors to the chrome edges of the fins. The car had a California rake and seemed to rear off its hind tires. The dashboard and front seat were padded with rolled and pleated white Naugahyde.

"My airmail special-delivery," Losch said when he pulled the door closed. "Eighty-six in second and rubber in all four."

"Did you build it yourself, Frank?" Conrad said. He felt dizzy, relaxed. The lights of the movie marquee diffused into a pastel neon glow.

"Bought it off some joker," Losch said. "But I keep her tuned right on the dot myself."

The rumble of glass-packed mufflers; Losch pushed the eight-ball shift knob forward into first gear. The acceleration thrust Conrad's head back.

"You sure get a lot of clowns on the beach this season," Losch said.

"I guess it isn't too bad," Conrad said. They took one of the dark side streets. Losch swung the car along Beech Street.

"Hey, I've been making it with this bunch from Long Beach. You know that beach club outfit," Losch said. "Man, they got 'Vettes by the yard."

"We're just buying a new Pontiac," Conrad said. "I'm taking ours to school in the fall. Not just weekends."

"What's it go like?" Losch said.

"Well, it's pretty fast."

"What's it make the quarter?"

"I don't . . . I never tried it out," Conrad said.

"Well, it don't go like this gun," Losch said, and slapped the accelerator pedal against the floor.

The hood of the car seemed to lift up before Conrad, and the rolls of stiff Naugahyde held firm against his back. A shriek of spinning tires; the Chevrolet lunged.

"What about that for legs, Connie?"

"I never saw—"

"A lot of balls, hey?"

Conrad put his hand on the chrome door handle beside him. When had he ever ridden in an automobile that moved with the shock of this one? When had his stomach ever been jarred that way with acceleration? He spread out in the seat. Losch slammed the Chevrolet to a stop.

"A party," he said.

But Conrad didn't see Julie at first. He saw Sally Warner with the freckles and the big chest cleaving her sweater. She got hold of his arm and this was Bob Murphy and Jerry Reimann and Susan Newman and Mandy Shilling and Hal Mark and Benny Spatz and Toinette Rees. Mimi Herzog was there with Irv Abelov. Lynne Zuckerman and Joanne Petrillo and Clark Jennison and Norma Ford. Mary Romig and Jeff Loria and Nate Milikowsky and Dick Zeeman.

Then Julie said, "Hello, Rick."

"Hello."

"How have you been, Rick?"

"I've been okay. What about you?"

"Pretty good. Nice party."

How had she changed in the last month? Her eyes were lizard-green against the suntan. Her small mouth. Conrad got hold of a can of Miller's. Someone turned the stereo up. Conrad was among the paneled Lally columns that held the house, on the squares of rubber tile of the basement floor, against the walnut walls. Conrad was jostled near her white turtleneck sweater.

Sally Warner's gleaming nose, peeled of freckles. "Richie, come on and dance."

"He can't, Sal. Rick can't do the Twist. Can you, Rick?"

The high, hollow punch of drums.

"Oh, Richie, you've got to be kidding."

"Tell, Rick."

"Well, I guess I can't, Sally."

Her pronged laugh. He watched Julie walk away, into the swirl of grinding dancers. She shot her hip his way. Conrad blinked with the impact.

"Man, I'm telling you, these punks knock me down," Losch said.

72

"Quit," Conrad said.

"Don't get your stones up, Connie."

"Just lay off, Frank."

"Okay." Losch put up his hands. "Okay already. Hey, that was the Julie broad wasn't it?" Losch had to shout over the music.

"What?"

"I wonder who's taking that piece of goods home," Losch said.

"Look, what do you say let's get out of here, Frank?"

"Sold."

At the car Conrad said, "Say, would you let me drive, Frank?" and Losch spit into the gutter.

"You handle a stick shift, Connie?"

"Sure. Like a champ."

The keys caught the glitter of the streetlamp, struck Conrad's chest.

"Let's head for Coney," Losch said.

It wasn't like the Pontiac at all. The accelerator pedal was steel, fit the shape of Conrad's shoe. The eight-ball of the floor shift fit close to his right hand and the bright face of an 8000-rpm tachometer stared back at him between the spokes of the steering wheel.

"Crank her up," Losch said.

Conrad said, "Listen, I've been to Brooklyn once today."

Losch lit a cigarette. "So let's cruise. Maybe we'll find some skin."

Conrad stalled the Chevrolet and Losch said, "Competition clutch. Juice her a little more," and sat back.

The car bucked, moved away to the street corner. Conrad turned in the direction of Lido Beach where Park Avenue spread out into four broad lanes. They were out of the business district, where the land narrowed and the water lay dark at the shoulders of the road.

"What a mess of finks," Losch said. "Man, I breathed free when we cut out of that Warner's place."

Conrad held the Chevrolet to forty-five. Half a moon above them and the cool wind running. The dead smell of the sea and the gardenia smell of Julie's cologne. Conrad pulled back into second gear, bottomed the accelerator pedal. The tires bit concrete. The tingling sense of speed with the engine winding 7000. The empty sense of speed. He stepped down on the brake pedal.

"Swing for that drive-in burger joint," Losch said through the noise of exhaust and wind.

They pulled to the railing around the glass face of the diner. A red-and-blue sign flashed DINO's above them; the litter of tissue paper and cups on the gravel parking lot. The swish of carhops in kilt skirts and white tunics. A dozen cars faced in to the railing. Conrad thought of Julie's white clamdigger pants, her sleeveless sweater.

Losch said, "Boy, if one of those babes asks me what I want to eat there's gonna be trouble."

Someone jumped up in the front seat of the Lincoln convertible two cars away from them. "Hey, Losch, you prick!"

"Jesus Christ, Critter, go to hell," Losch shouted back and gave him the finger.

"I thought you were in jail, you son of a bitch," Critter shouted. Conrad stared in the direction of his voice. Critter stood up tiny on the doorsill of the Lincoln and waved his bug-sized arms. In narrow dungarees and T-shirt, the shine of his brass belt buckle.

"Hey, come on over, you turkey."

Critter came bouncing across the hoods of the intervening

cars and squatted over the windshield of the Chevrolet. "So what you got there, Losch? Now, Richard Conrad, as I breathe and live. Ain't he cute?"

Conrad waved for one of the carhop girls. "You want a burger, Frank?"

"And he's taking care of you real fine, I see." Critter clung to the windshield and leered at Conrad, his long black hair sweeping his forehead. "What, are you two guys in love?"

Losch laughed and dropped his cigarette in his lap and had to scramble for it.

Critter said, "Look out, Losch, you'll burn your nuts off and won't have nothing to play with." He jumped up and down. "Let Conrad dig that out for you, Losch. He'd love it."

"Cut it, Critter," Conrad said.

"Well, won't you pardon me." Critter flitted his lashes; then he smiled hard. "Watch how you talk, Conrad. You're looking for a mouthful of Chiclets."

Conrad took a pair of menus from the carhop and when she turned Critter let out a howl at her and threw himself across the hood.

"Listen, Frank," Conrad said. "Let's forget this."

"You cracked? Critter's turned on, Connie."

"Get this," Critter said, when he crawled back up to his knees. "You know where Conrad's old man is right now?" His belt buckle, the edges honed sharp, scraped across the windshield glass. "Ten gets fifteen he's up to his elbows in my old lady. Conrad, that's a cheap fuck."

Conrad set the menus aside. He turned the keys in the ignition and the Chevrolet shuddered and caught.

Critter jumped down. "At least my old lady let the stiff get cold," he said.

Conrad threw his door open. Losch reached for him, but

Conrad was already on the other side of the car.

"Now, you start with me and you're done, fag-puss," Critter said. He touched the free end of his belt. Conrad swung with his right hand and missed, and Critter hit him in the face. Conrad swung again and missed, and Critter hit him in the cheek and Conrad tasted blood. Conrad put his head down and grabbed for the smaller boy; Critter moved back, wrapping the belt about his fist. The women in the car beside them began blowing the horn and one of the carhops screamed.

Conrad got hold of the front of Critter's shirt. The edge of the belt buckle cut into his lip and then his shoulder. Then he threw Critter against the railing before the diner and the belt jangled to the ground and Critter went to his knees reaching for the small of his back. Conrad kicked him in the face and Critter rolled underneath the railing, going for the belt.

Conrad ducked the railing. Critter scrambled after the belt. Conrad kicked him in the face again. Someone jumped out of the Lincoln convertible and threw a leg over the railing. Conrad hit him in the side of the head and he tumbled back.

A man in an apron came running around the side of the diner, shouting at Conrad. Conrad couldn't hear him. Critter's face was running with blood and his T-shirt dripped red. He got up on his hands and knees. Conrad kicked him in the face with the flat part of his sneaker and then pulled him up by the hair and kicked him in the groin. The man in the apron got hold of Conrad's arm, but Conrad pushed him away. Losch was screaming and the carhop girls were gathered against the fence and screaming. Conrad didn't see them and he didn't hear them. Critter tried to crawl under the fence and Conrad kicked him in the ribs. Critter went down, rolled away under the railing. Losch reached over and clapped his arms around Conrad; Conrad shrugged him off, climbed over the railing.

76

The boy who had been in Critter's car came around the other side of the Lincoln, swinging the belt. It caught Conrad about the back; the buckle crackled against his spine. Conrad grabbed the belt, pulled the boy toward him and sank his fingers into his face. The boy bit Conrad's hand, Conrad rammed his knee into the boy's groin and let him fall. Then Conrad turned around to Critter and kicked him behind the ear. Critter sprawled on the gravel and stopped moving. Then Losch was pulling Conrad into the Chevrolet and there was the sound of sirens. Without lights, leaving the road empty behind them, the car ran hard in the direction of Atlantic Beach.

IV

COULD IT have happened? Conrad looked at himself in the mirror. His lower lip was split in the corner of his mouth and clotted; there was clotting spread down the side of his neck where the belt had cut him. The back of his Yale jacket was torn and spattered with blood. He wiped the clotting away with a washcloth and balled the jacket and carried it outside and threw it into the wire incinerator and his shirt after it. He struck a match and held his arms across his bare chest while the flames grew.

His arms ached and his back was stiff with pain. He had no sense of his mouth. He tried to remember what it was that Critter Simons had said. Then he heard the sound of the Pontiac and he ran back to the house and slipped on a fresh shirt and buttoned the collar.

"The most disgusting thing I've ever seen," his father said. He poured some tea for Conrad and then sat down on the far side of

77

the table, folding the skirts of his bathrobe over his knees. "A perfectly lovely dinner party. Just a few of the people your mother and I used to know. And Mrs. Simons being so nice about getting us together. And the police drag her son in looking as though the house had fallen on him."

Conrad took two dots of saccharin, stirred them into his cup.

"In the denim pants and blood all over him. Just like a little hoodlum. And you can believe me that the police had seen him before," his father said. "Do you want the lemon juice?"

"No, thanks."

"You've got the start of a nice fever sore there, Richie," his father said. "Put a little vaseline on it or it'll be dry by tomorrow and you'll have to stay out of the sun for a week."

"I was going to get some before I went to bed," Conrad said. He held the brim of his cup against his lip.

"You look in the back of the medicine cabinet," his father said. "You'll find it."

"Okay," Conrad said.

"Naturally the poor woman was beside herself," his father said, and crossed his legs.

"Who?" Conrad said.

"Estelle. Mrs. Simons. The policeman said he picked a fight with someone twice his size in the parking lot of one of these drive-in places." His father touched his mouth with the edge of the napkin. "And had the living daylights beaten out of him. The policeman said it was bound to happen sooner or—"

"Do they . . . did they catch whoever it was?" Conrad said. He pressed his fingers against the side of the table to still them.

"I don't think they really care," his father said. "The owner of this diner or whoever it was . . . he's had the boy thrown out a dozen times. For annoying the waitresses and making a commotion. " His father smiled. "Of course, the little gangster claims it was half a dozen longshoremen."

Conrad put his cup down; he pulled the collar of his shirt against his throat. "I saw Julie tonight," he said.

"Well," his father said. "How has she been?"

"Okay, I think."

His father drank off some of his tea. "It's a shame there aren't any muffins," he said. "We could have breakfast now and sleep late tomorrow morning. Then have a brunch the way we . . . just the two of us," he said.

"Julie looked really nice," Conrad said.

"I'm glad to hear that. You two could see a lot of each other if you decide to stay the summer here." His father watched him a moment. "Unless you're determined to get a job and live in the apartment in Manhattan. I won't stop you, son. You know that."

Conrad put his spoon into his tea and stirred it.

His father said, "Son, why don't you see if there are any biscuits or anything in the bread bin?"

Conrad got up and went over to the counter beside the sink and pulled one of the drawers open. He held up a package of Graham crackers. "This is all there . . . What's—"

"Richie, come over here and let me see that lip of yours, if you don't mind."

"The . . ." Conrad touched the back of his shirt. It was soaked through and the redness clung to his fingers.

His father rubbed the corners of his eyes. "It was you," his father said. "It was you, wasn't it?"

"Dad, I was with—"

"Don't tell me anything that isn't the truth, son. Did you do that to the Simons boy?"

Conrad put the cracker box down on the counter. "Yes."

His father pushed his cup and saucer away. "Do you know that if it had been anyone else the police would be looking for you this very minute?"

"Yes."

"But you don't care?"

"I, well . . ." Conrad watched his father. There was not the slightest suggestion of anger in his face. "Yes, I care," Conrad said.

"But you didn't think of that earlier in the evening?"

"He was talking about you," Conrad said. "About Mother."

"That's not so and you know it, son," his father said. "Come over here and sit down with me, son. Please." His father folded his hands before him on the table.

"He said you were with his mother," Conrad said, and pulled his chair in behind him.

"And I was," his father said. "So what could be—"

"But doing—" Conrad put his fist against his mouth. He held his breath.

"I don't know if I should make you go to the police," his father said, and Conrad stared at him. "I don't suppose it would do any good."

"I won't go," Conrad said.

His father shook his head. "Well, you need rest," he said. "I'm sure you'll pull out of it, Richie. You'll be just . . ." His father blinked his eyes and took a long breath. "I'd better have a look at your back," he said, and stood up.

In the bathroom, Conrad held the tails of his shirt over his head. His father dabbed his back with Mercurochrome and taped a square of gauze. Then his father said, "Come along, son," and led him back through the kitchen and the porch.

"There's something savage in us all, Richie," his father said. "Sometimes, when we're in turmoil inside, that animal in us breaks out." His father shook his head. "When my brother Peter drowned I was even a little glad about it. That is, before I recognized my loss."

Conrad said, "But Critter was talking about you and—"

"The moment comes when you've just got to let all your frustrations go," his father said. "That's when you need to control your emotions. When you have to learn that it's mind that makes the man."

Conrad's hands began to shake; he couldn't make his father's face out clearly in the yellow light. "He was saying that you were—"

"You're going through a period of depression now," his father said. "But you have to keep a grip on yourself, son. You can't take our misfortunes out on someone else. Even if they provoke you or badger you or try to push you around. I know the Simons boy must have hit you or shoved you."

Conrad couldn't catch his breath. His mouth was dry. The membranes in his nose and throat were dry.

His father bent through the open door of the porch. He opened Conrad's hand. "This is sand," his father said. "Nothing but sand. But add mind to sand, and you get miracles," his father said. "You get glass."

The yellow light splintered by the etched faces of his mother's favorite goblets; the yellow light pouring all around him. His father's voice said, "I'm going in to bed now. Sit out here and think about that, son."

V

THE MOON was down near the rim of the western sky. Conrad didn't know how long after midnight it was. The white ridges of the waves ran toward him from the moon, curling on the beach.

Above and parallel, the Milky Way spread against the black sky. The muscles in his shoulders and his legs pulsed with effort. Had he been running? He didn't remember.

He jingled the coins in his pocket and the spray of the waves jingled on the beach. Every twenty-five yards, another house with lights in only one window. Had he killed Critter Simons? He didn't think he had, but he didn't care whether or not he knew. He wished he had some cigarettes, but he was always afraid to bring them into the house where his father might find them. Had his mother been dead a month? Was it a month yet? Almost six weeks already?

Julie's house with the glass-enclosed patio. The only new house in the row. How long had he been waiting? Probably she wasn't even home yet. He stopped walking. Headlights turned into the driveway and he dropped down behind the tide-line hummock. The sound of a car door. Was it the police? Conrad laid his head on the damp sand and shut his eyes. Soft laughter, the sound of the front door. An automobile engine starting. He lifted his face and the car had gone. Someone parted the curtains in the lighted window. Conrad hugged the sand again. Had his father said something about sand? The sound of the glass patio door and the yapping of one of the Yorkshire terriers. Conrad looked past the tops of the tide grass. Julie was coming his way with the dog skittering about her heels. Her white clamdigger pants twinkled in the moonlight.

She said, "Rick? I saw you in the headlights. I know you're here somewhere, Rick. Ricky?"

Conrad got to his feet, brushing the sand from his knees and elbows. She came toward him.

"I'm glad you came to Sally's party, Rick," she said. "I didn't know if you'd heard about it. I was hoping you'd come."

Conrad tucked his shirt back into the top of his shorts. He didn't say anything.

"I guess I owe you an apology for being . . ." Then she was directly before him and she put her hand lightly against his mouth. The Yorkie pawed Conrad's calves.

"Who did this to you?" she said.

Two dots of moon formed in her eyes. Her cologne came downwind to him. He couldn't feel her fingers where the nerves in his lips were dead. She put her palm to the side of his neck.

"You just stood there, didn't you?" she finally said. "You won't ever hit back, will you?" she said.

Then she was brushing the hair away from his forehead. "I'm sorry for what I did to you at the party, Ricky. I'm sorry I wrote to your father. Sit with me a minute, Rick. Talk to me."

The Yorkie hopped into her lap, stared at Conrad, panting. Julie kept hold of his hand and pulled her knees up. "I wish we didn't have to go on pretending, Rick," she said.

Conrad looked at the flat crotch of her clamdiggers. There was deep shade under her breasts.

"I hit back," he said, and Julie began to smile, vaguely, rolling her head so that her hair poured down with moon in it.

"It's all right, Ricky," she said. "I know."

"I really did," Conrad said.

"I didn't think your father would ever tell you, Rick. I was just afraid and I didn't know what to do."

"I hit him, Julie," Conrad said. "A bunch of them. They were all over and—"

"You just don't care about me at all any more, do you, Rick?" she said.

Conrad looked at her hand resting in his own. "Of course I do."

"Don't you ever want to see me any more?"

"Yes," he said.

"We have to start all over again from the beginning, Rick," she said.

"I know that."

"I want to, Rick. Don't you?"

"Yes."

Her eyes were wet. "You'll take me to the movies tomorrow night or one of those things?"

"Yes," he said.

Something fell off her face onto the sand.

"I don't ever want you to do that to me again, Rick," she said. "Stay away from me that way again."

"I won't."

"It's not fair, Rick."

Then she put his head against her bosom and she didn't seem to care. She was soft, warm through the thin sweater, and the Yorkie raised his face to lick Conrad's chin. Julie's arms held him and he could smell the dog's breath but he wasn't going to mind that.

"They hurt you," she said. "Didn't they?"

"Yes," Conrad said. He was thinking of the dry taste of cinders, the way he had covered himself with the dust of cinders in front of her and Greenberg and Morissey and all the rest. He thought of the pathetic way Critter Simons had tried to crawl through the gravel of the drive-in's parking lot. How beaten and frightened Critter Simons had looked.

"I won't ever let anyone do that to you, Ricky," Julie's voice said. Conrad nodded. He began to cry.

MICHAELMAS

──────────────────────────

THE WIND flung a handful of leaves in Conrad's face. For a moment he was blinded; he could see only autumn yellow and he dreamed that chipmunks' paws were grabbing at his cheeks and chin. He raised his gloved hands; a dried leaf stuck between his throat and collar, shattered into flakes, and the flakes scurried around under his overcoat and jacket and shirt and scratched down his chest. His chest itched; he had an itch in the small of his back; he ignored that.

It was cold. His breath swung before him like creamy smoke off piles of burning leaves. He smelled burning leaves. The forest of poplar and birch that ringed him was going up in crimson and lemon-yellow flames. The grass between the trees was dappled brown like trout. He looked at the sky through the spiderwork of birches that bent above him. The wind was in the clouds, driving them.

Toward the horizon, he could make out Connecticut College, dark against the sky, light among the firs that surrounded the

85

campus. He could smell chestnuts; he could smell evening coming on, and the firs and poplars and birches beneath the eastmost hills were already awash with darkness. He was thinking about Julie, and the fur linings of his gloves made him dream that he had hold of the reins of her hair.

There was an automobile on the narrow macadam road in the valley below him. The macadam was swamped with the corpses of leaves and as the car rolled it sent up a steady hissing noise like a scythe topping wheat. Conrad stopped where he stood behind a braided stand of birch; there was a puff from the exhaust pipe of the car; the car stopped; Conrad crouched; the driver's door opened; a man emerged.

The man was a priest; his round collar gleamed at his throat like a pearl choker. He went around the car, first one way, then the other, bending from the waist crisply at each tire. He kicked the rear right tire twice, and then began to kick away the leaves that inundated it. He kicked with his left foot, then his right. Then Conrad could see that he was moving his feet but that he wasn't kicking the leaves. The priest was doing a little jig. He raised his black homburg over his head, raised both his arms over his head. Leaves rose about the priest in clouds, in flights, in great roostertails of red and yellow leaves. The priest had his hands at his hips, kicked like a Follies girl, his bandy-legs limber like the birches, the toes of his shoes pointing straight up. Round and round. He began to spin. Leaves whirled. The priest danced on. Eddies of leaves formed, whirlpools, a kermess of leaves, spiraling, dancing. The priest clapped his hands; the hills rang. He kicked up his heels. He seemed ready to leap up on the roof of the car to tap-dance. Then, without warning, the priest stopped, fitted his homburg, re-entered the automobile, and drove off at high speed.

Conrad stood up. The last leaves were settling out of the slip-

stream of the automobile. The automobile vanished around a
bend in the macadam road. The wind picked up a tide of leaves
and covered the place where the priest had danced. Conrad
turned and went up over the rim of the hills, going crab fashion,
carefully, down the other side.

He could see the red tile roof of the kiosk among the woods at
the base of the hill. He knew that Julie was waiting there, that
she had been waiting probably half an hour. He knew that her
face would be glowing with the cold by now, that she would
show not a little impatience with him, that her impatience would
go well with the color in her face and on her fingernails. He slid
his feet along, crunching, feeling for roots snarled under the
mantle of leaves that covered the side of the hill. He held his
hands just away from his sides for balance.

He didn't know why she had called and asked him to come up
to New London on a Wednesday afternoon. He knew that he
should be back in New Haven, in classes, wedging notations into
the corners of his textbooks with blue pencil. He didn't know
why he felt he had to come. He didn't know why she'd asked
him to meet her at the abandoned kiosk. But it was right somehow. He had a sense of resonance, of harmony with the autumn,
with the season of change. He slid on down the hill, dodging the
trunks of trees, welters of ferns. He had a sense of gravity, of
momentum. He was on skates. Enormous masses were in motion,
like the winds and like the seasons turning over. The inertia of
the train ride up the Connecticut coast, with the rails just inland
from the sea. The taxi that brought him to the park's edge, a mile
of forest away from Connecticut College. How his tiny intelligence had guided his body seventy miles from New Haven to a
bull's-eye in an abandoned gazebo that almost no one knew
existed. How he had climbed a hill at just the tick of time that let
him watch a priest dance with leaves.

At first, when he reached the bottom of the incline, he didn't see her. The octagonal kiosk with its slender corner posts seemed empty. The benches that ringed its inner perimeter were vacant. He came forward uncertainly toward the small clearing, forgot to brush aside twigs. They struck him.

"Ricky, you're late. I didn't know if you were coming. I was almost ready to give up."

She was directly in front of him; as he had expected, her cheeks were flushed nearly to the color of her mouth and finger-nails. She had the hood of her green loden coat up and her dark hair cushioned it around the corners of her face. Wasn't she going to kiss him?

"I'm sorry," he said. "Do you want a cigarette?"

"You'd better not smoke. The woods are dry."

He already had the cigarettes and his lighter in his hands. "Well, I'll be careful."

"I wouldn't do that, Rick."

"Sure." He put the cigarettes away. He said, "You look nice."

"Thank you."

"Do you want to have dinner after?"

"After what?"

"After"—he shrugged—"after it gets dark or something."

"I'd love to," she said, and the sound of her voice said that she wanted to. "But I can't, of course. Mid-terms. How are yours going?"

"Over with." He leaned back against the gray trunk of a hem-lock. She didn't come to him. He watched her climb the rails of the kiosk and sit on the uppermost, locking her toes behind the one below. "Will you do all right?"

"I guess so. Did you pass them all?"

"Sure." He didn't understand why she was being so distant, as though they were in the same room with her parents. He thought about the dancing priest, but he didn't know what to make of that.

"I'm glad you could get away," she said.

"So am I."

"You don't think you missed anything?"

"Nothing I can't make up. There are reading lists."

She said, "I guess so." She was staring at him and almost smiling.

He said, "Well, I guess my mid-terms were okay." She watched him steadily. He said, "For a while I didn't think I'd be able to make it."

She said, "I'm glad you could."

Conrad shuffled his feet in the leaves drifted up about the hemlock's trunk. "I thought I might have to go to the physics lab."

"I have my first examination tomorrow," she said. She leaned back; the muscles in her thighs rolled under the stretch of her green slacks.

He couldn't endure the flushed, pleased look on her face. It had to be something. "Will you be down early Saturday morning?" he said. "There's a band concert in front of the library before lunch. You'd like it." He listened.

"I could get the ten o'clock train," she said. "That one gets to New Haven just after eleven. What time does the concert start?"

"Eleven, I guess."

"I guess the ten o'clock would be too late," she said.

"Probably." He squatted down, resting back against the hemlock. What he could see of the sky was darkening fast. The shadows of the trees were spreading around his feet, growing thicker.

"I'll make the nine-thirty. I don't know what time that gets in."

"I can check it," he said.

"All right."

"Is everything okay, Julie?" he said.

"Yes."

It had to be something. "You were saying the other day that your parents thought you ought to date around more."

"Oh, I'm not worried about that, Rick."

"Are you sure?"

"Yes."

"Because I guess you could."

"What?"

"You know." He rubbed his hands together for the warmth. "That wouldn't spoil anything as far as I'm concerned."

"I told them I was dating, Rick. And they let it go."

He raised his eyes to the place where she sat. "Are you?"

"Am I what?"

"Dating around?"

"No, silly."

He stood up; the cold had stiffened his knees. "It's getting dark," he said.

"I know it." She kept her place atop the railing of the kiosk.

He pushed up the sleeve of his overcoat. "It's almost six. You'll miss dinner. The dining hall will close."

"I'll make it in time."

She kept looking at him, evenly, almost tenderly; every now and then she blinked and he was sure that she was about to say something that would hurt him. "I saw a priest dance," he said.

She laughed. "What?"

"On the other side of the hill." He pointed out of the clearing.

"What do you mean?"

"On the road toward the college. He stopped his car and started kicking the tires. Then he was kicking the leaves and he started dancing."

"You're fooling," she said.

He was grinning; he felt ridiculous, but he didn't care. "No kidding. He got out of his car and took his black hat off and started dancing around."

"Ricky," she said. "You're a lunatic."

"No joke. Like this," Conrad said. He threw his hands up and scampered around letting out whoops, kicking up the leaves, spinning.

"Rick, stop. Please." She had her arms folded across her bosom, was bent over in laughter. "Rick. Don't. I'll fall."

Conrad began jumping in the air, clicking his heels, waving his arms. He felt a great release. The bitter cold got underneath his overcoat but his body heat drove the cold away. All around him dead leaves whirled, flew, sprayed in a glut of bright color. He shouted and threw up his arms. The whole forest seemed to spring about him.

Julie jumped from her railing and ran to him, laughing. He leaped like a deer. She put both her hands against his chest and shoved. He went down among the leaves, writhing. He seized two handfuls of leaves and let fly at her head. When the leaves fell away from her she wasn't looking at him any more and her laughter had stopped.

"What's that, Rick?"

"What?" He sat up, brushing the dust of leaves from his arms and shoulders. He knew he had made a fool of himself.

"Over there," Julie said. "By that big tree."

"Where?" He squinted into the branches. The tree was an elm and its branches were empty.

"On the ground," she said. She was walking toward the elm.

"Is it a snake? Don't touch it." He started to rise.

She was kneeling. "It's a bird's nest."

He said, "Julie, come on," and dropped back down. She

wasn't going to make any sense this afternoon.

"No, it is, Ricky," she said.

"Well, don't touch it," he said. "They're filthy."

"It has babies in it, Rick," she said. "Poor babies." She reached out her hand.

"Julie, let them be. They've probably been dead for months."

"They aren't dead, Rick." She looked across her shoulder at him. "There are three of them. And they're alive."

"Don't pull my leg, Julie," he said. "Birds only hatch in the springtime. In late March and April and May."

"Some hatch in the summer," she said.

"Well, this isn't summer."

"Come here, Rick. Please."

He got up and bent over her shoulder. Between her hands there was a ring of dried twigs and a few tiny feathers caught among them. In the center of the ring, three beaks like pen points moved and opened. There was a small noise, like whistling in another room. Her hands closed on the nest.

"Don't touch them," he said. "If the mother smells the scent of you, she won't come back any more."

Julie turned her head; she had her lower lip between her teeth. "I already did."

"Well, that's the end of them," he said. He went down on one knee beside her.

"They must have fallen with the leaves," she said, craning her neck up. "You'd think the fall would kill them."

"They're pretty hardy," Conrad said. He leaned down farther.

"They have no feathers," he said. "Can you tell what kind they are?"

"Nope." Each of the tiny birds had small wings pressed against its sides. That shouldn't have surprised him, but it did. They had no feathers, but were whole. Their eyes bulged, their slender beaks were outsized. Their skins were as thin as waxed paper and translucent.

"You can see their veins," Julie said. She brought her face down close to his, close to the nest.

Red and blue lines like pencil tracings on the birds' skins swelled infinitesimally and then subsided. They stretched their necks toward Julie; their beaks parted and closed. They shuddered up and down. Conrad felt a bullet of sweat skim down his back under his shirt.

"That's crazy," he said. "Birds don't hatch in October. They'll just die."

Julie put her head down on the leaves beside the nest, watching the birds. She closed her eyes and opened them.

"It's just wrong," Conrad said.

She looked up at him.

"Well, it is. They would have died whatever happened, mother or not." He dug into his pockets for his cigarettes. "Well, they would have, Julie."

She began to rise; she cupped the nest in her hands as she stood up, holding it close to her body, harboring it in the folds of her wide green sleeves.

"What are you going to do now?" he said.

"I really have to go, Rick."

"I mean with them. What about them?" He held the flame of his lighter to his cigarette and drew; he blew the smoke away.

"I'll take them."

"Back to the dorm?"

"Yes. I'll put them by the radiator."

"They'll only die. What are you going to do about food?"

"I have an eyedropper," she said. She had all her fingers curved back over the top of the nest. "I'll give them some milk."

"They don't eat milk," he said. "They eat worms."

"I'll heat the milk."

"They'll only die, Julie." He heard the high, scratchy crying of the birds and he thought of his own face pressed in her arms.

"I have to go, Ricky," she said. "I'll be there early Saturday morning. I'm glad you came, Rick. It's just so good to look at you sometimes."

He just stood where he was and watched her back moving away from him, growing smaller, less familiar, as the clearing ended under her steps and the trees began to close in around her and the darkness thickened. Then he couldn't see her any more and the forest was full of the sounds of leaves turning over and twigs coming down and the kiosk was empty and rotting and it grew colder. He said, half-aloud, half-defensively, as if reminding himself, "They won't live through the night." Then he ran to the place where she had left the clearing and screamed it after her.

WHEN I WENT
WHERE THE ACTION WAS,
HOW I WENT AND WHY

——————————————————————————

NEWPORT
August 12, 1960

DEAR JULIE:

You want to forgive me for being so careless about letters. Up here nobody does much of anything, so you put off. The sun comes up; it gets hot; you're on the beach; it gets cooler; the sun goes down and you're still on the beach. Greenberg is still here. He was going to leave after the 4th of July, but put it off. Then he was aiming at August 1st, but August 1st passed and he hadn't left. I asked him when do you think? But he said he didn't have a calendar and besides if he was bothering me he'd just get the hell out and I could go to the devil. I said look you don't have to get so goddam touchy. He said stand between me and the sun, would you please? and we dropped it.

We have broken into one of the beach-front houses on the shore drive with about eight other people. You really can't call it

95

breaking in because the house is in somebody's family, but it's about 30 rooms and the ocean is a couple hundred feet from the front door. The house has many roofs (rooves?) and dressing rooms on all the bedrooms that are like living rooms. The walls are stone and the rooms are usually cool and with breezes. There is no electricity and in the night I always expect the next noise to be the ghost of Scott Fitzgerald waltzing his Zelda under the string of darkened Japanese lanterns in the grove behind the house, across the patio's broken stones.

The jazz concert was exceedingly gauche. A plague of drunks descended upon us. We went into town, but you couldn't get near the stadium and the streets were paved with beer cans curb to curb. A great mob invaded our place around midnight the first day and we had to fight them off. Greenberg had a sock filled with sand but was thrown down the staircase from the second floor and lay in the foyer with a fistfight going on atop his carcass. The police came and were going to arrest us all before one of the girls identified herself and that the house was in her family. Then they picked out the aliens and herded them into the Black Maria and off to the Newport pokey which is rumored a pretty rum place. Greenberg had a knot on his head like a yarmulke—you know what that is—but I came out untouched by human hands and let him know what a fairy he was. We all had thought living in the deserted house was a caper, but that girl telling how her family owned it kind of took the edge off the place. Most of the people left in the next three days, along with the girl who left a letter of identification for any of us who wanted to stay the summer.

Right now there are three girls living next door in the master bedroom. There isn't any furniture, so they're sleeping on the floor just like us peasants. They are sophomores from Reed College out in Washington (Oregon?) and I believe they are in love and create an uproar every night. Greenberg and I are still solvent, although I can't see us lasting until Labor Day on what we have between us. We have been drinking Grappa (cheap)—that's a Greek (Spanish?) wine—and occasionally port, but not much of that, since it turns one's tongue blue. If you have a few bucks to spare—like twenty or so, less if you can't spare it—please send them to me care of General Delivery, Newport, Rhode Island. I will check General Delivery every couple of days until I hear from you one way or the other.

When do you go back to Conn College? Yale starts up on September 23rd.

About a week ago Greenberg and I went into town for dinner and just to see the sights. We drove out toward a place they call Second Beach. Greenberg said the action is pretty keen out there and you can really have a lot of laughs if you fall in with the right crowd, you get me? So I said well look I know you've got a pretty original idea of what's fun and what isn't. He said don't be a lady for Christ's sake Connie you are an incredible blue nose. I said look you know I can stand it if you can, but it's only a little tough to swallow sometimes when you get a few belts and start whipping off your trousers in company for a romp in the surf à naturel. There were some guys with guitars and lice in their beards. A couple of blue-jeans and T-shirt girls; nobody here wears a brassiere. Anyhow.

We park and I can just see my hubcaps are about to disappear since we're surrounded by aborigines. But Greenberg knows them mostly and gets a big hello. I'm his little roommate, he says. One of them pokes me, says you're cute. So I say listen Greens let's get back in the car and get the hell out of this nest of queens. Greenberg says it's better than the circus let's hang around and watch the show. I say Jesus this is a zoo. Greenberg says you've got no sense of humor. I say oh for crying out loud. So we stay.

Nothing worth mentioning happened anyhow. We had pretty stiff rain for the next two days. The roof in our bedroom and all the others leaked, so we bedded in the garage. Most of the windows in the garage were out and the wind came off the water in the night. The sky was blacked out and we heard many spirits moving among the trees and through the gardens decaying behind the house. The second night we went out and stood in the wind, waiting for ghosts. I told Greenberg I bet Scott Fitzgerald danced at parties here. He said you don't know that. I said so what? The treetops rolled; it was a regular blow; branches clicked against the old house. We didn't say anything but we kept bumping into each other. Then we heard music. The wind was kicking the Japanese lanterns around and we couldn't place the music. We walked around in the garden. Greenberg hit his knee on one of those wild wrought-iron benches that you can't possibly sit on without a cushion. There was so much wind and trees slapping each other and the water turning over that we couldn't hear the music and then we could hear it and then it was gone and back again. Greenberg went up into the house by the back way and shouted who the hell has a radio on at this goddam time of night? One of the three lezzies shouted down something I won't tell you, and Greenberg wanted to go up and pitch them out the loving window. We kept hearing this music off and on with the wind between like crying. I don't know. The whole patio was going up in wind, leaves were throwing, and against the sky we saw the Japanese lanterns straining at their lashings.

Greenberg came outside, we cupped our hands behind our ears and kept shaking our heads. We figured it was the gang living in the next house down the beach but that was half a mile and the wind was blowing the wrong way. We started figuring it from there, finally guessed to try the beach, and went down through the weeds in our front lawn.

Midway in the beach there was a fire going in a hole in the sand and we heard the music. We hid down behind the rushes at the tide line, peeping out. Some girl was bent over the fire. I thought she was praying. Greenberg said she was stoned. Her hair was blowing. She had one of these transistor radios up to full blast. Greenberg said your ghosts are dancing to WNBC the cha-cha. I said listen you want to watch that syntax. He got up. I said where are you going? and he said where do you think? So we went on down and stood over from where the girl was sitting. She had a blanket around her and looked ice-cold. Her knuckles showed where they had the blanket and her face, which was about 20 years old, very small. She saw us, took the radio under her blanket with her and the music was gone. Greenberg and I went over by the fire and she looked at us but didn't talk. She was right down by the water and I could feel the spray stinging my face.

Greenberg asked her what she was doing. I said we're staying up at that house. Greenberg said we hadn't seen her before. I wasn't sure she could hear us. The sand was hard and the fire was dying but felt pretty good since it was as cold as I said. I was damp through and the wind was strong and no help. Greenberg said what was her name? He was Greens and I was Connie. I said Richard Conrad. She was looking at us okay, but she didn't answer. After a while Greenberg said let's go back and we got up. I figured she might say something then, but she didn't. Greenberg whispered to me that she was a hipster and stoned silly. I said I didn't think so.

We went back to the garage and the ground inside was so wet

you couldn't sleep on it. We had some smokes and what was left
of some sticks of Italian sausage and split a can of beer. It
started to rain again and the garage filled up with the pattering
from the roof. I kept thinking about that girl and trying to figure
what the hell she was doing on the beach in that weather, freezing with a blanket and nothing on her head. Greenberg said she's
drunk and doesn't feel it. I said I guess from the look on her face
that she feels it all right. I said that didn't make any sense at all.
Greenberg said maybe she's waiting for a party that isn't going
to happen. I said I didn't know. Greenberg said there are lots of
lunatics up here in the summer. I said I didn't think she was a
lunatic. He said she was a hipster and that's the same. I said I
didn't know. He said well you can't understand any of their
hocus-pocus. I said that sure was the truth. We had ourselves
wrapped in blankets like two squaws. I said what time is it? and
Greenberg said 2 A.M. by my radium-dial Benrus. I said look,
we'd better see what the hell happened to that girl. He said you
go if you want to, but she can freeze solid for my two bits. I said
she probably would be pretty frightened by and by. Greenberg
said let's forget it, and the rain was going on the roof and the
wind was pulling on the hinges of the garage doors and you
could just about see the sky through the empty windowpanes
and I said come on and let's have a look down on the beach
again. He said hey you've got that girl on the brain. I said well
it's getting pretty stuffy in here with your fat perspiring hide. He
said go get some sack time, and I pulled off into my corner and
got both my blankets around me and curled up out of the draft.

You could hear the old house creaking from where I was,
shutters going slam-bang and the rain in the gutters, splashing
down off the roof onto the driveway. I smoked a couple of cigarettes. I could feel the rain hitting the other side of the garage
wall through my back and I was thinking about Gatsby's house

with the swimming pool out back and his big Duesenberg or whatever it was and how whoever owned our house must have lived up here with servants and the whole thing during the summers or whenever they lived here in those days. I was thinking about how when I graduate from Yale I'll get us a place like this with servants and deep rugs in every single room and a lot of those lamps with the stained-glass shades. Then we could come up just for our vacation and sit around on the patio and have whiskey sours and those little French after-dinner icing things. I was pretty sure I heard Greenberg get up and stomp around and then he came over and said, hey are you sleeping? I said what do you want? He said he figured to take a walk. I said that sounded okay.

The rain was still coming down and we kept our blankets over our heads and went around in circles across the patio and through the garden and over the lawn and around the side of the house. It was bitter, dark sky full of rain, wind up, you could feel the waves hitting on the beach. Greenberg said I guess let's see what the hell that goddam girl has got to. I said okay with me. We went over to where she had been sitting, but there wasn't anybody so we went down on the beach to make sure and found the hole where her fire had been and the rain had put it out of course. Greenberg was looking toward the water but you could hardly see it. I didn't see her blanket around. Greenberg said she'd probably reeled off in the wrong direction and jumped right in the ocean and drowned. I said how he was crazy and I told him to shut up. He said what was I getting sore about? and I said for him to go to hell and shut up. It was 6 A.M. by then so we kind of sat around in the rushes to watch the sun come up. It rained off and on. The girl didn't come back. It got a little warmer, but the overcast didn't break and it stayed dark long after we figured it was time for sunrise. We talked about driving back to New York after lunch. Greenberg said was I going to have the car at school in the fall? and I said sure. About 8 A.M. a man came by walking a collie dog. We had our blankets around us but they were soaked through and we hadn't shaved and looked lousy. The dog sniffed us but the man shouted at him and he ran off. Greenberg said there would probably be a party in one of the shacks off Second Beach that night and we should make it. He said there was no sense in sitting where we were and I said I didn't see the point in it. I said why don't we get some breakfast in town? So we got the car and left our blankets hung over the lanterns' wires to dry and got some eggs and toasted English and coffee at a diner on the Boston road.

We didn't see that girl at the party that night and we didn't see her again either. It wasn't much of a party with a couple of people just sitting around. I have been puzzling over what that girl was doing out on the beach in the rain and freezing when she could have been inside, even in our house, and nobody would have minded. It just didn't make any sense to me then and I can't figure it out any better now. Anyhow, I didn't mean to bother you with all this. But it sticks in my mind and I wonder if it makes any sense to you. That's all I remember. Greenberg if he were writing this I don't think he could tell you much more.

RICK

PACEMAKER

CONRAD HELD HIMSELF to the chrome stanchion and lowered the heel of his shoe against the edge of the dock. He straightened his knee; water sloshed up between the empty drums that buoyed the whitewashed planking. The dock dipped and rolled back up; the shoreline of Cos Cob yawed and pitched as the Pacemaker drifted away. He heard Julie's voice say, "I'm starting dinner, Rick," and then the sound of the cabin door slamming. He let the nylon hawser puddle about his feet, and then turned up the ladder to the bridge house.

Night was coming on; the land breeze had already filled the atmosphere above the inlet with green. At the eastern horizon the sky was turning the color of the water. Conrad put his tumbler of Scotch and ice cubes down atop the polished teak dash and switched up the lights of the instrument panel. The ignition keys were hung from a peg under the flare chest. Conrad pulled out the choke and pressed the starter. The twin diesels coughed and caught, spitting water from the exhausts.

The vibration came up through the deck into his legs until he eased off on the choke and the sound settled to warm humming. Conrad threw the toggle switches for the running lights and the spotlights and engaged the propeller drives. The huge Pacemaker shuddered, rolled with a thud against the dock bumpers, and then glided out into the channel; its low wash left a procession of tapered nun buoys dancing off to the port side and behind.

When the inlet closed down before opening into the fullness of Long Island Sound he could see the first lighted windows on the mainland. Connecticut was still surrounding him, closing in a peninsula from starboard toward the harbor's narrow mouth. The land breeze rose, cooling off, and Conrad closed the door of the tiny bridge cabin and put up the collar of his poplin jacket against the back of his neck. He tossed the strap of the binoculars over his head and sat up on the tall stool behind the steering wheel. Then the last buoy stumbled by and the Pacemaker slipped through the neck of the harbor and the winking depth sounder edged toward the luminous 100.

Conrad turned the dial below the circular viewing screen at his left hand and there was a dim grinding from high on the mast as the radar sweep began to rotate. He sipped his Scotch; he didn't much care for the taste of Scotch, but somehow Scotch went well in the cabin cruiser on an October night. A trail of brightness followed the clockwise turning of the radar indicator, and the screen showed the arms of the harbor receding behind him. Ghostlike, two blips drifted in from the southeast like shuffling footprints. Conrad raised the binoculars, leveling them on the gathering dusk through the starboard window of the bridge. His index finger adjusted the focus knob; two thousand yards toward the Long Island coast a brace of day sailers bent with the wind, their spinnakers ballooned, their needle masts heeling toward the water.

The radar screen showed him the pattern of power boats moored near the private docks that studded the Connecticut shore. Due east, a squared circle of light rose. They would be drawing under the lee of that island soon, heaving the sea anchor over the side, and he would be watching Julie across the dinner table in the cabin below his feet. The sky in the east turned toward purple; Conrad moved the throttles ahead until the tachometers registered 2500 revolutions and the spray kicked up above the bow like silver coins in the glare of the spotlights.

He had a vivid sense of Julie moving below in the cabin and pantry. The Pacemaker lurched and fell, planing against the coming water, and he knew the muscles in her back and legs were constantly reordering themselves for balance, just as his own muscles responded to the spilling. Conrad came down from the captain's stool and planted his feet apart on the rubber tiles of the bridge deck. He had a notion of a dance; they were moving in unison above and below. Their decks were parallel; their decks angled parallel and recovered parallel as the sea pitched up the Pacemaker and let it fall. He had the notion of a waltz.

That afternoon he had approved her dress for the February prom and he was thinking about it now. The dress was daring, had no sleeves, not even straps. She had refused to try it on for him. The part from the waist upward was pastel spangles that glittered like midday surf; the rest was shiny cloth that he guessed was satin, and fell in folds. The dress seemed longer than he thought her legs could be, but he didn't want to mention that and worry her. He had conspired a plan when she held that dress up before him, limp about its hanger.

The sky above Long Island Sound was coming black and bound over with heavy clouds. Beyond the windshield, the Pacemaker's spotlights paid out into the darkness without returning. The radar showed a four-inch span—fifteen hundred yards—between the image of the island and the boat's position at dead center of the screen. Conrad eased the throttles until the tachometers' needles fell to 1900 revolutions.

He had conspired great plans about that prom dress in the instant that Julie had swept it out from behind the closet door. He had gotten as far as asking her to try it on. Then she said no and his plans went bust. They had been inside her bedroom; he had been sitting on a window seat, staring at the lace canopy strung above her four-poster. The whole room had been pink: the window shades, the curtains, the area rug, her desk and dresser, all the doors, the ceiling, walls and floor. The canopy was a froth of dogwood petals. He thought of how she probably had on pink underpants and brassiere. Her skin was pink; there was pink in the highlights of her dark hair. The stark skirt of the white prom gown had splintered all that.

She would have asked him to go outside into the hallway while she changed. She would have said, Well, how can I change with you right in here, Rick? He would have shrugged and said, Go on, it won't kill you. She would have said, If you're going to be that way, and he would have said, Don't act like an infant all your life, Julie. Then, of course, she would have surrendered. She would have tried to act blasé, would have turned sideways, buttoned off her blouse. He'd let her get her shorts around her ankles, then he'd lift her off the floor with one arm behind her shoulders and the other under her knees. He'd have had her on the bed in another moment, the canopy would be floating above them and there would have been nothing to worry about any more.

Conrad heard the cabin door, heard her footsteps on the ladder to the bridge. He knew he should be planning how to fill her full of Scotch and get her into the stateroom after dinner. He eased the throttles further and the bow of the Pacemaker settled lower in the water. He felt a draft through the open door of the bridge, and then she went past him to stand against the windshield in her quilted yellow jacket with the hood and her yellow slacks.

"It's nothing but franks and beans," she said. "You don't mind?"

"My favorite dish in all the world," Conrad said.

"Let's run up the coast after dinner, won't we?" she said. "Up to Sherwood Island or one of those places. Don't you want to?"

"It's your boat," Conrad said.

She tucked the ends of her hair into the hood of the jacket and pulled its zipper up against her throat. "The summer's really over, isn't it?" she said.

"I guess so." He was thinking about her prom dress and how it would probably cling to her bust. He felt nearer to her when she wore slacks and casual things; sometimes he couldn't conceive of her in dresses that made her look so much older.

"Listen, will you really help me with Plato over Thanksgiving?" Julie said.

"Sure."

She put her hands in her jacket pockets. "I'll tell my parents not to let you stay the weekend unless you promise, Rick."

It was that kind of thing that made him angry.

She said, "How's Greenberg?" and Conrad said, "Why don't you ask him?"

She looked at him and then leaned over the radar screen. "You know, this is a silly machine. Did I ever tell you that?"

"What are you talking?" Conrad took a long breath; there

was salt on the air, and the air was cold in his chest, hurt him.

"You never know when it isn't lying and when it is," Julie said. She was bent from the waist and even in the half-light Conrad could see the rib of her panties' hem curling from her hip, under the fullness of her buttocks, beneath the drawn wool of her stretch pants.

"What?" he said.

"The radar."

"What about it?" She turned to him; he swung his eyes away too late.

"Oh, you just can't tell, that's all," she said, and smiled. She slapped the running-lights switch back and forth; ahead of them the bow light flickered.

"Look, let that alone, Julie."

"Why?"

"It's not smart. And it's against the law." She leaned toward the radar screen again, the wool of her slacks went taut, swung in his direction. He looked more closely for the line of her panties; it was not there. "Somebody is going to run right into us," Conrad said.

"Well," she said, "there isn't anyone but us around here."

Conrad said, "You don't know that." The line of her panties was there; then it wasn't there. He had heard Greenberg talk about girls that went on dates without their underwear and you lifted up a girl's dress and suddenly you had a handful; how that was always the genuine gilt-edged come-on. "There could be some boat out there somewhere," Conrad said, but automatically.

"Well, I suppose I can read the radar as well as you can." Julie drew a fingernail from one of the jacket's pockets and tapped the glass covering the screen and grinned at him.

He thought about that ridge showing through her slacks and

why it didn't show now. Often, he had seen it before—bowling, when she dropped a lipstick, slipping back into her sneakers— and every time, he thought of following its curl beneath her, to the warmest part of her. He didn't know why he couldn't see that line now; in the uncertain light he couldn't see the line and that cheated him of thinking about the place where the line disappeared.

"You like driving the Pacemaker, don't you, Ricky?" she said.

Conrad didn't answer. He looked past her shoulder at the screen. They were within a hundred yards of the island now and he swung the steering wheel hard to starboard and cut the throttles back. The diesel hum went down and vanished; the hollow slap of low waves against the hull replaced it; the Pacemaker rocked, but slowly. Conrad swept the spotlight over the wooded coast of the small island.

"That's a lonely place," Julie said as though for both of them. "Ever since I was a child I've wanted to build a house out there. But you can't. It's really not an island at all," she said, and leaned against him.

"Sure it is," Conrad said. He saw the outline of her profile between his eyes and the instrument lights. The sky and sea around them were solid under darkness.

"It really isn't an island," she said. "It just looks that way. It's only trees on rocks, and whatever ground there is is under water all the time. Even at low tide."

Conrad turned the spotlight toward the bases of the trees at the water's edge. He saw only a tangle of crawling roots, damp and shining, clinging to a scattering of boulders.

"It isn't an island at all," she said.

"Look, do you want to have dinner?" Conrad said.

"That's what I mean about the machine," Julie said. "You

just can't trust it." She turned her face against his chest. "I don't trust anything but you, Rick."

Conrad laid his arms uneasily about her and then his arms fell away. "Julie, what's the matter with you tonight?"

She didn't answer him; he could hear her breathing. There was the sound of the sea throbbing under the hull of the cruiser, a general stirring in the bridge about him as though he were moving, brushing things by in the darkness. "I'm hungry and dinner is going to be ruined," he said.

Her voice said, "Don't you ever want to just hold on to me, Rick?"

He touched her shoulders; her breath was going through the knit of his jacket, through his shirt and undershirt. He held her away. "We're going to drift right on to your island," he said. "Whether it's there or not."

"Okay," she said, and went away from him, through the door out of the bridge and down the ladder to the deck and gone into the cabin.

When he had the canvas sea anchor over the side he followed after her. The cabin was warm, paneled with mahogany. He ducked under the electric fixture that swung from the low ceiling and pulled his jacket off. They had plates of franks diced in with the beans at the table with a railing. He smelled the maple syrup in the beans. She had a bottle of Chianti open and she was picking at its wicker binding; she had her quilted yellow jacket off and her blouse glistened metallic blue against the deep brown walls and the leather upholstery.

"We'll go up to Sherwood Island," she said. "They have dancing on Friday nights. I'll show you off."

Conrad put his fork through the beans; the taste of maple syrup was oppressive.

She said, "I made them the way you like them."

"Yes. They're terrific," he said.

"Were you ever up to Sherwood Island, Rick?"

Conrad rinsed his mouth with the Chianti; it was ice-cold. "Did you have this in the fridge?"

"Of course. I was up there a couple of times this summer." Her fork skimmed and darted among the beans and pink cubes of frankfurter.

"Who did you go up there with?" he said.

"My folks. You didn't tell me anything about Newport. I was furious with you all summer long. One letter," she said.

Conrad raised his head; softly beneath him he felt the Pacemaker pivoting about the line of the sea anchor, turning to face into the north-running current. The electric fixture glazed the windows and he could not see the rocks of the island.

"You told me you didn't get out much this summer," Conrad said.

"No," she said. "A couple of the girls from school came over July fourth. We went to New York and saw *The Fantasticks.*" Julie drank her wine glass empty and let Conrad fill it up. "I guess there were a lot of parties in Newport."

"Not so many. A lot of fairies," Conrad said.

She touched her fork to her lips and then brushed the hair from her forehead with the back of her wrist. "You'd think there'd be lots of girls up there."

Conrad shook his head. "We didn't see too many."

She smiled. "I used to think how you were probably getting a lot of, well, experience up there."

"I'm sorry your parents gave up the house in Atlantic Beach. Did you like Southampton all that much?" Determinedly, Conrad slugged the maple beans down and sipped Chianti.

"Oh, if it weren't so hot," she said. She ran an end of rye bread through the sauce left on her plate. "Do you want some more?"

"No, thanks."

"I thought you were so hungry."

"My stomach's off," he said. "It's this boat." He rocked his elbows back and forth. "I can't eat with this—"

She put her plate on his and laid them behind her on the counter.

"I mean, did you have a lot of dates this summer?" Conrad finally said.

She had her hands on the table between them, one upon the other. "That's a silly thing to say, Ricky." She looked at her hands and Conrad looked at his wine glass and the Pacemaker moved gently in the press of the current.

"I guess that didn't sound the way I wanted it to sound," he said. "All I meant was, well . . ."

He chanced a look at her. Without the bulky jacket her bosom pressed to the glossy front of her blouse. Two dark, unmistakable points jabbed the cloth.

"I got a lot of phone calls," Julie said.

He looked away.

"But I always thought of you and said no, Ricky."

When he looked back she had slouched against the leather of the bench seat and the sheen of her blouse was uniform and still. "Look," he said, "Greenberg and I, we really kind of kept to ourselves, you know what I mean?"

She put her right hand flat on the tabletop and pushed it across the Formica until her fingertips were just touching his. "I know that, Rick."

"It was mostly a bunch of weirdos, you know. With the beards and the whole dirty bit. We saw some girls, but not like you talk to or and so forth." It was sounding compulsive, like a confession, but he didn't care.

"Let me have some more wine, would you, Rick?" she said.

He raised the Chianti bottle to her glass, poured. She reached for it, her nipples hit the front of her blouse.

"Don't spill it, Ricky."

"We went to a few parties. Sure. You had to, just about, to keep awake." He set the bottle down; better than half the wine was gone. "But it's the world's dullest place. No fooling. You thought yourself into a frenzy just lying down all day."

"I know how that can be. Cos Cob wasn't Vegas either."

"Yeah, I guess not." She had slouched again; the fall of her blouse assured him that she was wearing a brassiere after all. "I just wanted to tell you once and for all," he said.

"I'm glad, Rick," she said, and then had to cover her mouth with her hand. "Excuse me." Her glass was empty again.

"I think I'll get us under way," he said.

"Good. You do that. I'll polish this off and straighten up." She took hold of the long green neck of the Chianti bottle.

Conrad slid out from under the table and went through the cabin door before he remembered his sweater; when he thought of it, he didn't go back.

The hawser for the sea anchor rose knotted around a stanchion at the bow of the boat, bent over the guardrail and disappeared down into the water. Against the haze of moonlight that penetrated the clouds he saw that the island had already drifted a hundred yards to the south. East and north of him lay open sea. The night was a brilliant, pristine cold, and the moisture clinging to the nylon rope froze his hands around it as he pulled arm over arm. The bag of the sea anchor came up reluctantly, and the water from it clattered on the deck and soaked into his sneakers.

He was angry with himself and that made him haul the anchor around as if it weighed nothing at all. He never liked the way Greenberg talked about girls who didn't wear underwear and he knew Julie always did and he knew she wouldn't have gone to bed with him that afternoon if he had stood on his head. He really wanted to apologize and he was going to do that, and if he had wanted some he could have had plenty up at Newport, and he knew it and so did Greenberg. Julie knew he could have had all the experience he wanted and as long as she knew it that was all he cared about. Driving up to New Haven for the first day of freshman year his father had said it all. He had said, What does a dog know, Richie? A dog knows he wants to eat and take a drink and other things. You have to have respect. You'll meet lots of girls, some not so nice as Julie. I know what you think of Julie and if you have respect then, you can never tell, someday you and Julie might come to something. Conrad had understood that, and it didn't mean be a fairy, but just be a man about it and not an animal.

He threw the sea anchor into its locker beside the cabin and went up the stairs to the bridge again. He hit the starter and the diesels caught without hesitation, without the choke. He engaged the propeller drives and pressed the throttles forward to 3000 revolutions and looked down at the radar screen. The irregular circle of the island was fading behind them and toward starboard. They could run along the coast and turn in toward the shore at Sherwood Island, wherever that was.

Greenberg liked to brag and Conrad knew that, and when Greenberg ticked him off about Julie he wasn't afraid to tell Greenberg to shut the hell up, and that made him feel good. You couldn't let your senses guide you; it had to be your mind. You couldn't be an animal. He could have fooled around a lot and Julie wouldn't ever know a thing about it. But he didn't, and

Julie had to respect him and so did Greenberg and that was a better feeling than any cheap affairs. In his dreams sometimes he saw Julie naked but then her belly curved under unbroken like a mannequin's and so that didn't bother him. He shouldn't have thought the way he did when she showed her prom dress. And he liked to be able to tell Greenberg to shut up or else.

"Don't you want to come in closer to the shore so that we can watch for it?" Julie said. She hadn't put her jacket back on; Conrad could see her breath in the glow of the instruments. "Sherwood Island," she said. "I can tell it by sight but we won't be able to find it otherwise."

"We can't go in too close," he said. "It's dangerous at night."

She rapped her knuckles on the radar screen. "You've got your machine. What are you worried about?"

He could smell the Chianti on her breath. "Underwater rocks. The radar doesn't show them."

"You're a goose," she said.

He liked it when she called him that. "Better safe than sorry," Conrad said.

"It sees my island that isn't there and it can't see the rocks that are," she said. "Your silly machine." She swung the captain's stool out from behind him and perched next to him. "I like you, Richard," she said.

That was a familiar game and he swung easily into the catechism of it. "What do you mean?"

"I mean I'm fond of you."

"And what does that mean?"

"I mean that I feel close to you." She laughed.

"And what does that mean?"

"All right. I give up," she said. "What does that mean?"

He said, "It means you love me," and listened. He looked at her; she hadn't answered. Her eyes were pointed toward the windshield, and the reflection of the spotlights on the water rising about the cruiser gleamed in her eyes.

"I love you, Rick," she said.

"I love you, too," he said, but his smile slipped away.

She spoke louder, clearly, over the drone of the diesels. "You know that I was in love with you when I was seventeen," she said. "Three years is a long time. You'll be twenty-one."

"I always felt the way I feel, Julie." Her eyes glistened; he wasn't sure what to make of that. "Are you okay, Julie?"

"Sometimes I want you to touch me, Rick," she said. "This is a hard thing to tell you."

"Listen, you don't want to drink so much Chianti and eat your own cooking," Conrad said. He slapped her lightly on the back. What his fingers didn't find made him pull the hand away.

"You're afraid of rocks," she said. Her head turned in his direction, was half in darkness, half in the reflected, changing light.

He shrugged his shoulders, forced himself to face her. "That's just using your brains," he said.

"Are you afraid of other things?" Her voice became dim, was down among the sounds of the engines.

"Afraid of things like what?" The Pacemaker bucked against the water; together they held to the back of the captain's stool.

"I don't know," she said. "Spiders. The dark. Water. High places. Crazy things. Silly things."

Conrad watched her for a sign, but her face was calm, yielded no secrets. "None of those things," he said.

"What about snakes? Elevators. Little rooms. The number thirteen. The number nine."

Conrad shook his head. "None of those things either."

"Elephants? Are you afraid of mice, Rick? Lightning?"

"Nope."

"I don't want you to be afraid of me, Rick," she said.

He felt her hand come up, cupping the back of his neck. "Why should I be afraid of you, Julie?" He stood straight up, head up almost level with her own, his shoulders erect.

"I don't want you to be afraid of me, Rick," she said again, and her voice had become moist. Her free hand was among the buttons of her blouse and the blouse was coming undone. He held fast to her chair. "I love you so very much, Ricky, and I know you're frightened but I don't know why." She pulled the ends of her blouse out of her slacks and spread them; bared, her breasts poured toward him, moved at him. A nipple closed his eye, pressed to his eyelid. He felt the cold flesh grow warm in contact with his cheek; the nipple was a stone. He couldn't think.

"I want you touching me," she said. "I won't apologize. I won't let you apologize, Rick." She took his wrist, placed his fingers at the clasp and zipper of her slacks and guided them.

Then her slacks were open and she raised her hips and pushed them past her knees and kicked them aside. She brought his hands against her bare abdomen; her arms wrapped his face into her breasts.

Conrad felt the creases where her thighs began; she moved his fingers back and forth and that was the topology of where the rim of her panties lay. It was a familiar figure to him, fit neatly in overlay upon his dream of it. A well-remembered and a known thing, like the contours of her breasts just as he had imagined they would be.

She came off the high chair, drew him down with her against the icy rubber decking and covered his body with her own. She had his trousers parted and the cold floor aroused him. He had her body open and his own half-dressed just as he had always known he would. He wasn't worried about how they would feel about each other afterward. She was clumsy, but he didn't mind that, didn't hurry her. He felt himself against the warmest part of her and how her small muscles slowly gave. The slightest pressure, a very slight thing, and she so eager and so willing after all: to be viewed critically, with precision, with restraint. His mind gave him a crisp image of them locked in intercourse: his body smothering hers. Julie whimpered.

And then he had a vision of the Pacemaker, charging through the darkness of waters with its blind eye spinning atop the mast.

OUR WALTZ

——————————————————————————————

JUNIOR PROM NIGHT came white with snow; the parking lot and courtyard of the Three Judges Motel was buried under snow. The window felt cold enough to shatter under the pressure of Conrad's fingers and was dewy. Distant, ghostlike through the fall of snow, West Rock rose. The curlicues in the wrought-ironwork of the balcony railing had husks of ice; there were cocoons of snow in the corners of the window frame. Near the stairs and below, the Pontiac was drawn up, humpbacked with snow; snow lay in runners and risers on the steps. Conrad saw a man begin the steps. He was carrying a suitcase, and the brass lock fittings gleamed wet with the damp of snow. The man had his chin bent down into the collar of his overcoat. His breath curled. Snow edged his hat brim, lay in epaulets on his shoulders. The man's step was cautious, unsteady; he dragged his hand up the banister after him for balance and his glove sheared the banister's wool of snow.

Conrad reached through the parting of the venetian blinds; a blade's edge grazed his wrist. His palm turned the haze on the windowpane to droplets. The man came on. His suitcase had casters; at the head of the stairs he set the suitcase down and wheeled it beside him, leaning upon it. The chatter of metal and concrete came into the room with Conrad. The suitcase rolled, the man moved along the balcony, shuffling his feet and pushing up waves of snow with the prows of his shoes. He came past the window and did not look up. A fog of snow lifted off the roof of the motel office, wheeled twice around the blue VACANCY neon, and spun off to the northward, gone into the shale sky. The man went gliding toward the end of the balcony so that Conrad had to put his cheek against the windowpane to follow him, then around the turn, gliding down the far walkway, elegantly, gracefully, with his coattails ballooning after him. Then the man stopped.

Conrad squinted; the tip of his nose touched the windowpane, was frozen. Conrad hated that dumb, sodden feeling of cold. A rectangle of light glowed from the motel building into the snow. The snow crystallized, filled with needle points. He saw the shade of the man put the castered suitcase indoors. Then the man emerged from the room and came to the balcony's rail. He leaned out over the drifted cars of the parking lot. The man took his hat off and his head pivoted awkwardly on his neck as he turned his face up to the sky. He smiled and opened his mouth. A whirlpool of snow surrounded him, and his bald head glistened at the vortex. Conrad couldn't understand that; he couldn't understand how a man could love the cold that way. Then the man turned, seized his hat by the brim and scaled it into the room, followed it, and slammed the door.

Conrad let the venetian blinds go; they rang. He heard the sound of running water for the first time. He took a cigarette and

match from the night table and pulled the blankets up and bat-
tered the pillows on the bed erect. He stretched out, clamping
the cigarette in his teeth and pushing his hands in beneath the
elastic of his undershorts. His fingers were cold from resting
against the window; he tried to snare the hairs on his belly, but
his fingers couldn't hold them. He knew that the stranger's
fingers were frozen and he didn't see how the man could be so
pleased about that.

"Rick?" Julie's voice was thin above the rumble of the running water, small through the locked bathroom door.

"What do you want?"

"Rick?"

"What?"

"What time is it, Rick?"

"I don't know. Eight o'clock."

"Rick? Rick, please tell me the time."

He flung the pack of matches at the bathroom door; the
matches sailed, rising. Then they struck the door and fell, spinning, with broken wings. "Jesus, eight o'clock!"

"Rick?"

He sat up. "What?"

"Rick, are you getting ready?"

"Yes."

"I said, are you getting dressed?"

"Yes."

"Rick?"

He lay back, flicked the cigarette's ash to the floor.

"Rick?" The sound of running water stopped. "Rick?"

In the mirror above the dresser at the end of the bed he could
see himself laid out atop the blankets.

"Rick, are you out there?"

He heard the last drops of water tinkling as they hit the pool

121

in the bath. Over the closet doorknob he saw the tuxedo jacket covering the hanger that held the razor-edged pants. The tartan-blue bow tie was clipped to the jacket's lapel.

"Rick?"

In the mirror he saw himself stretched out in the tuxedo jacket and the pants with the stripe like an usher's or a bellboy's. He didn't think of the bath, of Julie's nude body. His eyes were shut in the mirror; his hands were folded calmly across his abdomen; his tasseled patent-leather shoes gleamed. He heard the sound of running water again.

The cigarette was gone in his image. His face seemed on the verge of smiling; the glow in his cheeks was rouge and his forehead and his chin were powdered smooth. He had just been shaved. His fingernails were manicured and lacquered.

Julie's voice began to hum. The song was "Belle of the Ball." A candle had replaced the night-light on the table near his bed. Julie's humming undulated behind a sound of shuffling feet. People were filing by him. In the mirror he saw their backs bent over as they passed him, their heads tucked down; he couldn't see their faces. Their footfalls pattered lightly, as if on marble— like the sound of snow against a windowpane. Julie's humming ended; he couldn't hear the water falling. He couldn't hear the sound of Julie humming. The snow was falling outside, hissing against the door. A single flake came through the roof somehow, swinging back and forth in the motionless air of the room. Like a microscope his eyes zeroed on that flake, discovering all its repetition of facets. The facets of it split the light up, then broke themselves into atoms. The flake was aimed directly at him, edged at him, sidled at him, swinging like a pendulum. He saw his shoes in the mirror; there was snow about the leading edges of his shoes, clinging like lichen. He saw the atoms in the crystal of the snowflake, rigid in the four corners of the rhomboid crystal like tiny solar systems. He was on one of the planetary electrons—in a New Haven on one of the electrons, in a motel room, laid out on a motel bed with a candle flame dancing at his right shoulder. There were men rolling a coffin along the balcony outside the room as they had once rolled his mother's coffin. A predatory snowflake was in the room with him, swinging toward him like a spider moving on its tangled prey.

Then the rhomboid crystal cracked. The snowflake was a falling drop of water, like the last dripping from a leaky bathtub faucet. The drop of water whistled, came down like a bomb and hit the candle flame and drowned it. Darkness broke like thunder. The motel room door crashed off its hinges, hammered down by snow. And white, lacy flakes of snow filled up the room with a numbing, torpifying death.

"Oh, Rick, really, please." Julie came to the edge of the bed; she had her frilled half-slip pulled up above the top of her strapless brassiere. Below the half-slip's trailing hem, her garters showed, her nylon stockings. The slip was snow-white and embroidered with flowers of ice. "Rick, that isn't fair."

"I'm getting ready," Conrad said. He rolled his legs over the side of the bed; the corners of his eyes stung.

"That isn't fair, Rick. It's called for eight-thirty."

"I know when it's called for." He held his fingers to his temples; his head was throbbing and his eyes stung.

"Well, Rick, you aren't getting dressed sitting there like that," Julie said. "If we're going at all, let's go."

Her stockings and her high-heeled shoes moved out of his sight. He heard the closet door open and the whisper as his plastic tuxedo bag brushed the wall. He heard the swish of skirts, like the sound of dancers brushing each other by. He had no feeling in his lap where his shorts pulled against his crotch. He had a sense of death. He shut his eyes against their stinging.

Conrad was dead. He was lying in state in the snarled motel room bed, stripped naked. The sheets were slush with his perspiration and stained. Someone was moving in the shadows of the room. Someone's quick fingers were deft with lipstick, nimble with mascara. Some fresh female thing was moving, lively in the dour room that held him, touching up the pallor of his cheeks with rouge and powder. A female thing was regenerated with his death, was rising from his corpse like a phoenix.

There were ritual cloths arrayed about the room: They were of silk and nylon and lace. A censer was gently swinging; its odor was Chanel. The room was a reliquary of erotica. In its focus his cadaver lay, slowly cooling, beyond passion. Beyond ever wanting to open Julie's narrow thighs again.

"Rick, do you want to go or don't you?"

"Cut it out." He struck her hand away. "In a minute I'm going to tell you to take your prom and go to the devil, Julie."

"It's your prom," she said. "And your tone of—"

"Shut up." He stood abruptly, pushed her aside, threw the bathroom door closed between them. Blindly, he went to the sink and turned the water on. It drove down on his hands from the neck of the faucet, hot, aerated, a torrent of bubbles. Steam rose, coated his face. His face felt slick, greasy. The water seared into his hands, burned his skin red. He brought up water in his cupped palms, flung it back at himself. He choked a towel. There was a small frosted window in the bathroom with him. It was the color and opacity of Julie's half-slip. He was going to smash his fist through that window, shatter it. He yanked the bathroom door open.

Julie was sitting in the chair beneath the drawn venetian blinds. The beaded top of her gown held her bosom rigid. Its skirt was white, draped in folds over her legs to the floor. The skin of her arms and shoulders glowed. Her dark hair was spun above her head; she smiled.

He hadn't seen her look that way before. He took the hanger with the tuxedo, sank his stiff fingers and tore the plastic away. "Well, I'm sorry, Julie."

"For what, Rick?"

"Nothing." Other times in a formal gown she hadn't been convincing, had looked uncomfortable, unnatural. The gowns had been alien to her, hadn't moved when she moved, had seemed like armor. Conrad bent and pulled his socks up to his calves; then he stepped into the ridiculous pants with the satin stripes, one leg at a time. "You look swell," he finally said.

"Thank you. You look tired, Ricky."

"It's okay," he said.

She said, "You should have waited."

He buttoned the black suspenders before and behind the trousers. "Waited for what?" He felt absurd without the confidence of a belt.

She was inspecting the polish on her fingernails; she didn't look at him. "Until we got back."

He tossed the plastic wrapping of the frilled, effeminate shirt aside.

"It just seems anticlimactic now," she said. Still looking down at her fingernails, she was smiling. "I guess that's a play on words."

Halfway into the shirt, he stopped to stare.

She said, "Let's dance every dance tonight, won't we? Even the waltzes."

He plucked his studs off the top of the dresser and held them out to her. "Do these." All the dances, watching her pretty face and not wanting her body against him.

When she bent beneath his chin with her hands clever with the buttonholes she said, "I'll hold the very edge of my gown and we'll stand far apart and let our heads swing."

"That's dumb," he said. "I can't waltz. Nobody will. We'll be the only ones."

"That's all right and you can so." She raised her face. "Rick, I know what's wrong, don't I? The edge is off it for you now, isn't it?"

"What are you talking?"

"You don't have to pretend with me." She buttoned his collar and clipped the bow tie to its wings. "It's crazy to have a prom in February anyhow," she said. "I despise snow. I always have."

"Next year. The senior prom's in June." He watched her step away from him and lift the folds of her gown, swinging toward the door.

"It's fine to wear a dress like this now and again," she said, and looked back at him across her bare shoulder.

He pulled his jacket on. The collar of the shirt bit his throat and the hard cuffs grated his wrists. The cummerbund did not satisfy him. He brought her tulle stole from the closet and both their raincoats. He turned to her and she had her head tilted to one side.

"Remember your high school prom and mine?" she said. "I couldn't stand them, Rick. We looked so stupid in the formal clothes. I wished we'd gone to the movies instead." She shook her head and the mass of her hair trembled. "But I think that jacket actually fits you, Rick. Haven't we grown up together?"

When he opened the door she looked out and then leaned against him and in the cold wind he felt the warmth of her body through the skimpy jacket and frilled shirt, through both their raincoats. "You may have to carry me to the car, you know," she said. He put the tips of his fingers against the side of her throat. "All this is part of it, too, Ricky," she said.

He did carry her at last, holding her tight against him. Down the stairs and into the parking lot, threading their way among the cars, avoiding drifts that blocked their path, doubling back, going around one car, and then another and another while the snowflakes spiraled down about them.

WHAT ELSE I DID
ON MY SUMMER VACATION

———————————————————————

DEAR JULIE:

I always thought that French postcards had pictures of naked women on the back. I know what the Eiffel Tower looks like. Send me some naked women instead and bring home some of those paperbooks with the orange covers that we talked about.

My father is out in the house on Atlantic Beach for the months of July and August, so Greenberg is of course staying with me at the apartment. He has to go up to New Haven for the start of football practice before Labor Day weekend, so I presume to be living alone for about a week. Greenberg says that you will probably come home with some run-down Count in tow. I am sure that you are behaving yourself and keeping your promises.

The way we work it is this. I buy the food and Greenberg is the cook and afterwards we split washing the dishes every couple of days. You can pretty much make anything in the world taste okay by putting it in a frying pan with a stick of butter and some of that pepper that comes in flakes. We have found a way to make fine iced coffee which includes saving what's left over and freezing that into ice cubes for the next batch. We are using the Chinese laundryman over on York and 77th, being cheaper. Our last load he wanted $10 for the whole batch and I was ready to pay but Greenberg told him at that price he could keep it and we started to walk out. So we paid $3 each.

A few guys from Yale are living down in St. Mark's Place which is around the Village and we ran into them at a bar called Gogi's (Googi's?) which is the best integrated bar in the city of New York. They walked us over to a place by the name of the Hair Club which is the dirtiest bar in New York with educated people in it. You don't want to drink anything but bottle beer in places like these and then you don't want to use one of their glasses but there isn't any choice. When we were leaving the Hair there was a police car outside with its cherry top spinning and the cops had two big colored guys, and a little Italian fellow was holding a handkerchief against his forehead. The cops had the two guys turn out their pockets on the hood of the police car. They had four or five wristwatches each and were shoved into the back of the police car which drove off like blazes. Over on MacDougald (sp?) Street later on I saw a man throw a bus stop sign at some other guy and knock him flat out cold and run away. Greenberg was saying how you can give me New York, give me New York anytime. I said how I thought New York City was not to be beaten and one of the Yalies with us said he'd stick with L.A. Greenberg said if you don't like New York why the hell don't you go home? and the guy said he sure would like to but he didn't have any money.

The other day a woman came to the door and said did we have any old clothes for the poor, naked Tunisians. Greenberg said sure I've got plenty of old clothes but I'm wearing them. He went out on the balcony and we drank a few Cointreaus. The tide in the East River was going upstream then and the air was clear all the way across Welfare Island into Queens and you could see the jets wheeling above Idlewild. Greenberg said he figured that if his father was still alive he'd be getting a car for school in the fall. I said sure but what would we do with two cars? He said we'd figure something. I said well would you want to buy half interest in the Pontiac for fifty bucks, and we'll put the registration in both names and you can kick in on the insurance. He tossed the rest of his drink over the edge of the balcony and said he thought he'd take his spikes over to Central Park and run the track a couple of times. I said that sounded like a good way to kill the afternoon. We made up some salami sandwiches and put a couple of cans of Miller's in the Scotch cooler with some ice and walked toward Fifth Avenue. We had our sweat shirts with the YALE on them and shorts. We hid our sneakers and the cooler in some bushes and took off on the bridal path for downtown.

Greenberg chugs along pretty good for a lineman and I can still run about the way I did when I was in training. We got a good sweat up by 59th Street and stretched out in the grass. Greenberg said we should have brought the sandwiches and the beer with us. I said I don't know how we could have done that. He said on our backs. I said you should have thought of that back at 76th. Some little Negro kid came by and wanted to shine our shoes but when he got a good look at them and our sweat shirts wanted to know if we played football. Greenberg said he did and I was on the track team. I said I used to be on the track team and I wasn't any more. Greenberg said how I could probably run a hundred yards faster than any man in the city of New York and maybe the whole state. I said I didn't know about that and the kid said his name was Eddie and he didn't believe that. Greenberg said that he was a lineman, a tackle. Eddie said did he play with the varsity and Greenberg said yes. Eddie said he wanted to be a sprinter but he liked football too. He said he was going to be a freshman at Boys High School in September and that he figured probably college after that and maybe Yale. Then he saw some potential customers and ran off after them. Greenberg and I walked back uptown. Our sneakers and the sandwiches and the Scotch cooler had been stolen, so we walked the seven long blocks back to York Avenue with our spikes scraping on the pavement.

That night my father called to invite us out to the beach house for the weekend and I said okay. Greenberg was in the shower when the phone rang and when I asked him afterward he said he was going home to Brooklyn and help his mother with her garden instead but thanks. Greenberg made minute steaks in the frying pan for dinner and we stood a can of corn on the stove's burners with its label ripped off. Greenberg made a pitcher of whiskey sours and we drank that and ate the steaks and corn on the balcony overlooking the city. Greenberg said how he loved New York. Evening, and the lights in Queens and in the hospitals on Welfare Island came on.

We got the doorman to have the car brought around and drove down to St. Mark's Place and rang for the bunch of Yalies but they were out. We tried them at the Hair Club and around but no luck. We hit a place called the Ninth Circle which has a barrel of peanuts in the middle of the floor that you just help yourself as long as you keep ordering drinks. We had a few beers, sat down with a couple of people who said they were all at the Columbia U writers' conference. Greenberg got cozy with one of the girls who was almost as tall as him and very skinny and peculiar with a synthetic British accent. She recited a poem of hers which was in fact by Randall Jarell (sp?) and which I studied freshman year in Structure & Style. Greenberg said that was a pretty fine poem actually and I said it was terrific and did she write "The Death of the Ball Turret Gunner" too? She wanted to know what I meant by that. Greenberg kicked me under the table and he's not as stupid as I thought. Her name was *Annice*—doesn't that kill you? She had to spell it out for us, but I think she got it off a cereal box really or out of Proust. Greenberg said he was a fan of William Carlos Williams and I said I liked Ted Williams. She said she admired Henry James and I said Jesse James. Greenberg said Nathanael West and I said Mae West. She said Ayn Rand and I said Remington. Greenberg said excuse me Connie listen I have got to talk to you aside a moment if you don't mind. We got up and went toward the men's and Greenberg said hey you really know how to hurt a guy don't you? I said listen you get tied up with the craziest broads in existence. He said mind your own business. I said you're my business and besides next thing she'll say she wrote the "Faerie Queene" and draws Little Orphan Annie. He said what the hell do you care if she says she owns the loving Brooklyn Bridge? I said well in light of your hyperbole I suppose you might say I couldn't care less and it doesn't make any difference. He said well then what about it Connie? I said look if you want to go to hell I won't stop you. We sat back down.

She started talking about Thomas Wolfe. I was going to say

Jimmy Foxx and Twentieth Century Foxx and Smokey the Bear but instead kept a dark silence. The whole place began to strum guitars and sing "She'll Be Comin' Round the Mountain." I shook my head. Greenberg asked for the car keys and I handed them over. He said wait right here and left with the girl. I sat for about one hour. One of the guys at the table wanted to talk about Malamud but I said I didn't know who that was. Then he wanted to talk about Tolstoi and I said who was he? The guy said don't you go to college? and I said no. He said what do you do? I said I was a barber. He said haven't you ever heard of Styron? I said was he a barber too? The guy said holy smoke and I said if he ever came by 46th and Lexington to stop in and I'd give him a trim at no charge. He said that was pretty square of me. I said well I'm just trying to be friendly. He was a little fat guy and his chins covered his tie knot but he was reasonably neat and just lonely. He said that he went to Oberlin and I said what was that? and he said a college in Ohio. I said I had been in Ohio once. He said what do barbers think about Blake and Addison? I asked him what poets thought about the White Sox' chances for the pennant. He said he didn't mean anything by that and I shouldn't be offended. I said what did he mean? He asked me if I wanted another beer and I said bring it on. He said it was just story material and that all his friends were writers and when did he get to talk to a barber? I said I didn't know.

He said once he had been in love with a girl who broke his heart. I said his story was very touching. He said he was writing a collection of poems about her and when it was published she would know what she was missing. I said I'd bet she already does. He said do you think so? I said don't you think she's probably writing a book of poems about you? He said he'd never thought of that, but maybe I was right. I said sure I was. When you're a barber you talk to so many people you get to know people pretty well. He said sure but only men. I said I was a hairdresser for a long time before I became a barber so I knew women inside and out. He thought I meant some double meaning by that and laughed and hit the tabletop. I said I was leaving and he said wasn't I going to wait for my friend? I said I'd just met Greenberg outside and come in with him. He said he'd be dropping up to Lex and 46th was it? I said come on in and I'll give you my supreme deluxe. We shook hands and I went outside.

It was one of those nights. Warm with cooler breezes. The city smelled clean, very well-dressed people were moving on the streets. Girls in bright-colored dresses. I had a pair of old jeans and a sweater on. Nobody stared. I waited by the curb for Greenberg for a while and then walked over to the subway and took the Lexington express uptown. About 2 A.M. Greenberg came home and we got a couple of beers for a nightcap and sat out on the balcony with the lights off in the apartment. We didn't talk much. I was watching the lights of Queens and started thinking about how Paris probably looks almost the same except Julie's there and I'm 3,000 miles east into last night. Greenberg said did I think that shoeshine boy had gotten our sandwiches and Scotch cooler? I said probably not him but somebody just like him. Greenberg said he thought so. He said he thought that was okay with him. I said I didn't care either. He said that the girl poet was living in a one-room flat below Delancey Street with one crummy chair, no sheets and a 10-watt bulb. I said I didn't think I'd want to live that way. Greenberg covered his eyes with his hands and said he hoped to Jesus he'd never have to live that way. I said that I was sorry as hell for what I'd said about selling him a share of the Pontiac that morning. He said to forget it. Then he said we were goddam lucky that we didn't

have to lie to anyone about anything and I told him to shut up.
We drank our beers and I told him that I could hardly wait to
see you again. Greenberg said it would be more like it when we
were back in New Haven.

RICK

ALL AFTERNOON
I HAVE BEEN DREAMING
OF A PARTY

————————————————————————

The GREEN DOOR closed behind them and they were in what seemed to be a cloakroom. Through the facing archway there were diners in separate paneled rooms off a center foyer. There was a din of plates and glasses and flatware. Julie preferred to carry her blue linen coat to the table with her; Conrad's father wasn't wearing a coat and neither was Conrad. Conrad's father said, "Well, I haven't seen the inside of this place for must be almost thirty years."

A balding, underfed waiter shuffled them through the foyer and to a side room and a tiny low table without cloth and three uncomfortable ladder-backed chairs. The tabletop was carved with an infinity of cursive initials, and years of stain and polish had soaked deep into its straight grain. Julie put her hands on the table before her; there were blue-and-white painted rowing sweeps hung from the ceiling and Conrad's father had his head thrown back and had put on his glasses to read the lettering on the paddles.

"I wish I'd been here before," Julie said.

"They don't let women in," Conrad said. That wasn't true. "Only in the summer," Conrad said by way of concession. Julie was busy with her hands along the whittled edge of the table. She wasn't looking at him. That was fine with Conrad.

"We could have driven up," she said. "It's not so far."

"What do you mean?" Conrad said.

"From New York during the summer." She was wearing a light gray suit with very narrow lines; the suit had a choker of dark gray and a stripe of dark gray down the front to the hem of the jacket, like a West Point cadet. "You know," she said.

"Look, they close most of the summer," Conrad said. "You can't tell."

"We could have called, checked."

"I'm very proud," Conrad's father said. He put his eyeglasses in a pocket of his vest and sat back, folding his hands in his lap with his elbows resting on the arms of the chair. The wall behind him was a montage of varsity team captains straddling a piece of the true Yale fence.

"I want you to know I'm very proud of you, Richie," his father said. He touched some perspiration away from his forehead with his napkin. "I wish your mother could have been here, but that wasn't the way it was going to be. So it wasn't." Conrad's father lit a cigar. "Mrs. Greenberg was down the other end of the row we were in," he said.

"I saw her," Conrad said. "She wished me lots of luck."

"She hasn't had much luck," Conrad's father said. He rubbed his napkin across the nape of his neck.

"I wouldn't have come," Julie said. She shook her head and

the chips of turquoise in her earrings glittered. "I would have wanted to be a million miles away."

"I don't know why the hell she had to come," Conrad said.

"She probably wrote for a ticket," Julie said. "Can you imagine that? I couldn't, I mean, writing for a ticket?"

"Well, I feel sorry for her," Conrad's father said. He looked at the end of his cigar for a while; a slip of thin smoke trailed from its perforation and rose among the rowing sweeps. "Benighted woman," he said. "One year the husband and the next year the son. Take a lesson from that."

"She made me want to cry," Julie said. "Honestly. Right there in front of everyone."

"We always think we've had our share of grief," Conrad's father said. "But then another—"

"I don't know what the hell she was doing here," Conrad said.

His father looked up at him. "All right, son," he said.

A waiter came by and handed them menus on small printed cards. Conrad's father ordered them all martinis but Conrad asked for a whiskey sour instead and Julie wanted a ginger ale. When the drinks came they touched glasses over the middle of the table and some of Julie's ginger ale spilled into the uncovered sugar bowl and curdled there.

"Here's to your new life, Richie," Conrad's father said. "Your life is beginning all over again. You know that, don't you?"

Conrad didn't say anything; the whiskey sour was dry, bitter. All afternoon he had been dreaming of a party.

"I think I'll have the rarebit, folks," his father said.

"I was thinking of that, too," Julie said.

Conrad didn't know what he wanted. The type on the menu

was too small for him to read and the menu was too heavy for
his hands and he put it down.

His father hauled his watch out of a vest pocket on the end of
a slim gold chain. "We want to get back to New York before the
rush hour," he said.

"I thought the ceremony was just elegant, didn't you, Rick?"
Julie said.

Richard Conrad was dreaming of a party. Greenberg was at
that party. He was nineteen, as he had been when Conrad had
met him, a great and powerful man, swollen in the arms and
neck and shoulders. They had walked out together through the
September dawnrise at the party's end; Greenberg had said how
they could grab a bite. They sat over toasted Danish and coffee
at the Greek's and spoke only of important things: Conrad
hoped to make the freshman track team in the dashes and
Greenberg threw the shot; why the upperclassmen were so surly;
how you didn't put a weekend date up in the Gaines Hotel.
Walking back to the Old Campus later on, Greenberg had told
him about his stamp collection and Conrad thought of the way
Greenberg's enormous hands had unfolded the napkin into his
lap as delicately as if it had been a flower.

Conrad's father ran his napkin around the collar of his shirt.
"I guess they could let tradition go long enough to install central
air conditioning," he said. "Julie, do you want another ginger
ale?"

"No, thank you."

"I don't know how you sit there in a wool suit and keep so
cool," Conrad's father said.

"That's my feminine wiles," Julie said.

A waiter leaned in beside Conrad's father. "Well, make it two
rarebits and what do you want, son?"

"Oh, the rarebit." Conrad passed the menu along.

"Then it's three." The waiter moved away.

"You haven't said much, son. Contemplating?" Conrad's father touched him on the shoulder.

Conrad nodded. He was staring at Julie and she was smiling with her face bent down over the ginger ale as if she knew he was staring and thinking about her. Her profile was sharper than it had been four years before. The jacket of her suit went forward at her bust and gently fell. Oversized curls of her dark hair clung to the side of her face. No perspiration shone on her forehead; her ease shook him.

"It's a shame your Grandpa Kelly couldn't have been here," Conrad's father said. "They ought to let you have three tickets instead of two."

"I thought they did, Mr. Conrad," Julie said.

"Well, I wish you wouldn't call me that," Conrad's father said. "It won't be too long now. You could call me Dad."

Beneath the table Conrad felt her leg brush his, then lean against his.

Julie laughed and said, "Oh, I don't know."

"You're afraid of jinxes," Conrad's father said. "Well, I can't say I blame you. Richie's quite a man. Not that I really approve of you quitting college for him. But it's just a pity that his mother—"

"Stop it," Conrad said.

His father paused just as he was, with his martini halfway from the table to his lips. "Now, Richie, you don't—"

"Just cut it out," Conrad said.

"All right, son. Whatever you say." Conrad's father took a mouthful of his drink; Conrad saw him look at Julie. "It's your day after all," his father said.

"And you looked so fine in your robes," Julie said. "When

Dean Maynard took you aside, what did that old goat have to say?"

"Yes, I meant to ask you that, son. What did Maynard say to you?"

"Nothing." Between them, Conrad saw the glare of the sun coming through the windowpanes in four blocks of yellow smoke. Outside, mute, the elms dotting the pavement before the Law School swayed like chanters with locked arms.

"Oh, he said something," Julie said. "I saw his lips moving and he had you there for quite a while."

"What did he say, son?"

"He said, 'Congratulations.' "

"Oh, he said more than that, Ricky."

"I don't know what he said." Conrad sipped off most of his whiskey sour. "I wasn't paying attention."

"Well, that's a fine thing to say."

Then the waiter moved around the table and Julie was cutting into the toast submerged beneath her rarebit and a forkful was gliding toward her lips. A tear of rarebit clung to Julie's mouth an instant before she struck it away with her napkin.

"Why don't you eat, son?"

"Rick, it's just marvelous."

Richard Conrad was dreaming of a party. Greenberg was at that party. A month after the party's end they met again and realized they hadn't spoken since the coffee and toasted Danish at the Greek's café. Both of them felt uncertain of themselves; Greenberg said something about the beginning of practice for the track team and Conrad said that he surely wasn't going to miss that. Conrad said that they ought to catch a movie at the Roger Sherman, but Greenberg had seen it. They took a bus out Whalley Avenue instead and hit some golf balls at a driving range and then grabbed a pizza at Joe Pepi's. Greenberg insisted that they have a couple of beers but the waiter wouldn't serve them so they drank Coke and talked about whether the mixer at Connecticut College would be any worthwhile. Conrad explained about how Julie was going to Connecticut College next year maybe and Greenberg said she must be pretty terrific from what Conrad said. Conrad said he guessed she was. Conrad showed her picture and Greenberg nodded several times and stuck his thick mouth together. Then Greenberg told about how he got pussy for the first time when he was a junior in high school and how he hadn't gotten any since. Conrad said something about traveling in Europe over the summer and Greenberg said that would cost a barrel of dough and Conrad changed the subject.

Walking back to the dormitories after, Greenberg said he figured that he'd be going to law school after graduation if he could get a scholarship. Conrad didn't know anything about scholarships, but said that he'd applied for one and been turned down. Greenberg said how that was tough and what was Conrad going to major in? Conrad told him chemistry but he didn't know whether to take a B.S. or stick it out for the five-year engineering thing. Greenberg said he ought to check some of the grad students at Gibbs Lab and see what they thought. Conrad figured he'd ask his freshman counselor. Greenberg didn't think much of his own freshman counselor. Conrad said he had an eight o'clock class the next morning. Greenberg thought he would get himself a malted down at the Buttery before he hit the hay. Conrad told him good-night.

"First, we're all packing off for a good two weeks on the Cape," Conrad's father was saying. "Provincetown or something like that. Maybe sleep a couple of days at Martha's Vineyard." He pushed the last of his rarebit onto his fork with the end of a seeded roll. "Julie, you can come if your folks will look the other way. Traveling with two bachelors, I mean." He laughed and looked at his martini glass and drank some water.

"That depends on Rick," Julie said. "If he wants to be alone or have me go along."

"Julie, you're being too polite with him," Conrad's father said. He rekindled his cigar. "Got to put your foot down, be firm. Tell him that you're coming. Don't let him get out of your sight. I wouldn't let him get out of your sight, you follow me?"

Conrad moved the tines of his fork through the cold rarebit in the pewter dish before him. A brackish crust was forming on the cheese.

"Do you want me to, Rick?" she said. "I mean to come to the Cape with you?"

"Tell him, Julie," Conrad's father said. "Go on, tell him, don't ask."

"No, it's up to Rick," she said.

The yellow fat from inside Greenberg's corpse spreading on the blacktop of Route 9. The Pontiac gutted to the color of petrified wood. My gigantic, delicate friend. Your rarebit viscera.

"Rick?"

Conrad felt his father's hand upon his own. "Now, Rick," his father said.

About them in the room, families knotted tables like their own. There were drafts of laughter; someone stained a tie. The men wore new suits, mostly herringbones. Some of the women wore sprays of roses about their bosoms and bright hats with collars of lace veil. There was a general congeniality; men shook hands from table to table. Women touched their fingertips to their lips and smiled.

"When I graduated from this place I remember feeling very empty," Conrad's father said. "I felt full of endings, Richie. Just like you do. I got over that." He balled his napkin and set it

143

alongside his plate. "There's so much to do. Get a job. Think about marriage. You know how I feel about Julie. You get caught up in new things. Your new life. This was only an episode. You'll see that in a couple of days, a week."

Julie brushed the trailing hairs from above his brow. Conrad was having a dream.

"I don't mean to run it down, Richie," Conrad's father said, and smiled. "You can't be a boy all your life, you know. You have to look ahead to your responsibilities."

Conrad was dreaming of a party. Greenberg was at that party. He was nineteen, had fists like bowling balls, a stupendous nose. They saw each other often during the track season, roomed together before meets when the team bedded down in a motel. Made up how they would be roommates for sophomore year and after that. Then Conrad missed Greenberg for a few days and the track coach said Greenberg's father had passed away. Conrad had wanted to send a note, but he didn't have Greenberg's address in New York. He got the address from the registrar and then he didn't send a note after all. And Greenberg came back to New Haven on a Sunday evening and they went out to the Old Heidelberg for dinner and a pitcher of beer.

They talked mostly about next Saturday's track meet with Brown. Conrad said he was meeting Julie in Providence; that she would see the races and so on and take the train back to New Haven with him afterward. Conrad thought of suggesting that Julie could bring a friend from high school for Greenberg, but decided to skip that, only it popped out of him and Greenberg said no he'd pass that up thanks. Greenberg had met Julie a while before and said he thought she was pretty fine and an honest person. Conrad said he thought that too. Greenberg said he was pretty sure Conrad would marry her and Conrad thought he was probably right. Then Greenberg drank off two glasses of beer, one after the other.

It got to around closing time and all the tables in the Heidelberg emptied out and Greenberg bought a fresh pack of cigarettes. Conrad wanted to tell him how he was sorry about his father dying, but he didn't know what to say. He wished that he had at least written the condolence note—even if he never mailed it—so that he could just say what was in the note and it would sound okay. Then Greenberg said he sure had to see the financial-aid department director first thing Monday morning and Conrad said he would walk him over after breakfast but Greenberg said that was all right. Then Greenberg told all over again about the time he had gotten pussy during his junior year in high school and Conrad nodded his head a few times and said, Is that right?

When the Old Heidelberg closed they drifted around the Old Campus and then walked up to the library and back by way of Sheffield Hall. Greenberg looked at the stars and said how he was going to take Introduction to Astronomy for an elective the next year. Greenberg said he sure wished to hell that his father hadn't died and Conrad said he sure wished that too. Greenberg said that things were pretty goddam mysterious and Conrad said they really were. Greenberg said they ought to get back and Conrad dropped him at his dormitory and went back to his own room. A week before summer vacation began, Conrad's mother died of Hodgkin's disease; he was pretty upset about that, but he didn't let on to Greenberg.

Conrad's father paid the check and they were in the cloakroom again and Julie was wrestling her blue linen coat and Conrad had the green door open for her. It was a good, warm June day and the elm trees were full of leaves and there were breezes among the leaves that made the humidity bearable.

"Morey's hasn't changed a dot," Conrad's father said. "The food. The selfsame menu I remember." He looked at Conrad. "Well, I suppose my memory is a little liable to suggestion."

"It was very nice," Julie said. She walked between them; they headed down York Street toward where Conrad's father had parked the station wagon. "And thank you," Julie said.

"This girl," Conrad's father said. "So proper. I expect she'll civilize you, Richie, in spite of your upbringing."

Conrad didn't say anything; he thought he saw his father wink at Julie.

"Well, I'll be leaving you," his father said at the station wagon. Conrad had Davenport College behind him; the room he had lived in was behind him and he didn't entirely understand what his father was saying. "I'll be scooting off," his father said. Julie was trying to conceal her smile. Conrad heard Davenport College behind him: the breezes among the petals of ivy, doors slamming, shutters banging stone, water running in the pipes between the walls, the grass in the courtyard grinding up through the soil. "You'll have to find your own way home," his father said, and pushed something into Conrad's hand.

Julie said, "Surprise!" and kissed him on the chin and pushed him around sideways. Something was glittering in his hand and tinkling. Keys.

"You're a Yale alumnus now," his father said, and grabbed the hand that held the keys and pumped it. "You should have transportation befitting. Well?"

The white Pontiac convertible behind the station wagon was new, had all the June sun on it, shimmered.

Julie laughed and poked him in the side. "He can't talk, can you, Rick?"

"That's all right, son. Thank me when you get your words

together." His father opened the door of the station wagon. "Julie drove the wagon up and I tailed her, so she's earned a kiss." He pulled the car door closed after him. "You two get a fancy dinner in New York and some dancing and I'll see you late tonight." He put the station wagon in gear, backed up, and then moved out into the traffic.

"Isn't it a bomb?" Julie said. The top of the convertible was down; she ran around to the passenger side and hopped in. "Come on, Ricky."

Conrad let the keys fall into the pocket of his jacket. "I'd better check we haven't forgotten anything," he said.

"Oh, we've got everything and it's getting late, Rick. Come on. Please. Let's get out of here."

"I want to take a look," he said.

"Rick." She tightened up her face. "Okay, go on and hurry up about it, will you?"

"Sure."

"And hurry."

He went up the two steps, under the stone arch. The street noise drifted and disappeared, the courtyard spread between the dormitory buildings and the college dining hall. He passed someone he knew; the boy spoke to him; he ignored the boy. He went rapidly. The broken fieldstone walk was familiar to his step. Through the door to the entryway, up to the first landing, left at door 1271, inside.

The stillness of it held him, the dust in the grooves of the bare floor, the empty fireplace. The peace of it: the simple whitewashed paneling. The bare staple furniture: two university chairs beside the desks, the striped and abandoned mattresses through the paired bedroom doors. He had been dreaming of a party.

Julie was at that party; he remembered that now. Greenberg

147

was at that party and there was a sloppy girl named Amy from Wellesley. Greenberg told him how he got bare pussy from her and that they were in love. Conrad said she was the genuine hard article. Greenberg drank a full pint of bourbon neat from a glass with the Davenport College crest baked on in blue and white. He told a joke about the women in the Salvation Army. Conrad laughed until he got a pain in his chest and that made him wonder again whether Hodgkin's disease was hereditary. Greenberg said was it all right to take the car because Amy had to be back in Boston before morning. Conrad said sure, he had just better put in gas and not regular or any junk like Super Jenny. Greenberg said what was he worrying about? Conrad walked Julie back to the Taft Hotel and the police knocked on the door of 1271 half an hour later and first drove him up on Route 9 and then back to Westville Hospital and took him down to the basement. They pulled back a sheet, but Conrad said he didn't know for sure and they wanted to know if Greenberg was registered for the draft so that they could check fingerprints. But Conrad told them that after all they didn't have to bother about that.

Conrad was dreaming of a party. Julie was at that party. She was wearing a lavender dress with pearls and her shoes were lavender. She had taken off her shoes for dancing and her bosom did not press very hard against the dress. Greenberg was dancing with Julie and she was tiny in the hook of his arm, very thin and almost boyish. Then someone came into the room and the phonograph needle squealed across the record and the music stopped. Everyone was looking at Conrad. Then they drifted off toward the sides of the room. A woman was in the doorway; a stout, short woman in a bulky black dress with white touches at the collar and sleeves. The woman was carrying a large leather handbag and wore flat shoes; she had no shape, but a roundness, an unpleasant nose.

"I'm glad to see you're still here, Richard," the woman said. "I didn't want to break right in on you after the ceremony."

"That's all right," Conrad said; 1271 closed stuffy upon him.

"I wrote Dean Maynard and told him," the woman said. She didn't sit down, but stood leaning at the doorknob. "I'm not interrupting?"

"No," Conrad said. He pulled out one of the desk chairs. "Won't you have a—"

"No, thank you very much. I have a train coming." She changed her pocketbook to the other hand. "As soon as I saw the ticket I knew. Even with no letter," she said. "You're a very generous person, sonny."

Conrad didn't know what to say; he put his hands in his pockets; the keys to the new Pontiac rang. "I'm glad you enjoyed it," he said.

"No, I don't say that," the woman said. "I thought of what should I be doing up at Yale now, after these last months. But I'll tell you I thought of your own dear mother in the grave and that broke my heart for you." She smiled and nodded. "Oh, sure, I know." Then she was coming up to him and her heavy fingers brushed his face. "It wasn't that, you think. So brave," she said. "You all are." She went back to the door and Conrad closed his eyes.

"Remember me to your dear father, please. And thank you and you'll always be in my thoughts. Goodbye."

His eyes opened when he knew that he was alone. Through the window he saw her going down the fieldstone walk toward the archway and Julie passed her coming toward him. Julie stopped and turned to watch her go.

149

Conrad sat down in the desk chair. He saw Julie's body beneath her linen coat and gray cadet suit; her body had filled, matured, had lost its slender, boyish stride, was alien. He had a dream of the new Pontiac with all its unfamiliar dials twitching and its foreign entrails clacking. Julie left his field of vision and he heard the entry door slam and her sharp heels snapping at the concrete floor of the hallway. He laced his feet tight behind the legs of the chair and he closed his fists around the arms of the chair and he sat there in the quiet before Julie came into 1271, with the dust in the corners of the windowpanes and the warm light filling up the room.

I AM NEVER MERRY WHEN
I HEAR SWEET MUSIC

I

Conrad emerged from below ground at 77th Street, on the corner of Lexington Avenue. The long shadows of late afternoon, early evening, floated above the sidewalk, cooling the city down. Escape from the glass and aluminum of Maislin Chemical, Inc. White-brick apartment houses, doormen with Plantagenet bearing, the dapper shops tucked cleverly into the buildings' hips. Friday night. Soon the lights would be coming on. Tinker's and Spark's Pub. Frey's Bar. All the pretty girls, all the young men in worsteds and rep ties. Conrad walked. The pale-faced white-brick buildings; fenced sidewalk trees, dwarfed with malnutrition, springing leaflets of green. Past Third Avenue where the urban renewal dwindled into renovated brownstones with a pretense of mosaic facing. Across the street. Auto horns and impatient faces, ties askew and wilted collars. The ritual of week's end. At Second Avenue he went under the humpbacked awning, into the black Formica and tufted red leather, the air-conditioned splendor of the Golden Star pizzeria and his father's table.

"So here he is. Son, you seem to need a bath."

"I'm okay, Dad."

"Do you want a beer? Have a Manhattan, will you, and shake the straw out of your hair." His father stretched back in the booth, yawning. His father's cord jacket and vest were lightning-blue, every crease razor-edged into place; his handkerchief and tie were gray and carefully matched. "Charlie, bring us on another two Manhattans, would you?" his father said.

"Oh, just a Miller's for me, Dad."

"Don't worry about it, son," his father said. "This is my party."

"That's not—"

"Payday," his father said. "Two Manhattans, Charlie. I'm for celebrating every chance I get." The dark, stringy waiter left them. His father lit a cigar. Conrad hadn't ever seen him in that suit; it hadn't been in his closet at the house on Atlantic Beach that summer. Conrad wished his father had talked to him before buying that young suit.

"We just had pure hell at the office today, Richie."

The air conditioning froze the perspiration in the small of Conrad's back, dried the moisture where his pants were wrinkled against the backs of his knees. "They're phasing me into planning the Denver facility now," Conrad said.

His father patted a tissue across his high forehead and then balled it in the ashtray. "One of the secretaries passed out at her desk," his father said. "Then we had vice-presidents by the rasher and the Drug Division is called for consultation and the poor kid is lying there with the Executive Committee trying to decide whether to call a hospital or the police."

"They may be sending me to Colorado for a month during the winter," Conrad said.

"That should be fun, Richie."

"I don't know if we're going to have to postpone the wedding for that," Conrad said. He didn't look at his father. "I'll have to check the dates I'll be away."

His father smiled. "I shouldn't think that would be necessary, son."

"Well, I mean for setting up the apartment. All that kind of thing."

"I'm sure George Maislin will let you take your bride," his father said.

Conrad lit a cigarette. "I don't know if I'll have the money," he said.

"I think under the circumstances you can expect some consideration from your firm on that score, son." His father fluffed his handkerchief. "I'll probably see George Maislin next week at the Yale Club. I'll mention it."

"Well, sure," Conrad said. "But I don't want them to think I'm asking for special favors. You know I—"

"Of course not, son," his father said.

Charlie put the drinks down before them; his red tunic and gold braid interrupted Conrad's view of his father. A bell rang on the back wall of the restaurant and a pizza tray slapped down on the window counter from the kitchen. More and more frequently they dined together in places like this one at his father's suggestion. The Golden Star was far more convenient to their apartment at 85th than, say, Manny Wolf's or LeCoq Hardi. The prices were more reasonable, too; but Conrad knew how little that mattered to his father. A week earlier, for no reason at all, his father had taken him out late on a Wednesday night to

Eddie Condon's; the captain had greeted his father by name and had given them a preferred table. Of course, Conrad hadn't seen a great deal of his father during his last year at college.

Once during the summer Julie and he had met his father at the bar at The Half Note. They had all been very pleased at the coincidence. His father picked up their check and then they stood together at a knot of phone booths on Spring Street and called a dozen other jazz places to see which group was playing that night. His father gave the pros and cons of each until they finally decided on the Vanguard and Wes Montgomery. Conrad hadn't thought his father would know anything about jazz.

"Well, here's to your honeymoon in Denver," his father said, and drank off a good part of his Manhattan.

Conrad stared at the long, slender neck of the cocktail glass before him. The Golden Star was filling up. All the young, star-bright people; animated people.

"We live at the bull's-eye of the universe," his father suddenly said. "Do you know that, son?"

"Sure, Dad."

"There are more things to enjoy in New York City than any other place on earth."

"Whatever you say, Dad."

His father put his cigar down in the ashtray. "Come on now, son. It can't be as bleak as all that."

Conrad didn't say anything. He tasted his drink; it was heavy with the sweetness of vermouth.

"Julie has to spend a weekend home with her folks now and again, Richie," his father said. "You appreciate that, don't you, son?"

"Well, yes. But—"

"I know just how you feel, Richie. Here's the weekend and no one to celebrate it with. Am I right?"

"Yes," Conrad finally said. "Yes, that's it."

"Well, then I'll tell you what," his father said. "Why don't you celebrate it with me? There's a party—"

"Oh, I think I'll catch a movie downtown and hit the hay," Conrad said.

"That sounds a little lukewarm," his father said, and got hold of his cigar again. "Why not—"

"I'm driving up to Cos Cob tomorrow," Conrad said. "Julie has some picnic nonsense on the—"

"That's more like it," his father said. "Give her folks my best, of course, and ask—"

In the booth across from where they were sitting, a small, redheaded girl faced a pale young man with steel-rimmed eyeglasses. They talked energetically, kept their hands folded in their laps. They had finished dinner and the black top of their table remained immaculate: not a flake of bread crust, not a droplet of Ruffino. Their flatware lay parallel on their plates; the girl had, demurely, left her veal unfinished. As for her escort, the remains of his ziti grew cold and he glanced at his plate from time to time. As she had set her knife and fork down, probably he had politely broken off his eating too. He had offered her more wine every time the level of her glass slipped, was probably asking now if she cared for a cordial, a pony of Cherry Heering. How long since Conrad had been as meticulously gracious with a woman, he couldn't possibly recall. How long since he had planned his converstion in advance from the advice of friends: She cares a great deal for opera; well, she's in her Monet period now, you might say; for God's sake, don't bring up the Republican party with that one. Had he ever done that at all, or had there only been a predictable Julie? How long was it since he had stood before a mirror, preening and impatient for the sky to darken? How long was it since he had delayed leaving

155

the apartment on Saturday night so as to be ten minutes late? When was it that Julie had stopped expecting him to come around and open her door to the car?

His father put his pen away and pressed a slip of paper at Conrad. "You'll keep this just in case," his father said. "It's the address. Just a small get-together of some friends, but you may enjoy it. I expect there'll be one or two men you might someday profit from meeting."

Conrad folded the paper away.

"And if you can't make it but get off somewhere on your own," his father was saying, "if I'm already in when you get home late . . ." Then his father explained that if Conrad found a book of matches on the marble table in the foyer he should go to bed as quickly and as quietly as he could.

II

THE BARTENDER'S HANDS were mottled with psoriasis and that made Conrad think about how he had stained his shirtfront with tomato sauce at dinner and why he had to keep his blazer buttoned.

"So okay," the bartender said. He was about Conrad's age and he had somehow lost every single hair on his head, even his eyebrows. Conrad wondered if the man shaved; if he had hair on his belly, in his nostrils, on the knuckles of his toes. The bartender had hair on the backs of his hands. No. That was the flakes of psoriasis flaking off and the caramel lighting. If he didn't have hair on his chest, he probably never went to the beach. Was probably moribund at talk of Santa Claus, gorillas, the Smith Brothers.

"Hey, partner, are you deaf or just loaded? You hear me?"

Conrad blinked. "Hair?"

"What?"

"I just walked in this minute," Conrad said. "How do you get a drink around here?"

The bartender wiped his nose on his wrist. He was headed for psoriasis of the nose. Then the flaking would look like sunburn. A compliment to a man in terror of beaches. "You ask me," the bartender said.

Conrad heard music. The bar was shaped like a railroad car; carriage lanterns let a tired light down on its English pub veneer. At the far end, through the dun pollution of cigarettes, was a jukebox with a television or something on top of it. The pictures were of flamenco dancers, were in Technicolor.

"For a drink," the bartender said.

"Well, in that case I'll have a Manhattan," Conrad said, and swung his leg up on the bar rail with some style. He brought out his lighter and cigarettes.

The bartender made a farting sound with his lips and Conrad stared at him. "Straight up?" the bartender said.

"On the rocks," Conrad said.

"Son of a bitch," the bartender said.

Conrad watched him go off down the bar. He didn't know why people in the service trades had to be irritable like that. Of course, he was getting used to it in New York. He didn't any more expect a decent Manhattan than he would expect a TV repairman to get his father's set fixed properly the first time around. There wasn't any sense in getting it fixed in one visit at $5.50 flat rate per call plus parts. On the other hand, Conrad was more than a little drunk now and he didn't give a shit for the bartender.

He started to sit down and the girl on the next stool said, "I wouldn't sit there, mister. That's Big Frankie's chair."

"Sure," Conrad said, and gave her the Burt Lancaster smile. The girl had shaggy, bronze hair, repelled him.

The bartender put a Manhattan in an old-fashioned glass on the bar and Conrad put a dollar bill down next to it. The bartender said, "Thanks a lot," and rang up eighty cents on the register and put the change in the pocket of his candy-striped vest.

Conrad wasn't surprised by that. He took his drink and went over to where a cluster of people hedged about the TV-jukebox. The screen lit up with the words COFFEE BREAK A GO GO in gold against royal blue and the jukebox sang, "Way down among Brazilians coffee beans grow by the millions," and Carioca girls with bare chests were dancing on the screen and singing to shatter glass. Some of the girls on barstools laughed as though their secret was out. They jiggled their knees.

The man beside Conrad said, "That one always knocks them cold."

Conrad said, "I never saw one of those before."

The man stopped smiling and turned his head Conrad's way; Conrad felt his blazer burst open and his stained shirtfront tails rip out of his pants and begin to snap like flags. He touched his breast pocket; it was empty.

"Excuse me," Conrad said. He looked down the bar. Was there someone seated beside the bronze girl? He couldn't make out the bronze girl clearly; he felt dizzy, had to lean against the wall. Suppose Big Frankie had gone back to his seat, wouldn't return his cigarettes and lighter? Conrad leaned against the wall; he dreamed that there was an enormous man in the stool that had been vacant a moment before.

Conrad shuffled his feet. He said, "I beg your pardon."

The bronze girl beside the fat man glanced at him. Her mane

of hair hid her ears and throat, her forehead and some of her chin.

"My cigarettes," Conrad said.

The girl looked away.

Conrad touched the fat man's shoulder. "I think I left my cigarettes on the bar right—"

"Get lost," the man said, but didn't look back. "Hey, Louie, will you get this lush off my ass before I belt him."

The bartender's cue-ball head rose over the coils of Big Frankie's neck. "Is that you again, partner?"

"Say, I guess I must have left my cig—"

"Listen, you can finish your drink and you'd better move along," the bartender said.

Conrad held up a cube of space between his thumb and fore-finger. "It's a little gold lighter. With my initials. And a pack of Kents."

"Cunts," the fat man said, and the girl bent her face forward and her hair poured and her back began to jerk.

"Drink up and blow," the bartender said.

The jukebox said, "A politician's daughter was accused of drinking water."

Then the fat man touched the flame of Conrad's lighter to a cigarette in the girl's mouth.

"Hey."

"Now, are you going to blow off or not, buddy?"

"Look, he's got my lighter right in his hand." The bartender bent through a door under the bar and came out next to Conrad. "He's got my—"

The bartender took Conrad's glass away. The jukebox said, "No tea or tomato juice." All Conrad could think of was how the bartender's whole body must be as slick as the palms of his feet.

"I've got to have that lighter," Conrad said.

159

"Come on," the bartender said, and got hold of his sleeve.

"Listen to me, would you?" Conrad said. "Please. It was a gift from—" The bartender was pushing him toward the door and all the faces at the bar were pointed his way. He saw Big Frankie's face, which was rather jolly. Conrad shouted, "Give me that lighter, you fat bastard."

The bartender stopped shoving and the fat man got off his stool and the bronze girl began to laugh.

"You take your problems outside, Frank," the bartender said, but the fat man pushed him away and got hold of Conrad's jacket and pulled the door of the bar open and dragged him out onto Second Avenue.

"Pretty smart fella," Big Frankie said, and held Conrad's jacket and hustled him up the sidewalk and around the corner and into a driveway, out of the streetlamps. Humid night.

"I'm going to call the police," Conrad said. The fat man had something in his hand, but the hand was like a baseball glove and Conrad couldn't tell what he was holding.

"You're not calling nobody." Delicately, by fingertips, Big Frankie held Conrad's lighter as though it were a butterfly. "I'm gonna smear you right down this wall."

Conrad cleared this throat. He felt drowsy with the night and the drinking. It was a warm night and traffic noise went by on Second Avenue, and lighted windows dotted the front of the apartment house across the street. Three blocks east, he had a notion of the dark river running upstream with the current from the Narrows, curling against Manhattan's dark flanks. Big Frankie took off his jacket and folded it across a garbage can, keeping himself between Conrad and the alley's mouth.

"Say, we don't have to fight about this," Conrad said. "You're Big Frankie."

"So what?" the fat man said. He was half turned away from

Conrad, rolling his sleeves back. He put the lighter in the pocket of his shirt. Conrad thought about the stains on his own shirt, how he'd have to fight with his jacket on. Big Frankie's shirt-front was pure virgin white.

"Well, everybody knows you," Conrad said.

"What crap is this?"

Conrad didn't know. He didn't have the vaguest idea why he was being punished. He was tired and his feet hurt and he itched with the humidity and began dreaming of a shower. Dozens of naked men were in the shower with him, all wearing spiked shoes. They were singing, "They've got an awful lot of coffee in Brazil." Conrad got out of the shower and put on his clothes; but his clothes were only running shorts and a shift; and the shift was stained red. And he couldn't understand how he had gotten into the middle of New York City dressed that way. He pushed himself away from the wall. The music had stopped. Conrad rubbed his eyes. He was holding an empty glass; and when he got back to his place at the bar the stool beside the girl was still vacant and his cigarettes and lighter were where he had left them.

"Boy, I sure wouldn't want to lose this," Conrad said and held the lighter up.

"Sure," the girl said.

"I guess I'll have another one of these," Conrad said to the bartender. "It's—"

"I know," the bartender said, and waved him silent.

"Hey, have you seen Frank?" the girl said, and the jukebox said, "Love me or leave me and let me be lonely," and the bartender said, "He wasn't in all week and he ain't expected. Wise up, Shirley, huh?"

"Can't you ask a goddam question around here?" the girl said.

The bartender went off and Conrad looked at the girl and she said, "Well, sit down, mister, go ahead."

"Thanks," Conrad said. "Oh, they're all the same way."

"Look, you want to go me one of these?" She laid a long, silvered fingernail to the side of the tumbler before her.

"I don't mind," Conrad said.

"Gimme a G and T, Georgio," the girl said. "Christ, I wish they'd lay off that goddam Scopatone." She shot her thumb over her shoulder.

"The jukebox?"

"Yeah. With the films."

Conrad looked at the jukebox. Inside the machine was a rack of film cartridges and a prismatic projector with a wide-angle, short-focal-length lens. He hadn't noticed that before; he hadn't seen anything but the metal skin of the machine before, the lights and the TV screen.

"Thanks," the girl said, and tipped her glass against the side of his. She took a mouthful and put the end of her hair away from her throat. "I wasn't being fresh before. Frankie was supposed to be here," she said. "The hell with him," she said. "You don't come around here, What's-your-name."

"Well, Paul," he said.

The girl squinted at him. "Paul what?"

"Paul Harper." Why shouldn't she believe him?

"Okay, Paul Harper."

Conrad put two dollar bills on the bar; the bartender left thirty-five cents in their place and Conrad looked at him. "Well, what's your name?" Conrad said.

"Oh, for Christ's sake, cut it out," the girl said.

Conrad drank some of his Manhattan. He put his hand casually against his chest where he was sure the buttons of the blazer were slipping undone. The jukebox was singing again, but he couldn't catch the words. Elbows and purses, fingers and shoulders, were against his back. He hadn't realized how crowded the bar had become. The girl was looking down into the drink before her and her long bronze hair spilled over her forehead and her head was bent down. Beyond the rows of bottles, in the mirror opposite them, they were reflected in the dark gleam of the carriage lamps: his bright face and the tailored fit of his blazer, and the girl with her shoulders crumpled against her ears. He didn't know what he was supposed to say. Above the bottles and the mirror of the bar was a pen-and-wash sketch of a naked woman climbing out of a bath. The girl beside him was crying and he had to do something about it.

"Are you all right?" Conrad said. "I mean, don't you feel well?"

She didn't move. "Have you got a car?"

He looked at the ice and garnet fluid in his glass. "I, well, sure. Outside."

She held her hand between his eyes and her own. "Give me a lift home, okay?"

"Okay."

She moved down off the barstool, and she was smaller than he had thought she was.

On Second Avenue he said, "This way," but he couldn't touch her elbow. It was still warm, but there was an edge on the breeze. He thought he should offer her his jacket over the thin yellow sweater, but that would show what a slob he was. Inside the car it was darker; a fine cold from the leatherette bucket seat into his kidneys, and her arms crossed about her bosom. He hadn't known how cold it was after all; he couldn't feel the cold. The stains on his shirt tickled his chest. The ignition wouldn't catch. "Look, take my jacket," he said at last.

"I'm okay," she said. She had her face turned to the far window and in the light the coarse bronze was gone from her hair and its fall to her shoulders was almost elegant. "I'm at Fifteenth and Third," she said.

The Pontiac finally began. They went south on Second. Many lights. There had been a sprinkle of rain and the pavement glistened with lights. Friday night. Orange and purple beads of rain on the windshield among the wiper blades. The gold-leafed windows of Tinker's Bar at 75th Street packed solid, people spilling out onto the sidewalk. Sweaters and slacks and sandals. Conrad had a woman in the car beside him. The woman wore denim slacks and her sandals bound her ankles; she was not Julie.

"You know Tinker's?" the girl said.

"No," Conrad said, but he knew all about Tinker's. Malachy's and Tinker's and Himself and the Guardsman and Dorrian's Red Hand and the Gordian Knot and Spark's and the Inner Circle and Frey's. The Ward Room, The Leaves, The Kennel Club, The Pillow Talk, The Flick, Outside-In, Joe King's, Brandy's, the Pink Poodle, The Pomp Room, Maria's, Chuck's. He had a woman beside him in his car. What more could he ask? The woman was wearing a yellow poorboy sweater, denim slacks, sandals; probably a bikini bra and underpants with a skirt of tassels; she wore plastic eyelashes and the scent of pocketbooks. A mysterious scent, and her eyelashes were not her own. Strange that a woman would pretend her brassiere was not there but that her eyelashes were. Conrad never understood things like that with Julie.

"You're not from New York."

"I've always lived in New York," Conrad said.

"I don't think that's true."

"Except for school."

There were a lot of things that Conrad didn't understand: why the girls came like deer to Brandy's and The Leaves, why they came alone to Malachy's and Himself. Tangled at the bar so much like the subway: immodest, unabashed. Like this woman, this girl with her change and elbows before her on the bar.

"I'm from Wichita," she was saying. "Kansas. You're from Massachusetts."

"I'm from New York," Conrad said. "The better part of Valerie is discretion. Why is a mouse when it spins."

"I don't know what you mean," the girl said.

He had charged through dinner to get away from his father; that was the genesis of the stains. He had wolfed dinner, had been too rushed to change his shirt, had raced to half a dozen bars. Coming into the last one from Second Avenue, he had counted the house, so to speak: Those two had arrived together and Rock Hudson couldn't pry them apart; that one looked to live in Queens—an hour to take her home and an hour back to the city—no dice; that one was drinking daiquiris, reeked of Bergdorf's—too expensive. Willfully or not, he had chosen this one of the denim slacks, as though it had been by design. What more could he have wanted? The Kafkaesque conversation, watching the clock tick along. Rush together to her apartment, clothes flying in all directions, the shock of intromission. Friday night on the upper East Side. What more could he have prayed for? What more was the conversation between the young, unfamiliar couple in the pizzeria about? What was all the politesse for after all?

"Oh, you passed it," the girl said.

"What?"

"Fifteenth Street. Back there."

"I'm sorry."

"You can turn around."

"Say, why don't you just walk it back from here, baby?" Conrad said.

"Well, sure. All right."

"No. Wait a minute," Conrad said. "Just wait a minute."

How could he be so rude, talk like that? He drew the car left into a side street, up to the curb, stopped. He lit a cigarette and stared at his lighter. His head was just beginning to clear.

"Well, I'll just walk back," the girl said.

"No, don't," Conrad said. He leaned back into the bucket seat, deep enough that his eyes were below the steering wheel. The windshield had dried, was streaked in arcs where the wiper blades had dragged, diffused his vision of the dark street, the tenement buildings and the zigzag fire escapes.

"It's just a block or two and I can—"

"Would you wait a minute, please," Conrad said. "I told you something that wasn't true back there in the bar."

"So what?" the girl said.

"About my name."

"What do I care?"

"I think you care," Conrad said. She was looking at him and her face was squared, tough.

"Hey, all I care about right now is getting home."

Conrad put the car in gear. At the corner of Fifteenth and Third he stopped again and the girl said, "Would you like coffee?"

"Forget it," Conrad said.

"Maybe you need it," she said.

He held on to the steering wheel. "Another time."

"I'd like you to come up."

He didn't want to look at her. He didn't want to have anything more to do with her.

"Come on," she said, and threw her door open.

He shut the ignition and followed her across the street, going under the marquee of a white-brick apartment house, across the lobby into the elevator. The operator nodded and Conrad jingled his change uneasily. He had expected one of the tenements, a single brown room.

When the brushed-aluminum door rolled back she led him down the hallway and then put her hand over the plate beneath her doorbell.

"I knew," she said. "About your name."

Traplike, the elevator door hissed shut behind him.

"From the initials on your lighter," she said. "Now we start even." The girl raised her face.

"Richard Conrad," he said. "Look, I'll go and let you be."

She put her key in the door; he didn't even glance at the nameplate. He went back to the elevator and jammed the button in and waited. Below him, through the floor of the building, he felt the elevator begin to rise. It moved dead slow.

"Come in, Richard," her voice said.

The door of the elevator opened and the operator was staring straight at him.

"Richard?"

"Can I help you?" the elevator operator said.

Then Conrad said, "No."

III

IN THE MORNING, he passed the door of his father's bedroom walking lightly. Not yet eight o'clock. With luck he could be in Cos Cob by ten. Conrad brushed his teeth and shaved. From the bathroom door he could see the book of matches on the marble table in the foyer. He got a cigarette from the pack on his dresser and struck one of the matches. Then he opened the wall of curtains that faced Lexington Avenue. Could he have chosen a prettier day? He put on chino shorts and a stretch polo shirt and tennis sneakers. He turned on the flame under the copper teakettle on the kitchen stove and sat down and put his heels on the Formica top of the breakfast table. The apartment was chill with air conditioning, but he rather liked that, hot as the day was going to be.

His father's door sounded and then the bathroom door and running water after that. Conrad swung his feet away and set twin cups and saucers, spoons. They used saccharin in a tiny silver bowl with a blue glass liner and reconstituted lemon juice. The bathroom door. He was putting a crease into two napkins and the kettle began to sigh. His father always read the maxims on the Salada tea-bag squares aloud as a sort of benediction for the day.

Conrad said, "I haven't gotten to the toast yet. We've got that marma—"

"Oh, hi."

When had he bought that black-and-white plaid robe for his father? Last Christmas? His father's birthday? Only February, at Feinstein in New Haven.

"Can you make coffee instead?" the woman said. She held the collar of the robe at her throat with pearl-tipped fingers; its belt hung from her waist in a ludicrous drooping bow. She had the sleeves rolled back past her elbows.

"Well, we don't keep it," Conrad said. "Coffee."

"Maybe there's some juice." She pulled the refrigerator ajar and bent to it. "What time is it getting to be?"

"About eight. Eight-ten," Conrad said.

"I didn't know Phil shared his place," she said. She had a

carton of orange juice when she turned back. "Let me have a glass and your kettle's boiling. You're a little young," she said.

Conrad gave her a tumbler from the cabinet above the sink and poured his own hot water, and then hers when she said, "Oh, you might as well."

"Isn't there sugar?"

"I don't . . . Somewhere. Let me—"

"Don't bother. Lord, that's poison," she said, and poured the glass full of orange juice again. "You can sit down, and what's your name?"

"Richard."

"I'm Karen. Good morning, and how old are you anyhow?" She went for more saccharin.

"You don't want more than two," Conrad said.

The woman stopped, staring.

"The saccharin. After two it gets bitter. Really. You—"

"Have it your own way, Richie. You're not even thirty, are you?"

"No," Conrad said. He poured out a teaspoon of lemon juice.

"Neither am I, but—Christ—I feel like it this morning."

Conrad took a mouthful of the tea; dull, artificial sweetness of saccharin. The girl picked one of his cigarettes and waited. Her hair was very black, cut close to the side of her face. She hadn't any eyebrows and that made Conrad remember the hairless bartender and the psoriasis on the backs of his hands. The woman's hands were whiter than the tabletop; she moved the cigarette among her fingers.

"Do you know Hazel deForrest?" the woman said.

"I don't think so."

"Over on Sixty-first?"

"No," Conrad said.

She pushed the strewn ends of her hair away from her forehead. "Hazel gives a party at the gallop," she said.

"I don't know," Conrad said. He began to stir his tea and then he realized the Salada bag, tag and all, was in his cup.

The woman pressed her hands to the sides of her face and put her elbows down. "Are you going to give me a light or not?" she said.

"Okay, sure, I'm . . ." Conrad said, but she wouldn't lean forward and he had to bend across the table with the match.

She blew the smoke away and tapped the ash into her saucer. "I guess you're the square one," she said.

Conrad didn't know what she meant.

"Well, they always say that when two guys live together it's opposites attract. Unless they're fruits." She brought her tea bag up in the spoon and wound the string about it, squeezing the last dark drops back into the cup. "You and Phil make a perfect pair. He's the swinger and you're the choirboy."

Conrad shrugged; twenty after eight already.

"Listen," she said. "Could you cook me an egg? I don't do any of that stuff."

"I'm kind of in a hurry," Conrad said.

"Oh, yeah? Well, forget it."

"No, that's all right."

"Well, just a boiled one, Richie."

"Okay. Soft?"

"Oh, Christ, no." She touched her throat and stuck her tongue out.

"I'll put it up for you," he said. "But I've got to go in ten minutes. You could just take it—"

"The hell with the whole thing," she said.

"Whatever you say."

"Let me put it to you this way, Richie," she said. "What do you guys pay for a place like this? About three bills?"

"I guess. I'm not sure. They keep raising—"

"You don't know what the rent is?"

"I don't pay any—"

The woman turned her face halfway. "Hey, what's your setup here anyway?"

"The—" And Conrad stopped.

"Well, this place is okay any way you slice it."

"Look, I've really got to run off," Conrad said.

"Don't worry about me," she said, and waved her hand; but she wasn't looking at him the same way any more. "I promise not to steal the family jewels."

He put his dishes in the sink and said, "Nice meeting you," and the woman said, "I'll see you again, Richie." He knew that when he had gone she would sit watching his empty chair and laughing.

IV

JULIE'S CONNECTICUT HOUSE: How often had he listened to the gravel driveway whispering to the Pontiac's tires? Always the trio of Yorkshire terriers wagging down the stone steps to surround him, their steel-blue coats trembling with excitement, their quacking barks and tiny, simpering voices. Summer opulence of willows pouring around him; a tangle of color in a bed of impossible anemones; and the lawn rolling away behind the house to dip into the Sound.

"Good morning, Mr. Conrad," the French girl said. The starched points of the bow in her hair; her heels ticking on the parquet floor and then, in the main hall among the carved paneling that rose around him like organ pipes, the deep burgundy rug closing over his shoes.

"How do you do, Richard?"

"I'm fine, Mrs. Dixon."

"And I'm quite well, Richard. Won't you join us in the study? Julia will be right along."

Particle of a woman, Hummel figurine. Every hair touched into place, the perfect gray suit and pearls, ball-bearing walk. Miles of leather books and random squares of stained glass scattered among the arched windows. The egg-and-dart cornice. A fireplace of venerable stones.

"Will you have some coffee, Richard? None of you young people seem to care for breakfast. And it is—"

"Well, Dick."

Would his father-in-law wear cardigans and ascots? Would the Yorkie dogs prance and fawn at this father-in-law's slippers and knees?

"Say, you take a handful of these Havanas back to your dad. Tell him they're the last of the very last and my best wishes too. You're off to a picnic, or so the grapevine has it."

"Julie and I were going to drive up to Tangle—"

"Just right," Mr. Dixon said. "And then you stop in at the Danbury Inn and ask for—"

After all. Conrad thought about how he had been warned to get a good look at the mother before. But what happened after he looked? He wondered if Dixon had ever laid a girl in black net stockings. He wondered if Dixon ever brought a cigarette girl home. He wondered if Dixon knew that his daughter would be coming downstairs without panties under her skirt.

"No, that's quite all right, Dick. You call me Dad any time you like."

"It's only that we, Mr. Dixon and I, Richard, we feel . . . well. . . "

Her flighty polite eyes.

"Yes, Dick. We were rather hoping for a large affair. You understand, boy. Julie's our only—"

"We didn't know how to put it, Richard. Your father isn't inviting anyone at all."

"I don't think I—"

"Mr. Dixon and I are afraid it may be a matter of . . . Harold?"

Conrad turned away from Mrs. Dixon's discreet eyes.

"We don't know what it is, Dick. And I daresay we don't know how to approach it without your help."

"I don't know anything about it," Conrad said.

"Oh, you see, Mr. Dixon and I called your father to ask . . . that is, to ask him when he'd be sending his address list. So that we could mail invitations for his . . . but he simply, that is—"

"You know what a sport your father is, Dick. He had a good laugh and said he'd make his invitations in person."

"We didn't have any idea what—"

"Then we had this note yesterday." Dixon slipped on his eyeglasses; they were of fine wire, reminded Conrad of Benjamin Franklin. Conrad stared at the glasses, blinked. " 'Dear Mary and Hal, Here's my guest list. Philip Evans Conrad & Son. That's just enough, don't you agree? Best regards, Phil.' So you see, Dick."

"We haven't discussed this with Julia yet, Richard."

"No, and I have the feeling she'll be more than a little upset when we finally have to. Unless, of course . . . I don't suppose this is intended as a joke?"

"I guess there isn't anyone else," Conrad finally said.

"Oh, but surely . . . your family . . ."

"Just my grandfather. And he's not well. And too old."

"But friends. Your father must have friends."

Conrad closed his teeth on the filter of his cigarette.

"We felt, naturally, that it might be simply some formality, Richard. But we could make whatever—"

"What my wife is trying to say, Dick, is that we feel your father may be courting."

"Richard, your cigarette!"

Had it burned the rug? Or did he have the whole red ash between his thumb and forefinger, searing him?

"Let me see that, Dick. Here. That's a nasty burn. Mary, call Loretta for that spray thing of yours. You know the one I mean."

Mrs. Dixon fluttered off. Conrad listened for Dixon's private tone of voice.

"I don't see why I can't talk man to man with you, Dick. Is there any reason?"

"No," Conrad said. But how could Dixon know that his father brought home fifty-dollar hookers and let him cook their breakfast?

"Knowing what I do of your father, the man is the personification of a gentleman, of course. And also tactful to a fault. Mrs. Dixon and I simply feel that he may be courting and may think it wouldn't be appropriate to bring her—"

"Don't say any more." Conrad covered his eyes.

"Is that burn really distressing you, Dick? Do you feel faint?"

"I'm all right." Nausea swirled in him.

"Oh, here we are now, Richard. Let me have your hand. Loretta, hold that towel under—"

The bitter, tooth-splitting cold, his fisted, frozen hand.

"You see, Richard, bringing a woman to your son's wedding is . . . well, it amounts to making your intentions public. You don't just bring a casual acquaintance to an affair like that. You bring a special someone."

"I can tell you, Dick, that a mature woman would feel, have

reason to believe, that an invitation of that sort meant that your father intended marriage."

"And he may not be certain yet, Richard."

"Men of your father's age are very circumspect in their personal affairs, Dick. Your father wouldn't want to endanger a lady's feelings by leading her—"

"We'd like to have her as our guest, Richard. We would send our car for her, and that way—"

It was a smell he didn't want to recognize; and he felt the cold through his arms and where his forehead was resting. The tile cut his bare knees and he clung to the white porcelain bowl as though it were his mother's bloodless corpse.

V

"MOTHER ASKED if you were often like that," Julie said. "Isn't she silly?"

Tanglewood Lake was in the valley beneath them and powerboats and water skiers threw long roostertails of white water. The forest of elm and maple went down their hill to the lake's edge. Barefoot, in white tennis skirt and blouse, Julie stretched on their picnic blanket with her wrists crossed behind her head.

"What are you worrying about now, Rick?"

"Nothing."

"I'm sorry you didn't want to eat."

"How long do you guess that lake is, Julie?"

She rolled over twice, holding her knees together, and ended with her face resting against his bare thigh. "I don't care how long it is, Rick."

"I was just asking if . . . stop that, Julie!"

She bit again.

"Julie, come on." The red smile of a welt rising on his knee.

"Don't you ever think about how it will be heaven when we're married, Rick? Honest to God." She pulled herself up against his chest, swung her arms about his neck.

"Who told you it would be such—look out, my sunburn!"

"Oh, let me have a look at it."

"Just quit."

"My mother gave me the spray th—"

"Julie, will you lay off?"

"Rick, you're the world's most boring man."

"Swell."

She pulled her knees up across the blanket from him, crossed her arms. Was any female thing ever as pretty as she? Conrad didn't know. Her white linen outfit, the blue band through her hair, her olive eyes. Did he want to kill his own father?

"Let me have a cigarette, Rick."

He looked at the matchbook. He had a sulphur taste in his mouth. The delicacy of matches on the foyer table. His father, the personification of a gentleman. The aging whoremaster and after-fifty cocksman. The sulphur smell of burning matches. The green smell of Tanglewood Park; and among the acres of green and artifical blue lake, a tiny, desperate flame.

"Julie, my father brought a prosti—"

"Where's your lighter, Rick?"

"What?"

"Your birthday lighter. The one I—"

On a pack of Kents beside that narrow bed. Scrambling in the darkness for cigarettes. Dressing quickly without a lamp *Will you call me, Richard?*

"I don't know, Julie."

"You didn't lose it, Rick?"

"I must have left it home."

"You lost it. I know you did. You left it somewhere. Rick, I could cry."

On the living room couch with coffee cups between them, Conrad had been charming, conscientiously attentive. The girl had explained how her parents were in Majorca, that she wasn't one of those girls at all. Conrad listened understandingly, decided that he was going to reach for her unknown body even if he choked doing it.

"Can't we go down to the lake, Rick? We could rent a boat. I could ski in these."

"I don't feel well, Julie. Can't we just relax?"

"Rick, you never want to do anything."

"Julie, my father brought a prostitute home last night."

Conrad waited for the outrage and indignation to rise in her face.

"Oh, Rick, you're kidding me."

"No, I'm not. She came out and sat down at the table with me this morning. Just like that. Like she owned the goddam apartment and everything."

"Rick, that's hilarious."

"What?"

"Oh, your father's a riot, Rick. I can just see him, well, wining expensive women all over town. Being so debonair and suave." She fell back on the blanket, laughing at the sky.

Conrad stood and went to the edge of their clearing. The artificial lake, miles long, creeping up the side of the valley, drowning the roots of the trees.

"You're such a prig, Rick," her voice said behind him. "I think it's a scream, and I know you. You think your father is a dirty old man."

"Shut your mouth, Julie."

"He's only human, Ricky. My God, did I want you to have me a million times before when we were on the Pacemaker! Were we obscene?"

"I don't know. Sometimes I wonder."

Her cool voice. "Sometimes I wonder, too, Rick. But I don't come out and say it."

She was getting to her feet when he looked back. "Listen, forgive that, Julie."

"Well, how did you know the woman was a whore?"

Conrad shook his head. "Julie, I can tell a prostitute when I see one."

"Can you, Rick?"

"Well, sure, I can."

"Do people know I'm a whore for you, Rick?"

He turned toward the water. "Don't talk that way, Julie."

"Do they, Rick?"

"Nobody knows."

Were there still trees in the bottom of that valley? Hidden trees, under the water of Tanglewood Lake, sprouting buds and birds' nests? Did he know before last night that some women's nipples only sprang after sucking? Had he guessed before last night that Julie trimmed her pubic hair? Hadn't he even known that?

"Oh, when we're married I'm just going to have you love me up every minute, Ricky. I'll never let you out of the bed. Not even for lunch. No more of those awful rubber things."

"Julie, for God's sake, will you shut up?"

She took his shoulders. "Rick, I want you to tell me right now. What is it? And not about your father either."

"Let me alone." He sat down with his back against a hand of birches. What would she do if he told her? Slap his face? Throw his engagement ring at his feet? Cry and cut his face up with her fingernails?

She came to her knees alongside him. "Ricky, don't you want to marry me?"

His hands were shaking. "I had another girl," he said.

"Did you take? In what way, Rick? I wish you'd—"

"I picked her up in a bar last night and took her back to her apartment and laid her." He broke off blades of grass, crumpled them between his hands. "That's where the lighter is, Julie. I left it in her apartment, on a chair next to her bed."

She stood up, brushing the dust of grass from her knees. "I think we'd better go get dressed for dinner now. Don't you?"

"Julie, I just had—"

"If you get the blanket together, I can put these dishes in the—"

He went after her, caught hold of her wrists. Behind her the sun was on the lake and drew a corona about her hair. "Julie, we need time to think about all—"

"There's nothing to think about, Rick. I don't understand why you tell me things like that. I don't understand why you have to concoct crazy stories like that just to annoy me."

A water skier between the trees, on the surface of the lake. Beneath the gleam of those skis, a hundred feet down out of the sunlight, Conrad saw the bare, rotting branches of drowned trees, beating in a black wind.

VI

CONRAD HADN'T EXPECTED his father to be awake that late: long after midnight. He hadn't expected his father to be home. All evening long he had toyed with the idea of how his father would be spending this Saturday night. He had dreams of the clubs he still shied away from: The Living Room, The Monkey Bar, Shepheard's, the St. Regis bar, the Oak Room at the Plaza, the Ritz-Carlton bar. His father and the wax hundred-dollar girls drinking brandy Alexanders.

What had he planned? To push his way into The Roundtable? To watch his father doing the Twist? To throw the left hook hard?

"Richie, have a nightcap with your old man, son?" His father in the black-and-white plaid robe under a dome of blue cigar smoke; the sweet sound of favorite Brahms. Lit with the last small lamp, the tweed living room.

"I think I'll skip that, Dad. I'm beat." Heading for the bedroom.

"I wish you'd come in and sit down a minute, son."

"Well, I—" Why was he hesitating now? Conrad didn't know. He didn't see any reason.

"Good, Richie. Do you want a touch of Cointreau?"

"Thanks." Cointreau like fine, colorless oil. The deep, cocoa-brown sofa.

His father sniffed delicately at the mouth of his rosebud glass. "I don't prefer any taste in the world to Cointreau. When I drink whiskey I sometimes forget that even C_2H_5OH can have a bouquet, a subtle flavor. None of us will ever make anything like this by hydrogenating esters." His father sipped. "Natural fermentation is—"

"We can make it if we want," Conrad said.

"Oh, I don't think so," his father said, and kissed his finger-tips where they were moistened with the liquid.

"The process is very simple," Conrad said. "Any moron can do it."

"I know the process perfectly well," his father said. "An ester—"

Conrad rattled, "$CH_3(CH_2)_{10}COOC_2H_5$."

"Hydrogenated," his father said, and set his snifter on the arm of his reclining chair. He squinted at Conrad. "Yields—"

"$CH_3(CH_2)_{10}CH_2OH$ and your ETOH. I don't understand why you had to bring that pig into our house," Conrad said.

His father straightened up the reclining chair. "You mean Karen, I take it?"

"No, I mean the man in the moon," Conrad said.

"How are the Dixons, by the way, Richie?"

"Great." Conrad put his head back against the wall behind the couch. The controlled, air-conditioned climate of the apartment eighteen stories from the ground; no traffic noise, no breeze. The super-perfect blue of Tanglewood's synthetic lake.

"Your mother loved Brahms," his father said. "I'd never heard of Cointreau when I met her. That was 1930, Richie, and Long Island was a farm all the way to my father's estate in King's Point. But New Haven was a fading town even then."

"Give me that bottle of Cointreau and I'll make you a wallet," Conrad said. "A plastic—"

"Son, I'm going to tell you only once—"

Conrad said, "Do you want me to come over there and punch you in the face?" He shut his eyes. "Don't pay any attention to me," he said. "Forget that."

"Richie," his father said. "Richie, listen to what I have to say. It's obvious to me, it's been obvious to me for a long time, what your relationship is with Julie."

Conrad put his chin on his chest.

"Do you understand me?"

"I didn't know that," Conrad said.

"When you're as old as I am you won't have to guess about

your own son," his father said. "As long as you're careful. Well, I wasn't put on this earth to judge you, son, only to counsel you."

Conrad looked at his snifter of Cointreau. It touched mint and orange to his tongue.

"There isn't any honorable way out for you now, son," his father said. He got up and went to the Lexington Avenue window and put his hands against the glass. "You're caught the way all of us are caught. It was very much with your mother and me as it is with you and your Julie."

Conrad raised his face. From the rear his father looked as small as the whore had looked in the black-and-plaid bathrobe: the sleeves bagging at the elbows, the bagging at the waist, his father's stalklike legs protruding at the bottom.

"You may find that hard to believe," his father said, "as you never knew your mother when she was younger and more handsome even than Julie is." His father turned around, but his eyes were luminous and weren't focused on Conrad. "I never wanted anything so well as your mother's body. And I went through hell before she let me have her." Distantly, his father smiled. "Of course, I was the dapper Yalie and she was a townie and pug Irish and it was expected. But she wouldn't let it be. And I starved with wanting her." His father laughed and lifted up his glass. "Naturally, after the fact I felt somewhat differently toward her. But we made out. And I loved her, later on, Richie, very, very much."

His father said, "In any case, getting married is a good deal of excitement and you'll momentarily forget that you— Where are you going, son?"

Conrad stood away from the couch. "What the hell do you care?"

His father leveled the index finger of his free hand. "Just

don't you project your own betrayals to me, son." Then his father shrugged and turned back to the window and the city lights.

Conrad felt all the dizziness and nausea of the morning. His vision was blurred and his balance failed him. He leaned with both hands against the back of the couch. "Do you know your Karen thinks you're a fag? Do you know she thinks I'm your pretty boy?"

"Single men my age, even widowers, are always suspect, Richie," his father said.

"But I'm not," Conrad said. "I'm not. Do you hear me, you mother-fucking son of a bitch? You goddam mother—"

Then his father's arms were about him and his father's face was pressed close to his cheek.

"Sit down, son," his father's voice said. "Right here. Let me pour you something more to drink."

Conrad covered his hands with eyes. He heard the tink of bottle and glass. "I picked up a girl last night," he said softly.

"I thought it might be that," his father said, and closed Conrad's fingers on a snifter. "Did you tell Julie?"

"Yes." Dimly, Conrad heard the music: his mother's favorite sweet Brahms. His father's face was sallow, crusted with wrinkles, growing old.

"I suppose it was right of you to tell her," his father said, and looked down at his slippers. "She must have been terribly upset, poor thing. This close to the wedding and all."

"She didn't believe me," Conrad said. Like wedding music. Music of his mother and Julie. Perfectly serene. Conrad scratched at the back of his neck and smiled. "I suppose I'll always wish she had."

EPITHALAMION

AFTERWARD, when they finally made their escape and the scent of trampled roses was behind them, they drove to the International Hotel on the outskirts of Idlewild. The hotel was garish and blue and behind it a Boeing jet was settling toward a landing with the glint of sunlight leaving its falling wings. They took the elevator. No one stared. Conrad told the desk clerk no calls, signed Mr. & Mrs. Richard Conrad, and Julie found a dozen tall carnations in a milk-glass vase atop the dresser in their room. The card said, "May the wind be always at your back and may God cup you in the palm of his infinite hand. Dad."

Julie had changed from her gown before leaving the house—the wedding had been under a green-and-white-striped canopy erected on her parents' back lawn; a small wedding of thirty guests. Now she took off her suede coat and kicked her shoes away and shut herself into the bathroom.

"Rick, don't listen," she said.

They had served Taittinger champagne with dominoes of wedding cake; the minister had been from Julie's childhood church, and seemed agitated, checked his watch repeatedly, and barged off after a mouthful and a single round of congratulations and sly cautionary remarks. Conrad hadn't thought very much of the minister—he had the look of an Elizabethan toady with his choke collar and perspiring face. Conrad's morning suit didn't fit him evenly, wouldn't come down to rest on his shoulders. Conrad's father looked extraordinarily splendid and had a diamond pin through his cravat.

Mrs. Dixon had begun weeping promptly at 2 P.M., the very instant Conrad and his father came through the door. Her elegance deserted her; she became a rickety, hollow woman, and her sobbing made a high, chirping sound. Mr. Dixon stood beside her, whispering to her, and gave embarrassed, brief grins to his guests and failed to mount even one conversation through the balance of the afternoon. Mrs. Dixon would not stop crying; and every time Conrad turned around, she seemed to be at his shoulder, squashing a soggy handkerchief against her nose.

Later on, toward five o'clock and after the ceremony and the cutting of the cake, there was some minor dancing on the patio behind the low brick house. One of Julie's aunts caught and turned her heel in a hole that usually held a clothesline post. A violinist and an accordionist played. The men queued up and kissed Julie and held Conrad's elbow when they shook his hand.

At one point Conrad's father asked him aside and took him through the arboretum beside the house, around front and inside, downstairs into Mr. Dixon's den. The room was a converted wedge of cellar, paneled and with cellar-style windows where the ceiling met the walls. The walls were done in books. Conrad's father lit a cigar and offered one, but Conrad refused. Conrad's father sat down in the heavy leather chair behind the

desk and Conrad sat down opposite the desk and smoked a cigarette and drank from his champagne glass. Conrad's father said
that he was sitting in a very fine chair and that the inlaid top of
the desk was quality work. He made that sound like an assess-
ment of Julie and her family.

Then his father put his fingers into the pockets of his gray vest
and took out his gold watch on the end of the gold chain. He
said, "Fathers are supposed to give sermons at a time like this,
Richie. You know that."

"I've heard that," Conrad said.

"I'm not going to give you a sermon," Conrad's father said.
"I'm going to leave that to our visiting apostle."

Conrad knew he meant the squirming minister and they both
had a laugh.

"I never told you about the birds and the bees and I'm not
going to start making speeches now," Conrad's father said. He
studied the end of his cigar and Conrad said, "Okay."

His father said, "I never made any kind of speeches to you
after all. Did I?" and Conrad said no, he never had really. Conrad's father said he didn't know if that was a mistake and Conrad said he didn't think it was and Conrad's father said one
never knew about that kind of thing anyhow, so why worry,
right? Conrad laughed and so did his father.

"I never had many long chats with you," his father said. "I
never got to know your passions."

Conrad wasn't sure what his father meant by that.

"You went through high school and college, never had any
problems that I know of," his father said. "Is it that you never
had any problems or did you just not let on?"

Conrad said nothing in particular had bothered him.

"You're a very urbane young man," his father said. "You
know that word?"

Conrad drank the rest of his champagne and said, "Sure."

"Well, you never seemed to have much to say to me or anybody else," his father said. "Why was that?"

Conrad said he didn't know.

His father ran his hand back and forth over the length of gold chain that spanned his vest front. "We should have had this chat months ago," he said, and then tapped the ash of his cigar into a wastebasket beside the desk. "I've wanted to talk to you. I've waited for you to grow up and I suppose I've waited too long. You don't understand that."

"Of course I do," Conrad said.

"You don't understand that," his father said.

There was noise and they looked up and Julie was bent over the window from the garden, rapping on the glass. She wagged her finger at Conrad's father, and Conrad's father smiled back.

"You've got your wife now," his father said. "I won't tell you how I feel about having children right off or contraception and why living in Queens is better than in Manhattan. Or vice versa. You never talked much to me and that's all right. I never talked much to my father either, but he was a different kind of a man and those were different times. Does that strike you funny?"

"No." Julie went away from the window; Conrad's smile faded.

"Oh," his father said.

"Julie hasn't talked about children much," Conrad said. "I guess we'll just let nature take its course."

"Well, Maislin Chemical is a good firm," his father said. "You've got a decent start and good opportunities to get ahead."

Conrad hadn't slept well the night before and his deep chair was easy against his back and shoulders. He was glad to chat with his father about whatever his father had on his mind, but he was wishing that his father would get to it and then let him rest a moment. He didn't know most of the people at the wedding; he had only his father.

"You can't make head or tail of a marriage easily," his father was saying in his parochial style. "You can think of it as a business deal or making two people one before God, but that's all nonsense and hocus-pocus and was dreamed up by blushing brides." Conrad's father reached into the pocket of his morning coat and handed over three books of American Express checks.

Conrad said, "Thank you," and put them away.

"I just want to tell you that I'm sorry you're leaving my house," his father said.

"I'm sorry about that too," Conrad said. He watched his father before the wall of books that backed the desk; it struck him that his father's rented morning clothes fit no better than his own, that they were far too large across the chest and baggy in the pants. He was wondering how his father hid that misfit so well as he danced.

"Two things can ruin a marriage," his father said. "Too little understanding and too much. There's got to be some mystery." He puffed hard on his cigar. "Well, that isn't much of a benediction," his father said, and got up and came around the desk toward the stairs. He said, "Let's go back to the fray," but Conrad thought he was going to say something else and then had changed his mind.

In their room at the International Hotel Conrad heard the water go, and Julie came out of the bathroom with her dress over her arm; she wore only a half-slip and brassiere. She unsnapped one of their suitcases and took her quilted yellow robe out and pulled it around herself; the robe had white fur trim around the wrists and at the throat and lower hem. Conrad drew back the long curtains before the window that faced the airport.

A jet liner came up from the nearest runway, rising toward the coral sky with four dark trails of vapor streaming behind it.

"I'm just beat," Julie said. Conrad heard her on the spring of the double bed.

"Me too." Conrad put his hands into the pockets of his trousers and felt the three American Express checkbooks.

"This time tomorrow we'll be in Palm Beach. You weren't in Palm Beach before, were you?"

"No," Conrad said.

"Oh, you'll like it a lot, Ricky."

"I guess so."

"You really will."

"Are you hungry?"

"How do you mean?" she said.

He didn't look back at her. "I mean dinner."

"Now? It isn't even six."

"If you're hungry, so what? We used to eat at five-thirty," he said.

"I'm not," Julie said.

"Not what?"

"Not hungry."

"Okay," Conrad said. He sat down on his edge of the bed to watch the sky fall and the planes among it like gulls.

"Your father sent the flowers," Julie said. She took his pillow and put it under her heels. "He's one of those people."

"Which people? Listen, will you start a conversation from the beginning for once?"

"What's the matter with you?" Julie said, and propped herself on an elbow.

"Look, for Christ's sake, nobody can talk to you. You've got to talk to have a marriage. What are you, stupid or what?"

Julie looked at him and then she looked at the ceiling.

"Okay. Just forget it," Conrad said.

"Your father's one of those thoughtful people," Julie finally said, "who never come empty-handed and always send a note after. What was that babbling just before, Rick?"

"What?"

"About marriage?"

"Holy cow," Conrad said. He got up from the bed. "I'm going down to dinner," he said. "If you don't want to come, don't."

"Oh, you go to hell," Julie said.

Going out, Conrad slammed the door. He took the elevator downstairs to the bar; the bar had a wire mobile above it that symbolized flight. Conrad had a Manhattan and then another, and when the barman passed him a third time, he touched the rim of his glass and said, "Do this again, will you?"

The barman was a long, redheaded yahoo. He swirled the vermouth and whiskey with bitters. He poured and said, "Newlywed, huh?"

Conrad stared at the man; his white tunic seemed to float, and the man seemed to float, hovering above his glass. "What is it that gives you that impression?" Conrad said.

"Sign back of your car," the barman said.

Beyond the bar a window opened on the hotel parking lot. Conrad squinted after the Pontiac. On the side of someone's Buick convertible was scribbled: "This may not be the Mayflower, but tonight she'll come across."

"Not my car," Conrad said. "We have a Pontiac."

"Know it," the barman said, and floated off.

Conrad went back upstairs. Julie had the reading light on and a copy of *Mademoiselle* open across her knees. She looked up at him and said, "Who on earth are you?" and Conrad said, "Lay off."

He went over and stretched out on his half of the bed and crossed his legs and shut his eyes.

"Jesus, you're romantic," Julie said. Conrad heard the copy of *Mademoiselle* hit the floor.

Probably his father was home by now in the apartment in Manhattan, and probably he was thinking about Conrad and Julie. Conrad wondered what his father was thinking about him.

"I'll skip dinner, if it's all right with you," Julie said. She drew the curtains.

"Say, forget it, would you, Julie?" Conrad said.

"I should have held out on you," her voice said. "I should have made you come in here crawling. I knew we'd go to bed like old friends."

"What are you talking?" Conrad said.

"Oh, I told you to go to hell once, didn't I?"

"Hey!"

She yanked his blazer out of their open suitcase and flung it in his face. "You take me out dancing, you son of a bitch, or I swear you'll never see me again."

But they didn't go dancing. They split a Chateaubriand at the airport's Golden Door restaurant, shared a bottle of Bollinger. Then they went out on the observation deck of the terminal building for ten cents apiece and walked down to the farthest railing. A jet taxied to a stop below them, blue flame glowing in its exhausts. It was chilly and Conrad put his blazer around her shoulders.

"Tell me what you're thinking, Ricky," Julie said, and got between him and the railing.

"I was talking to the bartender," Conrad said.

"You did more than talk to him," she said.

"All right. He said we had a sign on our car and I looked and we don't."

"He was playing with you, silly." A jet leaped away and its thunder wrapped them; she clung against him, away from the noise.

"I don't see why he did that," Conrad said. "Julie, this isn't the way I thought it would be."

He felt her arms move, and when he looked down, she had her knuckles pressed against her mouth. "Rick," she said. "Why can't you ever leave anything to the imagination?"

NOT EVERY MAN HAS GENTIANS IN HIS HOUSE

I

"I'LL HAVE A DOZEN, Mr. Schwartzwald," Conrad said. "No, make it a dozen and a half. And very fresh." He watched the Thermopane door roll; the clusters of refrigerated flowers rustled with pink and orange and a vivid, near-black green. The handful of carnations emerged a dewy, shimmering white.

"You've never seen carnations like these," the florist said. He let his eyeglasses drop on their halter. "Only an hour ago, in they came. Sweet as milk." He held the lot under Conrad's nose. Every scalloped petal stood starch-crisp.

"Very nice," Conrad said. He smiled and nodded and reached for his billfold.

"Oh, I shouldn't even let you pay me," Schwartzwald said, and spread the green tissue on the counter and laid the carnations down with shafts of fern. "Nobody can buy beauties like

193

this. Flowers like this have to be stolen. But," he said, and winked at Conrad, "in the interest of propriety, four-fifty for you alone."

Conrad laid a bill down; Schwartzwald turned to his cash register and swung the hand crank. Sound of merry bells.

"But you must pay the forfeit, too," the florist said. He put two quarters in Conrad's hand and rested his palms on the marble counter top. "Tell me what's the occasion."

"Well, I'm being promoted. Into the research department at my place," Conrad said.

Schwartzwald flourished a handkerchief and breathed his eyeglasses to frosted gray. "This is good?" he said, and began to rub with industry.

"I don't know," Conrad said. "Yes. We've been hoping—"

Schwartzwald shut one eye, held the glasses toward the fluorescent fixture. "A big raise? A new car? You'll be a millionaire yet."

"Well, I don't know about that," Conrad said. He couldn't be impolite to Schwartzwald. But he couldn't wait to see the expression on Julie's face when he told her.

"Then I'll tell you, Mr. Conrad, if you don't mind, since I'm a few days older than you are." The florist wired the glasses back over his ears. "Even when you're a millionaire, better carnations than those you won't find at any price. So think of me."

"Yes. I will."

Walking toward Central Park West with the first spring green of the park going into brown in the fading light. Half warmed, half brisk and the tails of his trench coat flying behind him. Conrad cupped the cone of glossy paper tenderly under his arm. Cloudless, twilit sky and the first evening star. Toward 71st Street, through the open doorway of the apartment house and into the elevator. Rising into the sweet smell of apartment house hallways. Key in the lock. On the brink of whistling, he shrugged his coat away.

Dented cushions of the tweed couch; he could ignore that. The *Times* askew on the black-and-gold plaid rug. Did he care at all? A single coffee cup jammed with cigarette butts; the heaviness of stale smoke. He threw open the windows, ran up the venetian blinds. He slapped the door of the fridge closed and went to the bedroom threshold.

Julie had her dark hair up in a gaggle of pink foam curlers; beneath the net, without makeup, her face was bare, simple, lovely to him.

"You're late, Rick."

He swung the bundle out from behind his back. "Why don't you guess what's in here?"

"I give up," she said, and shut the paperback book on the bed beside her.

"Well, you'll see," Conrad said. "And then I'm going to let you guess why George Maislin called me into his office at five o'clock."

"To make you late for dinner," she said; but he paid no attention to that.

He went around the corner of the bedroom door and back into the living room, tearing the wrapping paper and tissue away from the carnations. He stuffed that into one of the garbage bags resting against the wall of the pullman kitchen. Then he went for the crystal vase that stood on the dining table.

"Julie?" Conrad said.

"What is it now?"

"Julie, where did you get these?" Carefully, he lifted the vase in his hands. Dark red and blue, tawny purple flowers bent away from the center of the tall swirled vase, their tubular petals translucent and heavily veined.

195

"Get what?"

"These," he said, and went to the bedroom door.

"You'll spill it all over the rug, Rick."

"Where—"

"On the dresser. Rick, put them down."

He did, stepping back and pushing his hands down into his pockets. When had he ever seen such flowers as these?

"What are they, Julie?"

"Gentians," she said. "I got them over at Romano's."

"Well, they're quite—"

"They just make me shake all over," she said, and stood away from the bed and went to the dresser where the vase rested, nestling her face among them. "Aren't they marvelous, Rick?"

"Well, I thought we agreed that Schwartzwald had the best fl—"

"Oh, him," she said. "He has all that sentimental junk. He tried to sell me roses last . . ." She lifted the neck of one of the gentians with the back of her hand, rubbed her cheek against the trailing edges of its petals. "But I love gentians."

"I guess they must be like olives," Conrad said.

"Take your hand away, Rick."

"I was—"

She put her lips softly to one of the deep, livid petals. "You can't touch gentians," she said. "The way they bruise. And then they all curdle and die."

Conrad loosened the knot of his tie and undid the tab collar of his shirt. "I suppose I can just throw the carnations away. Julie? Julie, listen, you could at—"

"Oh, Ricky, don't have one of your moods," she said, and shook her head at him.

Conrad took off his jacket and hung it away in the closet. He went out into the living room and shuffled the *Times* together and sat down on the couch and kicked his loafers away.

"You were talking about Maislin before," Julie said. When she reached to undo the curlers, the lace hem of her slip showed beyond the quilted housecoat's edge.

"Nothing," Conrad said. He set the paper on his knees. "Don't you think you could find a minute to set this place in order?"

She turned for the open window.

"I'm sorry, Julie, but it simply has to be said."

When she bent forward, leaning out over the sill, he could see the backs of her smooth calves, the beginning of her thighs. "Julie?"

He set the paper aside, stared at the ceiling and the single brass fixture with its walls punctured like a sieve. Did he really care about the way the apartment looked? Did it matter to him how little she cared to cook a meal for the two of them?

At the beginning, it had been something else again: the fresh, cool sheets three times a week, the bucket of ice waiting beside the bottle of dry sherry, and anemones in the dining table centerpiece. Somehow, almost without his noticing, the apartment had slid into chaos. The sheets grayed. The dry sherry and ice vanished from the glass top of the bar. With every flake of anemone that fell, another facet of their lives gone to tarnish.

Conrad took out his pen, cocked the *Times* against his knee. In the margin he wrote:

$$
\begin{array}{c}
CH_2 \\
\parallel \\
CH \quad\quad CH_2 \\
\mid \quad\quad\quad \parallel \\
CH \quad\quad CH-CH=CH_2 \\
\diagdown \\
CH_2
\end{array}
\longrightarrow
\begin{array}{c}
CH_2 \\
\diagup \quad \diagdown \\
CH \quad\quad CH_2 \\
\parallel \quad\quad\quad \mid \\
CH \quad\quad CH-CH=CH_2 \\
\diagdown \quad \diagup \\
CH_2
\end{array}
$$

Then he wrote, "Or polymer. High MW.

$$CH_2 = CH - CH = CH_2 \longrightarrow (- CH_2 - CH = CH - CH_2 -)_n"$$

"Are you back to that goddam chemistry?" Julie said. She pulled the newspaper out of his hands, slung it. The pages crackled, filled and spread across the living room floor.

"Look, Julie, do you mind if I keep my job and get ahead a little in this world?"

She put her index finger to the belt of the housecoat. "And what about me in the meanwhile, Rick?"

Conrad scratched his head. "Julie, I swear you— All right," he said, and got up. "I'm sorry. I just want to make sure I know exactly how—"

"If you spent as much time wondering what I do all day in this rattrap, we—"

Conrad put his hands on her shoulders; they were the size of apples. "Julie, if we're going to live well we've got to—"

"You mean you've got to." She turned her head aside.

"Eight hours a day just isn't enough, Julie," Conrad said. "Try to understand. All the rest of the guys go home and dig out the books and study. I haven't even got a master's and I'm moving into research now with . . . That's right. Maislin told me this af—"

"Dreams," she said. "Rick, when are you going to come down to the practical?"

"Julie, this is—"

She pushed her face up toward his. "I've got a life in the present tense. Or don't you know that?"

Conrad let go her shoulders. He went over to where the linoleum tile of the pullman kitchen began.

"It would help if you spoke to me about something other than chemistry," she said behind him.

Conrad shut his eyes. "I'm sorry," he said.

On the drainboard alongside the refrigerator the carnations lay, their flowers drooping into the sink. White, frilled petals, whiter than the appliance enamel. "Let me see if I can poke a little supper together," Conrad said.

"Rick," she said. "You and I are having dinner with my parents. My God, Rick, have you even forgotten that?"

Conrad laced his fingers and held his hands tight against the buckle of his belt.

II

NO ONE had to tell me," Julie's father said. Impeccable in the black herringbone, he held up a manicured, tapered hand. "I saw bright days ahead for Dick the first time he came calling. Here comes an enterprising young man, I said to myself, to carry off my baby daughter. Hal, she's as good as gone right now. That's what being enterprising does for you."

At his right, his dainty wife gave her clam smile. She turned the handle of her demitasse a few degrees on the gold-leafed saucer.

"Ricky's going to be the greatest research chemist in captivity," Julie said. She grinned and slitted her eyes toward Conrad. Above her violet sheath, the cleavage of her breasts supported a double strand of pearls. "We won't talk about his marriage."

Was her mother going to dive headlong into the demitasse? Her father looked at his wristwatch.

"For Pete's sake, Mary, it's after midnight.

"Oh, I hadn't realized." Julie's mother touched her sequined purse. "Really. We must start back. An hour drive and—"

Julie's father pivoted in his chair, raised his index finger for the waiter. Most of the tables among the papier-mâché walls of the synthetic grotto were already empty. The check appeared instantaneously.

Julie's father touched Conrad's arm, leaned toward him. "I have a feeling we've overstayed our welcome, Dick."

"Now, just give me a moment to see to my face," her mother said.

"You go on, Mary," Dixon said. He glanced at Julie.

"Come keep me company, dear," Mrs. Dixon said, and Julie stood with her.

Dixon put his American Express card down on the check and handed it away. "What the hell is going on with you two, Dick?" he said.

Conrad fanned away the smoke of his cigarette. "We had a little commotion over some flowers this afternoon. That's all."

"That's not all. You two are at it every time we get together."

Conrad shrugged. He had slipped his loafers off under the table and he was groping for them now. "I don't know," he said.

"Everyone expects a few weeks of getting used to things," Dixon said. "But this is going on a year and it's becoming intolerable."

"There's nothing wrong," Conrad finally said.

Dixon sat back in his chair. "Dick, I know the kind of man you are," he said. "You always showed our girl all the respect her mother and I could ever pray for. May I tell you what frightens us, Dick? Your self-control."

Conrad drilled his cigarette out in the ashtray between them. "I don't have any prob—"

"I'm sure you don't," Dixon said. "What worries us is that your patience is . . . Dick, let me explain something to you," he said. "When I hear my daughter snap at you I can't help thinking, What has that son of a bitch been doing to our little girl? That's how fathers are. But Julie has to grow up and that job belongs to you."

Conrad looked into the bottom of his coffee cup. Dixon was an impossible bore. How could he let him know that he wouldn't discuss Julie with him now or ever? Dixon's counterfeit, ridiculous fairness.

"We let you marry Julie when we did," Dixon said. "We let her quit Connecticut College even though her mother had always . . . Look, the hell with all that," he said. "You kids are too damn young, but you've got to make a marriage out of this if it kills you both. I want you to remember that, Dick."

Conrad stared at his father-in-law's rigid face. "I'm doing the best I can," he said.

"Then do better."

They saw the Dixons to their car and then took a cab to Central Park West and 71st. When he put the key in the door of their apartment Conrad said, "I've never seen anything like that, Julie."

"Why, thank you," she said, and went past him into the living room and tossed her coat across the couch.

"I don't know what your parents think."

"The hell with what they think," she said. She went into the bedroom, out of his sight.

Conrad went to the far wall of the living room, pressed the switch for the light above the sink and picked a tumbler from the cabinet. He turned on the cold water. The carnations lay wilted over the edge of the drainboard and a clutter of filthy dishes welled to meet them. Conrad slapped the tumbler down.

"Will you just tell me, Julie? Will you just tell me what I'm doing that's so terribly—" Beside the dresser she knelt with the violet dress pulled up about her knees, her eyes closed, her face buried in the gentians.

"Julie, for Christ's—" He put his fist against the wall. "Just for once, Julie," he said. "Please. What? Will you just—"

She looked up to him and moistened her lips. "Pick me up and throw me on the bed and lay me, Rick," she said.

"I will not."

"Rick, why haven't we got any friends?" she said.

"I don't know." Conrad waved a hand in her face. "Julie, I'm too goddam busy for all the nonsense that you—"

"Why don't you ever take me anywhere, Rick?"

"Look, Julie—"

"Rick, I've got to have a life. Don't you know that?"

"Julie, if I don't make good at Maislin you won't have a home or clothes or anything."

She got hold of the dresser's edge. "Well, will you believe me if I tell you that I don't care?"

"No," he said. "And if you had any sense—"

"I just want to be thrilled with something again, Rick," she said. She looked down at the floor. "Just once more I want to feel—"

"Julie, you talk like a ten-year-old child. Do you know that?"

She raised her face. Conrad could see the lacy edge of her brassiere beyond the scoop of the violet dress, the warm hollow between her breasts. He turned away.

"We've got to start talking to each other again," he said. "We just can't live like this. I love you so very—" When he turned back she had lifted her head to the bowl of gentians, was pressing the flowers lightly to her face.

"God damn it, Julie!" Conrad shouted. "I'm going to smash those flowers to—"

Her eyes closed down. "You'll do nothing of the kind."

Conrad took a step back. "I'm telling you. I'll throw those—"

She began to get to her feet. "Rick, if you—" She stumbled

and her hand struck the vase. When it hit the floor the purple of the gentians seemed to run in the water among the shattered pieces of glass. She bent forward and put her elbows on her knees and burrowed into her hands with her face.

"Julie, I'm sorry," he said. "Julie, please. I didn't mean to make you—" Then he knelt beside her and kissed her on the forehead. "Love, you don't—"

She let her hands down and he was surprised to see that her eyes were dry. Without speaking, she began to sweep the flowers and the glass together.

"Don't, love," he said, but she pulled her hand free. "You're just going to cut your . . . Julie, watch out, the—"

An angular, ragged fragment of the vase lay in her open palm. She was looking directly at him while her hand shut tight to a fist and the first red drops appeared between her fingers.

Conrad couldn't move to stop her and he couldn't speak. He saw her opposite him on her knees in the purple sheath, a dark and closing flower.

MY LIFE IN MOVING PICTURES

I

I T WAS A LONG DRIVE from Manhattan, but even before they were through Jamaica, Conrad was certain he detected the saline and decaying scent of the ocean. That brought him back to recollecting: The Pontiac's radio was playing, but he didn't hear that; Julie wasn't saying anything. He remembered the chafe of sand between his belly and the elastic of his old swim trunks. They never went ocean bathing any more; the sun was too strong for Julie's skin and the sea air chapped her lips and took the set out of her hair. He remembered coming home and pouring the sand out of the heels of his sneakers when he was a boy, into one palm and then from one palm to the other, back and again, and finally flushing it away down the toilet. His mother had always insisted on anointing him with a terrible ocher grease; whenever she succeeded in cornering him with that tube the sand clung to him like burrs, breaded him. Too early in the season or too late, the beach fell dizzily into the surf from the tide line and the stripped underskin of sand below the waves was thorny with fragments of shell. The late-season waves struck him like a belt lash; a low, brass sun; the kelp beards along the jetty rocks that would soon become ice chains; the concrete sand. Every season's end, the cheer of their beach house thinning out, his family had clung to the dregs of summer. No one spoke of packing back to the city until even sweaters were futile. Then one day, instinctively and lemming-fashion, with a near hysterical flurry, they simply left.

Julie said, "I don't see the point in this. That doesn't matter to you." She had her knitting in a clear plastic bag on the floor beside her legs; she picked the bag up and then put it down again.

"You don't have to make it sound like that," Conrad said. "It's—"

"It's a pain in the ass."

Conrad dropped his cigarette butt away in the draft of his open window; he was wearing a short-sleeved white shirt and the October sun was hot and cold on his elbow. Julie closed her eyes, slouched.

"You don't—"

"First thing it will be one thing and another and then the traffic all the way back to the city," she said. "And then he won't want to go."

"He's all packed," Conrad said.

"A lot that ever meant to your father. He'd live out of his hat if he had the chance."

Conrad swallowed. "Look—"

"I never saw such a disorderly man," Julie said. "Since you stopped living with him."

"Look, you don't really have to talk that way, honey," Conrad said. "You know that."

"Rick," she said, "if I were a con man, I'd want a hundred of you for patsies."

Conrad eased the car right, out of the passing lane. "Julie, does it always have to be riddles?" He listened, but she didn't answer. "Julie?"

"It's father and son," she said. "Let me have a cigarette."

He drew one, put it to his lips and pressed the lighter home. "Do you want to talk about whatever it is?" he said.

She blew a breath out. "I can't talk to you, Rick. Don't you understand that?"

"It's not because I don't want to listen," Conrad said.

"I never told you that."

"Well, I want you to know I want to listen, Julie."

"Rick, just drive, would you please?" she said.

He signaled to pass, tapped the accelerator. The car moved smoothly with a hiss of the exhausts. "If only I could." He broke off there. She laughed, but he ignored that. "What were you going to say, Julie?"

"Is that the racetrack?"

Conrad looked through her window. "I don't know. I guess so. Sure."

"You're two of a kind," she said. "Like about the sympathy. You're two people who have got to hear it."

Conrad touched his tongue into the corners of his mouth. "I don't understand that."

She shrugged. "That cigarette's mine," she said.

He put the lighter back into the dash and passed the cigarette along.

Her voice was breezy. "Like when I'm supposed to say, I love you, Rick. You're supposed to know some things without getting hit in the face with them. Didn't anyone ever tell you that? Don't you know that, Rick?"

He didn't understand what she meant; he didn't know what she was saying. He could always tell, coming home, when she was tired, when her back hurt. He could watch her hips beneath her clothes, the way she walked. He knew whenever she had taken too much to drink; she seemed to look through him to the back of his brain. He knew when her period was due by counting the pills left in her dispenser. He knew her brassiere size, why she had to have her slacks made to order, how she couldn't flip an omelet over. He knew when she didn't change to her nightgown in the bathroom that she wanted him to love her; he knew when she had felt an orgasm and when she was pretending so that he would go on for himself.

"Adult people shouldn't have to hear it, Rick," she said. "They know."

"Please, Julie—"

"Rick, you're going too fast."

"Julie—"

"Rick, you're going to get a ticket."

He stared at the dashboard; the speedometer's needle was edging toward 70. He pressed the brake too hard. He felt his buttocks leave the seat.

"Rick, for Christ's sake."

The speedometer's needle held at 45. A Cadillac passed them, two new Fords in tandem, and a Volkswagen. They passed a shopping center on the left-hand side with cars swarming like termites. The radio was belting out rock 'n' roll.

"You'd better know your father's never leaving that beach house ever again," she said.

Conrad drove; the radio played on. The Cross Island Parkway rolled like waves. The sun bounced up and down. Through underpasses, going south the width of Long Island toward the ocean. Then there was more yellow in the grass and the trees were pared thin. A lack of houses, fewer automobiles, narrow highway with its pockmarked, ankle-high divider and weeds coming through the seams of the concrete and the bone-white broken line worn to gray. Tollbooth and the Channel Bridge. Down the sweep of the parabola toward Atlantic Beach. Kornbluth's delicatessen with its steam-and-grease windows. The drive-in with the speaker stands coming up through the sand like quills. Light-years of picket fence; scrub grass. The bang of aluminum screen doors, so distinctive, singular, familiar.

Conrad would bang in through the screen door; his mother would look up, wiping her hands in a striped kitchen towel. Season's end. The roses smell of cabbage and corned beef. His chair at the table too low and his hands reaching up to touch the green oilcloth. His mother's sloppy kiss. The general cold of air and water entering their beach house. The honey taste of the hot cabbage leaves.

"Cemetery," Julie said.

"What?"

"Nothing, Rick." She rolled her window up, pulled the lapels of her sweater across her bosom. "I said we'd be better off apart."

He stopped for a red light; the car's turn indicator clicked incessantly, an arrow beneath the speedometer flickered. "You don't want to talk like that, Julie," he said.

"I've said it before, Rick. I've meant it every time."

"Stop, Julie."

"Put the heater on, Rick. The fan, too." She touched his shoulder. "You don't see it my way, do you?"

He turned his head. "What's so funny?"

"Oh, you are, Rick," she said. "I ought to take pictures of you so you could see your expression when you get exasperated."

His hands were hurting him; he let the steering wheel go, flexed his fingers.

"Well, what are you waiting for?" Julie said. "An invitation?"

The light was green and he swung the car left; the lanes of concrete ran dead east from there through Atlantic Beach to Point Lookout and the beginning of the sea.

Often lately she spoke that way and always in the same even tone. She never lost a tear when she mentioned separation, was never close to the bottom of a bottle of Scotch. She never spoke of it when she was tired or busy, never when they were in a hurry. Always the thought seemed to come to her in her moments of greatest peace and lucidity, at times when her mind was clear and undisturbed. That was the terror of it for him.

It had begun, of course, in passion: when they were at daggers with each other. She had threatened divorce; he had told her not to talk nonsense. She had answered that he was straight out of the comics. That had made him shut his fist, draw his arm like a bowstring. And then he hadn't struck her. Opposite his fist she had stood breathless, waiting for the blow, her tongue caught between her teeth, her eyes closed, her hands held away from her body and her fingers clenched. He thought then of the first few times he had kissed her: the summer of his high school graduation, the pitch of his sailboat over the gleaming sea. Her eyes had been closed then and she had held her hands out of his way. Instead of her cheek, he caught her skirts in his fist, threw them back over her, pulled her down to the cork tiles of their apartment's kitchen floor, buried his face in her thighs. For the few seconds that he knelt like that, not a muscle in her body moved; even her breath stopped.

"When we're divorced, I'm going to live in Capri," she said. "You'll send me a check every month."

"Don't talk drivel," Conrad said. He knew all the whitewashed houses: those with the green shutters and those with the blue, their red tile roofs; the white stucco Beachaven Hotel with its infinite tiny windows. In snatches, between the houses in the bystreets, he saw the darkened cabana clubs.

"Oh, this can't go on forever, Rick," she said. "Your literal mind."

"Just forget about my mind and keep the house neat and be thankful," Conrad said. He wasn't really talking to her and he recognized the danger in that. He knew he had to be careful not to say the wrong thing and set her off. But at that moment he didn't care.

He knew every house, every tit on every red fireplug, all the stunted trees and all the crumbling porches. He had known the pizzeria as a private home, as a deli, as a bar and grill. The shutters on most of the houses were drawn closed and the pizzeria's windows were boarded over for the winter. He had seen all that, the aftermath, the leavings of the exodus, a dozen times before. He cherished these shards of the season; he hadn't realized that before. Down every street, something peculiar to his family and his family's own. Always they had been the last to leave, and his valedictory glimpse of their summer asylum was this bare one. It was this memory, this particular aspect, that he nurtured through the winter months with the radiator banging in the corner of his Manhattan bedroom.

He would straggle across town from public school with the slicker coat heavy and the tapping of the winter rain on the visor of his cap. His mother would see him change his shoes and socks and give him grilled cheese sandwiches and a bowl of brown potato soup. He would hold his face over the bowl and let the steam swell around him, looking into the frosted windows running with rain. There it would appear to him again as it had been in the moment that his father pointed the Nash northward across the Channel Bridge for Manhattan: Atlantic Beach through the rear window and across his shoulder, tucked into the curve of the green sea, drawn up on the coast of winter.

So it was through the winter: the snow transmuted into sand, waves in the bathtub water, books on sailing from the Children's Room of the library at 79th and Third. Whenever his mother baked, she left him the trimmings of crust and three fingers of apple. In a tapioca glass he baked his own small pie and watched it swell through the window of the Tappan range. His pie browned and the oven became too hot to touch and Conrad thought of the last days on Atlantic Beach with the cold sun and the particles of surf that burned cold.

They turned at Maxwell Street. The scrub grew thick on the shoulders of the concrete and Conrad's father's house sat apart from the rest, one floor and the peaked roof above the attic where he had first touched Julie's breasts, a veil of smoke curling from the chimney. Past the house the sand went away, narrowing into a vanishing point far short of the horizon, and in three directions the sea lay. He had his window open and the salt air chilled his elbow and his upper arm: a sensation from the prehistory before his earliest recollections, a bitter sensation, his own by birthright and his own by heritage.

In the yard with the sand pouring in over the tops of his shoes, he stopped her and said, "Please, Julie, don't start a commotion in there."

She had on a yellow dress with a full skirt; that was his favorite color against the color of her hair and eyes. She took the skirt in her hand and swung it like a young girl, and didn't answer him.

"I don't care what you say to me," Conrad said. "But not in front of my father, Julie."

She grinned and let her head roll. "Ricky, you should know

me better than that by now," she said. "That's one of them."

"One of what?" Conrad said.

"One of the things you don't have to say."

He heard the screen door. His father said, "Well, I'm glad you finally made it, Richie," and shook his hand and kissed Julie. "I'm sure you had lunch, which is good because you well know the way I cook."

Julie said, "Better than I do, Dad," and Conrad's father said, "Listen to this flatterer. Don't you know that once you've married the heir you don't have to banana-oil the old man, Julie? Why don't we go in?"

They did go in; through the foyer where the abrasion of sand had bared the flooring of its paint, across the braided bull's-eye rug that puddled in the hall. In the sitting room there was a tall console radio, two facing settees with squat, bent legs and funereal chintz curtains beating softly before the open window.

"You'll want a drink to get you started," Conrad's father said.

Julie said, "Scotch-and-water straight up," and Conrad said he'd skip it.

Conrad's father went out toward the kitchen and Julie took one end of the settee near the radio. "Look at this junk," she said.

"Julie, don't, please," Conrad said. He didn't sit down.

"Dry up," she said.

Conrad went out into the kitchen; his father had the cabinet above the sink open.

"Hello, Richie," he said. "Let us have a tray of ice cubes, son."

"Get them yourself," Conrad said, and pushed through the back door onto the porch. Two hundred yards away the water of the ocean turned a white lip. The sand at the edge of the porch looked like the surface of the moon. He heard the refrigerator door bang closed; a gull wheeled above his head, crying. Westward toward the land's end, he saw a man and a dog running after the horizon. He stepped off the porch and sank to his ankles. His father opened the door behind him and spoke to him, but he didn't hear that. He walked away. He heard the door close and kept walking; his shoes grew heavy with sand and he couldn't hold his ankles straight. The man and the dog were running his way. The man and the dog were on a collision course with Conrad, and Conrad didn't give a good Goddam. The man and the dog ran by. Conrad looked at the ocean, but there weren't any boats. He kicked the sand until his cuffs were full and then he turned his cuffs out. He walked back to the house and stood near the sitting room window and put his ear close to the sill.

"He didn't take his mother's death well," Conrad heard his father's voice say. The curtain flapped.

"I don't know what I can do about him," Julie said. "He has no nerves left, no feeling."

"Well, I know you'll weather it."

"I don't know if I will," she said.

"I know you will. You see, his mother was the sort of person—"

Conrad began to shout. He couldn't hear what he was shouting. He beat his fists on the windowsill and reached through the window and tore at the curtains. They broke like cobwebs in his hands. Julie and his father came to the window, but Conrad kept shouting at them. Then he put the heels of his hands against the underside of the windowsill and, while his father and Julie looked on, tried to push the summer house over.

They pulled a supper together from his father's larder of canned vegetables. They ate quietly in the kitchen on the table with the green oilcloth and Conrad's father drank two bottles of Miller Highlife and Julie drank one. Julie said that she was going to get the dishes done so that she could pack them and the flatware, and Conrad's father said that he and Richie were going to have a drop of Cointreau and a smoke and take the night air. They went out and sat in two wicker rockers on the front porch that overlooked the end of Maxwell Street. It was chilly, but a bright, pleasant evening. Conrad sat perfectly still; his father rocked easily.

"Julie was telling me how well you're doing at Maislin Chem," his father said. He was smoking a cigar and chewing the end to tatters. "You got a raise in August and you didn't mention that to me."

"It slipped my mind," Conrad said.

"Well, that's all right, son," his father said. "Do you like what they have you doing? I mean now that you've been in research for a while. I suppose you don't get to meet too many new people, stuck in the lab all day."

"They're okay." Conrad recognized the patronizing tone in his father's voice; he hadn't heard his father speak that way to him in a long time.

"Are you happy there? I don't think you're really happy with what you're doing," his father said. "You know, you're not locked up there. Not at all. You could change. You know?"

He'd had it in mind to push the beach house right off its foundation. There wasn't any doubt about that. He had the soreness in his shoulder blades. He was going to push the whole thing over and let it shatter into rubble. He didn't know what had made him think he could do that.

"You can get a thousand jobs," his father said. "I've practiced as an engineer for twenty-seven years. I've got the connections if you just say the word, son."

"I guess I'm well off where I am," Conrad said.

"Just say the word and you can go in with Allied or Monsanto. You name it. Well?" His father blew two trails of cigar smoke through his nostrils.

"I'm okay where I am."

His father went on rocking. "Julie and I had a good talk, son," his father said. "Julie said you were only twenty-three and that's right, you know. You don't have to pitch right in at twenty-three. You've got time."

"Sure," Conrad said. "I see that."

"The point I'm making is that you don't have to start hitting the stone wall for a couple-few years yet, Richie. I know what it's like and it's no picnic."

Conrad said it wasn't so bad.

"I have a friend—" His father broke off there and got up. "All done, Julie?"

"Done and I packed them in the hamper with the pots."

"Then we're all set but the cellar," Conrad's father said.

Julie let the screen door go. It whirred against its spring and drove home against its frame.

Conrad's mother had let him bake his own pies in the tapioca dishes; she had also taught him how to sew, and he made his own apron that he wore for baking. She had sat beside him on the settee in the living room of the beach house and she had put her arm around him and together their hands held the cloth and needle. He watched her clever fingers. Together they sat at dinner. When his soup ran down his chin, his mother made droll faces. Going to bed later on, he always listened for her moving about in the hall after the house was darkened. He would hear the heels of her slippers leave her feet and slap against the linoleum floor. He would hear her heavy breathing.

At first, his father spent only the weekends with them. In subsequent years, it was all the weekends and two full weeks of the summer besides. Then it was three weeks and the whole month of August and then, at last, in the three years before college, it was the whole summer. Mornings, it would be surf bathing; Conrad didn't swim well and his father made a point of teaching him. Afternoons, they watched the softball games in the park. But what Conrad loved most was the rainy days toward the season's end when the clams were fit.

Along the surf line he would follow his father to the very toe of Atlantic Beach, where the island ended. He'd wear his mackinaw and only slacks underneath, rolled to his knees. The sand would be cold and the rain would get past his slicker hat and under the collar of his mackinaw and run down his back. They'd stomp the tide beach for telltale squirts of water and dig after them with the hooked clam rake. For the length of the afternoon they'd caper together, tromping on the beach like dervishes, filling their bucket. The dwindling afternoon made all that sweeter; and they would linger until all of the sun was gone.

"Don't let me interrupt you," Julie said. She sat on the porch railing behind Conrad and put her hands on his shoulders, kneading them.

"We were talking about Richie's job," Conrad's father said. "I was saying how he could change over if he didn't like the spot he had."

"I don't see why he couldn't," Julie said.

"Of course he could. He's not stuck, are you, son? Anytime he wants, why—"

"Your father was telling me about a friend of his," Julie said close to Conrad's ear. "Did he tell you, Ricky?"

"I was getting to that," Conrad's father said. He struck a wooden match on the bottom of his sandal and rekindled his cigar. "There's a man I know named Otis. You don't know him. He was a CPA, did some business with my firm. I met him."

"He's in business now," Julie said.

"He's in the shoe business," his father said. "Nothing spectacular yet but a lot of growth potential. He has a couple of stores in Queens, one in the Bronx."

"He needs a new manager for one of his stores," Julie said.

Conrad's father said, "Well, not a new manager exactly."

"But someone with management potential," Julie said.

Conrad turned to her; she touched his cheek and looked away.

"We were thinking that would suit you better right at this stage, Richie," his father said. "Give you a chance to meet people, stand up to people on your own two feet." His father chuckled. "Shoe business and your own two feet. That's a joke."

Conrad didn't pay him any attention. He was watching Julie, and Julie said, "I think that would help you, Rick. You'd feel better. You know what I mean. I don't want people always to push you around. I don't want you to see the world by numbers all the time. I want you to have some sense of things."

"You see," his father said, "it's when you deal with people every day, you get to know they're all pretty much like you."

Conrad said, "Everything she told you was a lie."

His father took a look at his cigar, then leaned back into his rocking chair and pushed away from the floor with his toes. Julie's fingers worked the muscles through Conrad's neck and shoulders. Conrad's father began to hum; Conrad couldn't place the tune.

II

FINALLY, they decided to spend the night, to avoid the city-bound evening traffic and get an early start Sunday morning instead. Conrad's father brought the blankets back in from the car. They agreed not to fuss with the sheets and pillows. Conrad's father had had the electricity turned off that morning but, the way he put it, candlelight would add to the romance of things. They parted by candlelight from the sitting room: his father to the master bedroom and Conrad after Julie to his old room behind the kitchen.

With the door shut behind them, the yellow cone of flame dappled the room and the high iron bedstead. Julie sat on the corner of the bare mattress with her back against the wall and kicked her sneakers away. The light glowed and ebbed in her face. She covered her legs and the skirt of the yellow dress with one of their blankets.

Conrad touched a cigarette to the candle and drew. "I don't know what you said to him. You shouldn't have done that."

She put her head back against the wall. "It wasn't me that stood at the window and screamed," she said. "What was that all about?"

"Lay off," Conrad said. He leaned into the straight-backed chair that stood with his old desk; the chair was too narrow and its ribs drove into his hips. He didn't know what that business at the window had been about. When he had begun shouting it seemed as though someone else were shouting; and he couldn't hear what he was saying because of the racket.

"I just want to know," she said, "now that we're alone and Daddy isn't here. If you wouldn't mind."

"I wish I could tell you," he said. He rubbed his fingertips against the lids of his eyes. "I don't know what I was thinking."

She said, "Your literal mind."

"I'll tell you this," he said. "I know what I'm doing a lot more of the time than you do."

"Of course," she said.

He stared at her grinning face. More and more often he seemed to get things confused. He'd make dinner dates with her after work and stand for almost an hour, waiting for her and losing his patience. Then she'd arrive and remind him that he'd said six o'clock instead of five and he couldn't be sure what it was he'd actually said or meant to say. His shirts came back with starch; she'd remind him how he asked her to have them starched. He knew he never had his shirts starched, but he wouldn't be able to remember what he'd told her.

Two weeks ago—the fifth of October—he'd brought the traditional box of birthday chocolates with the appropriate card. She took it for a joke at first; then the confrontation came: "November fifth, Rick. After all . . ." Small tears. He was prepared to argue with her until she cried. He had actually been prepared to argue the date of her own birthday with her.

Conrad remembered that readiness. Maybe he had been living too close to the formulas and the calculators of Maislin Chemical. He thought about how they had driven down to take delivery on the new Pontiac, how he insisted that it would be her car really, even though he had signed the contract. He thought about how they had been waiting for a signal light to change and how she had laughed at him and said, Well, I think a red car will do us both some good. Waiting for the light to change, the perspiration had run behind his ears, circling his shirt collar; coming into the showroom, she put her hand uneasily upon the glowing yellow skin of the car, and the way she looked at him made him understand that she knew his secret.

"You know what I've been thinking?" Julie said. Her smile was gone.

He knew: that he had made one mistake too many; that the only solution was psychiatry, a job selling shoes, fewer dreams, less esoterica, more substance.

"I've been thinking about all the boys I could have dated," Julie said. Beneath the blanket, she drew her knees to her chest and wrapped them in her arms.

Conrad crushed his cigarette away. He lit another one. "What about them?"

"Oh, I don't know. Just who they might have been. Places I could have gone."

Conrad looked at the tops of his shoes on the bare wood floor. "I guess you missed a lot of big times."

"I was thinking that," she said. "We never had anyone but each other, you know."

He was afraid to look at her face, to see what she was leading up to. "I guess we never did," he said.

"That was a mistake," Julie said. "The experience. We might have saved ourselves a lot of heartbreak."

He knew her speech about why didn't they have any friends? Why was it he never took her anywhere? Why was he so much to himself? Occasions past, he had answered that her ideas of the glories of night life were ridiculous, even juvenile. But he had never even convinced himself that he wasn't simply "hiding," as she put it; that it wasn't just a matter of being shy, of being terrified.

"I'm alive," Julie said. "You haven't seen fit to ratify my existence."

He glanced up.

"I want something I can feel," she said. She had her fingernails against her temples. "I don't want only to know it," she

said, "have it in mind. I want something I can touch." She put
her elbows on her knees and cupped her face. "You've always
been frightened of women, haven't you, Ricky?"

Conrad knocked his cigarette's ash away. "Well, I don't
know," he said. "I don't think so. I wouldn't say—"

"You have." Her voice was light, charming. Her smile came
on.

He shrugged. "That's dumb."

"It's a struggle just to get you to have me," Julie said.

"What do you mean? Listen, I—"

"Didn't your daddy ever tell you, Ricky?" she said, and
laughed. "It's a battle trying to have a baby without your coop-
eration."

He shook his head; her expression gave no hint of what she
meant. "I didn't know you wanted— Listen, you keep taking
those pills to . . . well, I thought—"

"Rick, you're a goose—"

He loved the sound of that name, reveled in it.

"Rick, I haven't taken anything for the last three months."

She was laughing and then he was laughing.

"I didn't . . . you should have told—"

"Well, you're supposed to understand these things after being
married better than a—"

"How many months are you?" Conrad said. He should have
known that, but he wasn't going to worry now. He thought about
the niche in their medicine cabinet where the pink dispenser of
Ortho-Novum had always rested and how that spot had been
empty now for more weeks than he had realized. He remembered that very morning; how he had been half asleep digging
for his blades and razor, how he had dislodged her powder box
accidentally and how the box had fallen, spewing powder on the
bathroom tiles. The space for the dispenser behind the powder

box had been empty after all. He hadn't recognized what that meant, what he was seeing. Then he remembered how foolish he had felt patting up the powder from the floor with a damp face towel. Then he remembered how carefully he had wiped the powder from the pink plastic dispenser which had also fallen; he remembered being afraid that she would see the traces of powder on the tile and laugh at his clumsiness.

"What do you mean by months?" Julie said.

He shut his eyes. The dispenser had been there. It had been round in his hand, slick with powder. "Months pregnant," he said.

"Oh, I'm not pregnant yet, Ricky," she said. "Goose," she said, "I just want you to know that I'm available."

He visualized that dispenser. Half its pills were gone, the rest were pale yellow under the clear plastic top. He had balanced it carefully against the back wall of the medicine cabinet, folding the instruction sheet pasted to it. He drew heavily on the cigarette and the heat through its filter hurt his fingers.

Fantasy. That's all it had been. For some reason he must not want her to have a baby. It was, really, a struggle for her when she wanted him to have intercourse with her. He complained so often that he was tired, that he'd had a rotten day, that his shoulders hurt him. And he always managed to make himself believe that he was tired, or that his back was sore. He made her leave him alone, go back to her own bed. He understood that now.

"You want to have children, don't you, Ricky?" she said. "You like them."

"Sure," Conrad said. "But I don't think—"

"There isn't any reason to wait, Rick," she said. "I'm not afraid." She giggled and shrugged her shoulders. "Oh, I was, of course, when we first got married. What did I know about that kind of thing? But I'm in love with you and I'm not afraid any more and I think it might be the answer for us."

"I don't know about that, Julie," Conrad said. He lit still another cigarette with the butt in his hand.

"Well, for goodness' sake, why not? We are married."

"It's this whole thing," he said, and drew a circle in the air between them. He couldn't discuss it right now; not right now and with her.

"What whole thing? Rick, make sense."

"The world," he said.

"What?"

"Jesus, you know they're sure to blow it up one of these days." He didn't care how absurd he sounded.

"Oh, Rick, that's idiotic," Julie said. She held her knees against her bosom, peered at him.

"Well, it's true," he said. "All that jazz. You know. Bombs. Christ knows what else." It rose in him, strangely, for no reason. "We're stuck with it. The finger is on the trigger right this minute." It climbed in him and he spoke louder; he had something else besides his mother and his wife in him. "If you knew anything about how far science has—"

"Oh, if they blow the world up I won't care, Rick."

"You take the speed of light times itself," he said. "Now, listen, Julie. And you multiply that out by the mass of a lousy little acorn and—"

She shouted, "Well, if they blow the fucking world up it'll be people like you that do it, Rick."

He got up. "No, don't be a jerk, Julie." He couldn't stop smiling. "I just crack raw petroleum into gasoline and vaseline. Knock a few bonds apart. These guys that work with the fissionable stuff, they know—"

"What the hell do they know that I can't grab up and hold?"

"Oh, Julie." He opened up his arms. "There's a whole universe out there. Quasars and thermodynamics we've never dreamed of. You can't keep your whole mind earthbound."

"I can," she said. "And I will."

He stood as he was, arms raised toward the ceiling. She was looking at him, but through him, not seeing him.

"I don't believe what I can't feel. It doesn't make any difference to me, all your bonds and logic and galaxies and what else, Rick." Her lips were pressed together. "I don't understand all that, Rick. I only know I've got to live and none of that makes any difference. It's what I feel and after that, when I'm dead, it's nothing." The curtains across the window moved, and beside her on the desk the light of the candle flickered, moving across her eyes. "I can't cope with all the things you understand, Rick. I don't know about bombs or any of that. I'm just a woman."

He let his arms go slowly down; he heard from beyond the house the sounds of the ocean and, close to him, the sound of her weary breathing. "Julie, you can think about it and—"

"I can't think about it," she said. "All I know is what I can touch. You can't prove all your dreams to me. Anything I can't touch"—her voice grew smaller—"I can't believe." She touched her breasts. "I have to touch. I don't know why. It has to be in my sense. Sense is so much more real than mind."

He started toward her, but she didn't seem to notice that.

"You don't really believe it, Rick," she said. "No more than you can love me really. I hear you in the night," she said. "I hear you in your sleep, Rick." She stared at him. "I hear you calling out, Rick."

He stopped. "Calling what, Julie?"

Then she was pushing the blankets away from her legs and her knees were up against her chest, buoying her skirt, and she opened her thighs and she had no underwear.

"I want you, Rick," she said. "All day. I can't wait. Even the way you were at the window."

Her *mons* spread darkly where her thighs met; he turned his face. "Cover yourself," he said.

"I hear you calling in your sleep, Rick," she said. "Often. All the time."

"Stop, Julie," he said. He couldn't control the tightening beginning in his undershorts. He heard the zipper front of her dress. "Cut it out, Julie. Right now."

"Prove it isn't true, Rick," she said behind him. "Let me know one thing for certain. Prove it isn't true."

"Prove what?"

"Greenberg," she said.

He turned around; she had unhooked her brassiere and put it aside. Her breasts swelled toward him, jabbed toward him. Her thighs were open, her back curved against the wall, her fingernails thrust out to him.

"What about Greenberg, Julie?"

"The way you call for him in the night," she said. She kept shaking her head. "I don't care. I won't care. The way you screamed for him at the window—I'll forgive that."

Conrad put his hand over his mouth.

"Your letters. From Newport. Even then I understood, Rick." She came forward to the edge of the bed, reaching for him. He stepped away. "I don't care what went on, Rick."

"What went on? Nothing went on. Julie, for—"

"I don't care," she said. "Believe me." She stood up. "It's what I feel about you now right now that matters, Rick."

She came toward him, and he backed from her. "Listen, Julie, you're—"

"I don't care, Ricky. Please. Stick it in me and I won't—"

He grabbed the door open; she reached for him, missed; her

hand slapped across his face. Then she had bent her head forward and covered her nose and mouth. Through the crying she said, "Oh, you fag. You rotten fag."

When he had gone through the kitchen and outside, he looked back at her through the screen door. Dry-eyed, she was watching him. Then he heard his father's door open and she slammed the one between them.

III

FOR WHAT SEEMED a long while Conrad sat where the beach fell away into the ocean. There wasn't any moon and he couldn't see the water, but he had the fine spray falling on his face and on his arms. Quietly, he spilled a handful of sand back and forth and thought about Greenberg and New Haven and Yale. Of course, he had to explain it all to her. There hadn't been anything like what she had suggested. But she was the way she was and he couldn't expect her to understand the way he and Greenberg felt about each other. A manly affection; Conrad didn't see anything wrong in that. He'd never touched Greenberg. Not intimately. He'd thought about it occasionally.

He had thought about it. He had, but never really seriously. The way he thought of anything else, a whimsical notion. He'd tumbled that thought around. Greenberg slept naked, his morning urinary erection was impossible to overlook.

Conrad picked up another handful of sand. He'd seen Greenberg's erect penis; the first time surprised him. Greenberg's penis was no larger than his own. Greenberg towered over him, outweighed him by seventy pounds, but there was nothing extraordinary about his penis. Conrad thought about that; he rubbed the handful of sand between his palms until it spilled away. Greenberg's penis had a collar of rough, curly hair, its left testicle sagged beneath its right. That was very much like Conrad's own organs, and nothing very remarkable.

He wondered whether he had ever felt sexually stimulated by the sight of Greenberg's penis in the morning. He supposed he had. He thought about that. He had seen Greenberg's erection and been stimulated himself. Was that odd? Conrad didn't know. He looked at the sand cupped in his palms; the sand poured like water, was a true fluid. Not a true fluid, really, but fluid to the naked eye. In his intelligence he saw the sand was billions of tiny pebbles with sharp, irregular edges.

An erect penis meant sex, was a symbol for sex. Or was it only a symbol of an erect penis? A monolith was phallic, symbolic of the erect penis. Then an erect penis. Cock, dick, pecker, prick. Bird, man's name, bird symbol, needle. That didn't help him very much. He'd left his cigarettes inside. Julie would want to go on quarreling and he could do without his cigarettes until she went to sleep. He wasn't nervous. What she had said was too remote for shame or anger; objectively he dealt with it quite easily.

Cunt. He didn't know the etymology of that word. It certainly didn't symbolize railroad tunnels for him. Bush, muff. Those were obviously from form. Pussy. Julie had long fingernails; was anything more lithe than a cat? Snakes were, he supposed. They were phallic, though; little girls were supposed to be afraid that snakes would crawl up inside them. When they grew up they were frigid. Conrad had heard that somewhere. And he certainly didn't think of shoving his own penis into Greenberg when the sight of Greenberg's organs had aroused him.

Member. That was too polite. Conrad kicked his loafers off, peeled away his socks. The sand was cold between his toes, but that was a pleasure. Member was a word for . . . It was almost a euphemism. Mass as matter in terms of inertia. Prick was an emotionally expressive word, but limited in imagery. Speed was distance as a function of time; time was distance as a function of speed. That made a hell of a lot more sense than cunt.

Conrad was working it out for himself, and neatly. Greenberg's penis made him think of intercourse. He had never thought of Greenberg having an ejaculation. At night in his room at school when Greenberg was out, Conrad had masturbated. He invariably thought of Julie while he rubbed himself, unless he had met some attractive girl that day and glanced down the front of her blouse or between her knees while they were sitting down. Occasionally, since they were married, he had masturbated; but then he thought of Julie usually, or one of the girls in the office.

Cunt was a peculiar, clipped word; pussy had more the notion of a vulva—the sibilant helped conjure damp, a sliding movement. Conrad had stopped wondering whether he was queer or ever had been. He ran the number 3 through the circuits of his brain; it breezed through cubes and squares. The word cunt thumped like a lead penny. Odd language, but somehow better than seeing sand as fluid when he knew perfectly well it was crystalline. Someone was standing beside him.

"I guess I won't be butting in," his father said.

Conrad got up, holding his shoes.

"You'll catch cold," his father said. He was wearing slacks and a sweater.

"I'm sorry I woke you," Conrad said. There was a light burning in the kitchen of the house; he couldn't tell whether or not Julie's door was closed.

"I wasn't sleeping," his father said. "Take a walk?"

"Sure, Dad."

They turned eastward, toward the land's end, going around the rushes that grew at the tide line.

"I couldn't sleep, Richie," his father said while they went. "I know you're troubled and I want to help you. Julie's told me you've been confused lately." His father looked over at him. "Only about little things, naturally. But she's distressed."

"It's nothing I can't straighten out," Conrad said. He felt relaxed, easy with his father near him. "I've been preoccupied, I guess."

"Well, that's the way business is, son. You should appreciate that by now. It's not just nine-to-five."

"I know that."

"You can only get ahead if you give it twenty-four hours a day."

"I know."

The sand came to an end with the darkness of water surrounding them on three sides. There was a chilling breeze. They sat on the hull of someone's overturned dinghy. Conrad couldn't see his father well. He thought about his shirts that shouldn't have been starched and about the Pontiac that was yellow instead of red and about the contraceptive pill dispenser that wasn't there.

"I don't want you to get the idea I've flipped, Dad," Conrad said. "They've had me up to my ears and I've just been absent-minded lately."

"Oh, I know that, son." His father lit a cigar; in the gleam of the wooden match Conrad saw the grizzle on his father's face, the lines of age, the hollowness. "I just thought the shoe business would give you a breather. Let's not worry about that any more, shall we?"

"Sure." Conrad dropped his loafers to the ground and put his bare feet into them; he stuffed his socks into a back pocket of his pants.

His father puffed at the cigar and its tip glowed, but not enough to illuminate his face. "I learned something from you today, Richie," he said. "Remember when you were in school and you wrote home to us that you were going to break the Ivy League record for the hundred-yard dash?"

"Yes."

"Have you thought about that lately?"

"How do you mean?" Conrad said. The question was almost funny; he wondered what the hell it was he had been thinking about lately.

"I mean, any regrets?" his father said.

"Not really." Conrad put his hands in his pockets; the air was very cold about him, but he couldn't savor it the way he always had. He remembered how he had felt while he was talking to Julie; he remembered what he'd said about the universe. "I don't think that was very important for—"

"It was important to you then," his father said. "What about now? Don't care much?"

"Nope."

"Well, I must tell you something, Richie," his father said very softly. "You know I had a brother named Peter. You opened his trunk in the attic once, remember?"

"Yes," Conrad said. "He drowned."

"That's right, son. You know when that was?"

Conrad heard the rasp of the back of his father's hand across the stubble of his face.

"That was more than forty years ago. Can you imagine that? That's ancient history, almost," his father said, and laughed.

"Nineteen twenty-one. I was a boy then, just thirteen. You can't imagine me a boy, can you?"

The idea tickled Conrad. "I guess not, Dad. Were you pretty much of a pest?"

"You can bet I was." His father reached out and touched Conrad's arm through the dark. "I was thirteen when my brother drowned. He was swimming in front of the house and I was playing in the sand and he called to me. Screamed to me, you know. And I just stood there and watched him scream and go down and come up until he didn't come up any more. Then I ran into the house."

Conrad didn't move; his father's voice went on evenly, quietly.

"My dad and I got into our surfboat and rowed out to where he was floating and brought him back to the house. He was dead. Your mother knew about this," his father said. "Are you still with me, Richie?"

Conrad shuffled his feet. "Yes," he said.

"Well, I stood out there and watched my own brother drown," his father said. "You may think I didn't love him, but I did, very dearly. And I cried afterward. Because we were very much in love, he and I, and very close for the ten years' difference."

Across the water Conrad saw the beginnings of the moonrise, faintly, spreading on the waves.

"I mourned my brother Peter until today," his father was saying. "As I suppose you mourn your mother."

"Yes, I do," Conrad said.

"And I puzzled over him. Whether if I had run into the house or jumped after him into the ocean I could have saved him. You follow that?"

231

"Yes."

"That troubled me terribly," his father said. "I guess that until today I belonged to the past. Now I'm giving it up. You have to do that too, son."

Conrad thought of his mother's hand and his, together stitching the cloth into a baking apron. "I can't do that, Dad," he said.

"You have to abandon that past. That's all you can do, Richie."

"I can't," Conrad said. "I can't do that."

His father cleared his throat and spat. "It was my fault, son. Because I didn't think you were old enough to know that your mother was dying and there was nothing in heaven and earth to be done about it. I don't know why I thought you wouldn't guess," his father said. "Children understand so much more than their parents want to believe."

"I always knew," Conrad said.

"That she was dying?"

"Yes."

"Well, I just want you to know that there was nothing you could have done about it," his father said. "You couldn't have done anything that would have saved her, not if you turned the world upside down. I want you to believe that. No more than I could have done anything to save my brother from drowning," his father said. "I know that now. I believe it. And you must, too."

Conrad had to turn away. He looked back at the house and it was as it always had been at season's end, lonely on the land's end, gray in the first moonlight.

"I'm selling the house," his father said beside him. "I'm giving up on the past, and I want you to give up, too, and be a man. Have children with your wife and just forget about that house and everything that happened to you there."

The moon lit the beach house, and nothing beyond it. The house stood out, glowed with the presence of Julie.

"It won't be easy, Richie," his father said, and put a thin arm across his shoulders. "But you've got the ability and Julie has all the courage to help you. Forgive her if she seems oversensitive. She's only apprehensive. She'll stand by you, whatever comes, if you keep trying."

Conrad realized they were walking; the house grew before him.

"She's a rational, brave girl, son," his father was saying. "She'll help you a lot if you give her the chance. And try to forgive me," his father said.

The arm about Conrad's shoulders warmed him against the cold breeze. "For what, Dad?"

"For keeping this house so long and making you come back to it again and again, son. I didn't realize what I'd done in my selfishness until I saw Julie's face when you were standing out at the window and screaming that you wouldn't let your mother die."

At first, Conrad was going to say something; but then they were in the house and his father was telling him good-night and he couldn't think of what he ought to say. When he opened the door of his bedroom, Julie had a blanket over her, and through the darkness her eyes were watching him. He went back to the kitchen and sat down at the table and blew out the candle his father had left burning there.

ENTROPY

——————————————————————

"No, Ricky, wait," she said. "Please won't you just . . . just a moment. Touch this," she said. "Not the glove."

Conrad didn't want to, but he couldn't endure another scene. He shrugged out of the leather; the cold cracked down across his knuckles.

"Now here." She took his wrist. "Up and down."

The slender trunk of the birch was sheathed in ice, like oiled gunmetal under his fingertips. The texture of the tree was gone, hidden; the places where he could see the coated bark peeling back were only dimples and nodes in the ice. He looked from the tree to her.

"Now touch this." She thrust his hand between the parted front of her leopard jacket, underneath the cashmere sweater. "You can't feel anything, can you, Ricky?"

"Of course I can. Don't be smart."

"My skin," she said. "You can't feel the grain of my skin, can you?"

"Your skin hasn't got a grain. Don't be ridiculous. It's smooth."

"Like ice?" she said.

"It's—"

"Like ice?" she said again, and leaned the weight of her body against his hand. Her breath was smoky beneath his chin; the wind was in her hair and blowing it across her face. "Is it like ice? Really? What do you know about my skin in your mind?"

Conrad blinked his eyes. Over his shoulder he saw the gas station attendant's freckled, hooded face staring their way.

"Give me your other hand," she said.

"Julie, please stop this. Make sense."

"Give it." She caught at the hem of his other glove. "Take that off and touch me. I want to prove to you that my—"

"Julie, the whole world's gaping." Conrad was fumbling the bare hand back into the glove.

"Bashful." She was laughing. She got her fingers in among his, snarling his with the glove, defeating him. "You're embarrassed. Aren't you a fool?"

"Well, all right." He ripped the glove free and turned away. He heard her laughter and her boots with the same abrasive noise on the gravel of the filling station. There was a bubble of sweat sliding in the small of his back like a needle. The cold had burned his fingers; it was stiffening the muscles under his eyes. The air about him stilled and his breathing covered every other sound. He was sucking his tongue against the rage and he felt helplessness jelling his body, setting it like plaster. Then she slammed in through the door of the car behind him, and the explosion of that sound cleaved the air about him like a melon.

Conrad was paying the attendant; the dollar bills were brand-new, adhered to each other. He couldn't manage them through the black leather. She was watching up at him through the sealed windshield. All of Vermont, the white and green of Vermont, was reflected on the glass with her face spectral behind it. Her leopard jacket lost its yellow in the glass, and her eyes went down to green. Her skin was gray, her mouth went down to green. Her hair was green. The yellow of the car's paint had turned green like dollar bills and he ground the dollar bills between his thumb and index finger. They had no fiber, were slippery against the glove leather. The attendant was concealing his sneer badly. Conrad wanted to slap the attendant's face; he felt he could do even that to protect her.

In the car, he snapped the seat belt across the front of his quilted nylon windbreaker.

She looked on, amused. "Do you feel entirely safe now, love?" she said.

He twisted the ignition key, and the hammering of the V-8 brought the Pontiac alive. In the rearview mirror he saw the attendant leaning in near the open window of the station wagon, sharing a smirking confidence with its driver. Conrad took the transmission to first gear, punched the accelerator against the fire wall, let the clutch spring up. The torque hit the macadam of the filling station with a whoop of tires, spewing back gravel like shot. And the Pontiac lurched onto the roadway, a blind and an overpowering thing.

The snow had been plowed up on either side of the two lanes to the height of a man. The shoulder markers thrust above the peaks; the tassels of cotton cloth that measured a seven-foot depth were plastered down with frost, did not rise in the slipstream of the Pontiac. The seams in the concrete thudded up through the tires, through the links of the suspension and the frame of the car with the mesmerizing regularity of a pulse. The speedometer's pointer jabbed and stuck at the 5 in 65 as if pinioned. There was a steady, hypnotic whistle of draft across the automobile's canvas top.

"Did you have your revenge on those people?" she said. "Aren't you a baby?"

Conrad said, "You could put the seat belt on, you know. It doesn't cost you anything."

"Why should I?" she said. "Give me a good reason. Go ahead. Just . . . Rick, for God's sake, you're getting so stuffy."

"It's my brain," he said. He put a cigarette in his mouth; she took it. He brought a second one from the pack on the dash and thumbed the lighter in.

"What's the matter with your brain?" she said.

"Statistics," he said. He was going to explain it; but he stopped himself, and made a joke of it instead. "The seat belt raises my chances for survival. I can't keep from reasoning." He wasn't saying it right; he wasn't saying it lightly enough. He glanced over toward her. "Excuse me for having a mind," he said, but his voice died out in despair.

"Machine," she said. She plucked the lighter and put it to the end of her cigarette until the tobacco glowed orange with the lighter's coil. She lit his. "Take your right glove off," she said, and blew the drag his way.

"Don't start that again." Conrad wound his wind-wing ajar; their fine smoke vanished through it, and the roar of the wash sucking was a tone higher than the hiss of the canvas top.

"You don't want reality to charge in here and bust up your neat little bigotries, do you?" she said.

Conrad slouched in the grip of his bucket seat. "Look, we're almost there," he said. "Behave."

"Go on and take your glove off." She pushed the front of her jacket open and freed the cashmere sweater from the top of her slacks. "Ricky, do it. Please."

He knew he couldn't refuse her. He threw the glove at the crotch where the windshield met the dash and thrust his bare hand into the grasp of her miniature two.

"What do you think now?" she said. "Ricky, what?"

His fingers felt the swell of her belly, the pit of her navel and the furrows that poured into it. The skin was smooth as he had said it was. He thought of the ice winding on the birch tree. The ice was smooth. Then her skin was non-smooth, rough. The gravel driveway of the gas station had been ragged, rough. Her skin was non-rough. Ninety-eight-point-six. Ectoderm. The sense in his fingers rose until it was razor-fine. Her belly tingled upward through the nervework of his arm in pointillism. Cobbles of tissue. The seams in the concrete registered like fists beating on the Pontiac's hood, the wind sighed, whined through the crack in the open vent. She pushed his hand down under the top of her slacks. Warmer. $NaCl+HOH+NH_4OH$. Sweat. Slick. He clung to the steering wheel with his other hand. The frilled fringe of her pubic hair. Fur:rough. Skin:smooth. Gravel:rough. Ice:smooth. Semi-rough. Demi-smooth. Grain and texture. Define.

The roadway was like a channel between the walls of snow. Like the harbor of her snow-white thighs. Platitude. Her milk-white thighs. Platitude. Her non-white thighs. Thigh-white. Belly-smooth. His own hair-darkened thighs and belly. His thighs were not thigh-white; his belly was not belly-smooth. Then her thighs were: her-thigh-white. Impossible language. Her her-belly-smooth belly. Absurd. Wind shriek, engine scream, gearbox chatter, concrete rumble, *boom, bam, bang, whizz, pink, crack, clunk, clank, ting, pow, zip, hiss.*

"Rick, do you love me even now?" she said.

She said:

"Riky, dew yoo luff me?"

"Rickee, du yew luv me?"

"Riquie, doo yu loff mi?"

The noises of the car in flight were: *boom, bam, bang, whizz, ping, crack, clunk, clank, ting, pow, zip, hiss.* Onomotopoeia. Valid language.

His fingers parted her labia, touched heat, dampness. There was a sound, he knew, a splash when his fingers touched that wet. He wanted to hear that sound. He should put his ear to her vulva. A finely tuned ear. Hear that sound that was like no other sound in the universe. Hear it as he heard the road sound through the balls of his feet, as he heard the wind sound that was partly the tingling of the draft on the hairs of his auricular canals. Like the singular color of her thighs and belly, an unreproducible sound. An index-finger-touch-vulva-damp sound: *I touched the moisture of her vulva with the tip of my index finger.* Dry language that somehow turned loose a Niagara in his brain.

And dimension also: not merely vulva-damp. Vulva-love-damp. Vul'və-luv-damp. All their lives together compiled by a monosyllable. Hello. Courtship. Carnations. Satin dresses. Hair spray. Brassiere. Language like incantation. Phonemes to morphemes. Sounds to conjure with. Our waltz. Cointreau. Cigarette. Music. Scotch-and-water. Affair. Clasp. Clench. Kiss. Loss. Hip to hip and thigh between thigh. You were right, love. You were right, love. My history with you is packed into the sound between my index finger and your dampened vulva. Splash.

Conrad heard that sound. Like the car noise, the wind noise, the road noise. All the sensations whirled in him in a grand cacophony, and the muscles in his bowels folded shut like a fist. His body trembled and he sucked his tongue against the agony of wanting her. And the memory of the sense of helplessness at the filling station came back to him in resonance with his desperation to ram his body into hers. There was a truth in her that was beyond logic. And the rage to have her and the rage to protect her were identical, inseparable. The same. They were the same and, he knew, irreconcilable.

In the ski lodge her cheeks were pinch-pink before the glow of the fireplace. The night pressed solid to the high glass windows, impenetrable as the color of her hair. Mountains and trees moved in the darkness outside, bending and swaying while the wind swam among them like whales. Her skin was smooth in apposition to the fireplace brick; even the nubs of her sweater seemed smooth. The stretch of her ski slacks ran without a crisis from where her body became legs to the snares of her calfskin boots. She was holding a Manhattan and its color matched her mouth.

Conrad had watched the sprawling blond boy of twenty or so edging across rooms all afternoon, homing on the bare ring finger of her left hand. In range at last on the couch beside theirs, the boy said, "You'll love the hill. Try the Vista Trail." He was sitting so that Conrad could see the ski patrol patch on the shoulder of his white sweater.

"I know I'm going to love the hill," Julie said. "Ricky, don't you love hills?"

"I don't know," Conrad said. He didn't want to be belligerent, but he couldn't have the boy involved. "I guess I don't care much for hills, Julie," he said.

"Who's your friend?" the ski patrol said, and flexed the muscles in the neck.

"That's my ex-husband," Julie said. She looked at Conrad out of the side of her face.

"Please, Julie," Conrad said.

"He follows me around," Julie said. "He starts trouble wherever I go."

"Well, that's not quite true," Conrad said. His palms were becoming sticky; he held both of them to his glass.

"You see, he's afraid I'll have affairs," Julie said. "He doesn't want to lose me. He doesn't believe in divorce, even when two people have no future together. Do you believe in divorce?"

"You bet," the ski patrol said.

"You are a horse's ass," Conrad said to the boy, and immediately felt a fool.

The ski patrol sat back. He put his highball glass on the polished oak floor. "Say, hold—"

"Don't pay attention," Julie said. "Ricky was an athlete once and he's very dangerous to fight with."

The ski patrol looked from Conrad's side of the couch to hers. "He doesn't look as tough as—"

"That's the secret," Julie said. She stretched out, resting herself on one elbow so that her hair poured into Conrad's lap. "He doesn't look it, he doesn't want to face it, but underground in Ricky there are alligators and spiders. Devils. Violence."

"Julie, it's late," Conrad said.

"Devils and violence," she said. "Under the veneer of rationality. A primitive thing lives in Ricky. But he has corsets on his mind to hide it."

"Well," the ski patrol said. "All the same. He looks—"

"Like an orchid," Julie said. She set her glass down on the floor and leaned toward Conrad, arching her arm over her head to put her fingers in his hair. "He won't admit to anything he feels," she said. "So he's a madman. A maniac."

There was a yoke of perspiration under Conrad's shirt and turtleneck, bracelets of perspiration where they closed at his wrists. The instant the boy seemed hostile, Conrad would have to strike out at the base of his sternum, double him over, slap him across the ear.

"Break something for our friend," Julie said to him. Her voice was liquid, coaxing.

Conrad cleared his throat; he made a pass at gaiety. "What, for instance?"

"Break a chair. Chop through a tabletop. Split a board with your elbow. Then tell us what it's like."

The ski patrol picked up his drink. He seemed to be gathering himself to rise.

"Wait," Julie said. "You've been stalking me all night."

The boy blinked; shuffled his feet.

Conrad said, "We'd all better turn in."

"But he has been stalking me, Ricky. You saw him."

Conrad opened his hands. "Julie, it's midnight. We want to get an early—"

"Suppose I told you that this man here is annoying me?" she was saying to the boy.

The ski patrol looked at Conrad and then, cowed, away.

"Suppose I told you, 'Help me, would you, please? This man is being terribly rude.' What would you do?" She smiled at the boy. "You know that people like me, people like me always give their boudoirs to their heroes, don't they?"

"Well . . ." The boy shrugged.

"I'm not worth a broken nose?" she said, straightening. "Are you going to sit there saying I'm not worth a black eye and a headache?" She wheeled on Conrad. "Ricky, are you going to let him say those things about me?"

"Julie." Conrad fingered the wool of her sweater. "Julie, it isn't going to work," he said.

She subsided against the couch. Conrad looked across at the ski patrol. "What's your name, my friend?" Conrad said.

"Gerry Lynch."

Conrad felt the perspiration pouring around his neck and into the gullies above his clavicles. "Go to bed, Gerry," Conrad said softly. "It's almost midnight." He motioned with his head. "Go on."

The ski patrol stared at him.

"Go," Conrad said, and waved the back of his hand.

The boy looked at Julie.

She closed her eyes, settled on the couch and raised her heels to the edge of the elevated hearth.

"Go ahead," Conrad said again, and a silence lingered in the emptiness the boy left.

The groups that had been chatting in other corners of the room began to drift downstairs to bed and Conrad was alone with her. The fire sank away to ashes and a final glowing fringe on the charred logs. The heat dissipated, the light fluttered and passed. The sitting room of the lodge settled into quiet, and darkness rolled under the beamed ceiling, filling the room to brimming. The lamps had been extinguished, and there was only the dim gleaming of the lobby beyond the rear door. Their shadows slowly crept down the room's rear wall. At last the fire failed.

Julie hadn't moved. Conrad wondered if she were dozing. He reached toward her and his hand was trembling like tiny bells. Just in the instant before his fingers would have collided with her lips, her mouth pulled back and she said, "Standstill."

Conrad hung as he was, reaching from God to Adam.

"Will you love me even now, Ricky?" she said.

Conrad didn't answer.

She said, "I know you're here. Even without my eyes open. Don't make me open my eyes and crash all this as if it were china dishes."

"Julie, I'm doing the very best I can," Conrad said. "The very best."

She smiled; her mouth grew narrow and long in a meticulous bow. "You're a poet, Ricky," she said. "Like Oscar Hammerstein was a poet. You have absolute laws and so you have fine sentiments. You have certain knowledge. You're stuffy and soporific. You're a believer. And honestly, Rick"—her face rolled his way, but her eyes remained locked—"that's a tedious way to live."

"Because I believe in keeping promises?" he said. The darkness was cooling off. Even the last electric bulb burning in the hall outside the sitting room seemed to be wavering. "In things like keeping your vows?"

"You're discussing marriage now, aren't you?" she said.

"That's right."

Her face rolled away from him. "Ricky," she said wearily, "you will surely dance among the angels."

Conrad didn't say anything.

She sat without movement for a while. Then she said, "You're crying, aren't you?"

Conrad couldn't say anything.

"You think I'm out of my mind, don't you?" she said.

He couldn't talk. His throat was swollen closed. Gummy saliva filled up his mouth. His nose was running. He couldn't make out her silhouette clearly.

"Ricky, I want you to know that no one but you ever laid me."

"There's nothing wrong with—" Then his voice split in the middle of the words, and the muscles in his legs pulled and he was standing. "I'm just a human being, Julie. I'm just an average man," he said. "I can only take so much."

"You're a chemical engineer," she said. "You're well paid and you're attractive."

"If I can't always cope with you it isn't because I'm not trying," he said. "But I'm used to reason and to logic. I've earned everything we own with logic."

"Machine," her voice said.

"I have to reason," he said. "I have to plan, to understand things." Then he brought his hands in front of his face and drove his fingertips into his forehead to dull the thumping.

"Assumptions," her voice said. "You're always making assumptions. Come to bed and screw me in the present tense and I wouldn't give you one drop of spit for all your assumptions and plans."

Like a cat he turned to her place on the couch. He didn't want to grab into her like an animal, but his arms were moving and his legs were moving. He was going to debase himself if he touched her like this, shame himself, humiliate himself. He fought his appetite, fought back whatever was primitive in him. He couldn't let himself revert to savagery; he couldn't let himself be destroyed.

His foot struck her glass, crashed it over in shatters. He tried to adjust his balance, lost his equilibrium. He was falling. He tried to recover, stepped sideways, slipped again. Then he let his body go and fell at her place on the couch with all the force of his frustration.

His chin smacked down on the wood of the couch's frame. She was gone. And then her presence was beside him, so close that he could feel the heat of her through the chill of the room. "No suffering you can do can make any of your stupid plans or assumptions holy," her voice said at his ear. "Come to bed with me, Ricky. Let that be enough in itself. Come to bed with me."

She took his hand and led him toward the light in the doorway.

He followed arkwardly: threading his way between the sliding planes of shadow that were draped over the furniture of the sitting room. There was a throbbing in his chin and a sympathetic swollen feeling over the back of his head like a skullcap. In the lobby of the inn the single electric fixture seemed to swing from the ceiling like a pendulum, as if his visual acuity had trebled so that he could discern the sixty-cycle-per-second beating of the element in its bulb. He followed her down the bare, complaining stairs with the veined, splintering weft of the dry wood coming through the rubber soles of his après-ski boots; along the corridor through the hips of the inn where the recessed spotlights poured yellow on the deck paint of the concrete floor; silently to their bedroom's door with the notion of her hips ricocheting between the walls of his thoughts with the *ping* of an overinflated basketball. The cobbled texture of your skin. My pebble-grained love.

Her sweater was over her head, suddenly a formless, weightless tangle of animal fibers in the passionless embrace of a chair. Her brassiere with its stressed cups and halter like the high ironwork of a bridge. The latticework of pain in his jaw. The cones of her bosom brought to conformity by the elastic stitching. $\frac{1}{3}\pi r^2 h$. Volume. Her stretch pants, now listless, shapeless. Her straining nylon stockings and the stays of her garter belt. The pounding over his head like an umbrella.

"Rick, you don't look well."

Her naked body.

"Ricky, why don't you take your clothes off? Did you hurt yourself?"

The trellis of pain in his jaw.

Her hands were scrabbling down his chest like the feet of

squirrels. The turtleneck up over his head; a dark journey, like dying. The pile of slacks about his ankles, hobbling him. Naked, naked. With the whole lifeless room of dead artifacts about them. So that they became alien, the only breathing, heat-giving things in the room. And they moved about, making no real contact with the room or any of its parts. When the lights were put off, they drifted.

Conrad shut his eyes and tried again. But the darkness had no structure, no form, was inexpressible, resisted language; it was the cold, meaningless darkness of entropy. Her fingernails went through his back like talons.

He lay awake long afterward and found that his judgment had been hasty; there was light in the room after all, off the snow outside, through the netting of curtains. There was enough light for him to see the shape of her body rippling under the blanket beside him.

There was a numbness throughout his maxilla that had replaced the pain; the hurt had left the parietal area of his skull. His eyes were open. He could make out lamps, a dresser, a desk, closet doors, doorknobs. He knew the world by doorknobs. He was relaxing. He eased his head against the pillow; the springs of the mattress reapportioned their thrust to the configuration of his body.

The light from outside threw the pleated pattern of the curtains on the ceiling like the bars of a graph. The crests of the pleating were umbra, its troughs were fair, contained even the beginnings of color. Upstairs in the light of the lamps and fire-place of the sitting room, Vermont had seemed a country of blackness, imperturbable, incomprehensible. Now, in his own blackness, Vermont gave Conrad light, radiated, became intelligible.

247

He lay there, observing. The pattern of light and shadow made the plane of the ceiling discrete. Fine dark lines, finely etched lines. His mind filled up with numbers, like the functions of numbers on the x and y axes of a graph. *The locus of an equation in* x *and* y *is the collection of all those points in the plane whose coordinates satisfy the equation, and no other points.* $S = k -$ Boltzmann log P. $PV = 1/3 Nmv^2$. $KE = 3/2 nRT$. Conrad was singing himself to sleep. $P = (Nmv^2)/V$. He was sinking away. Numbers danced along the graph. Pure, path-of-a-point lines without measurable thickness. $\Delta p \Delta x \approx h$. All his neurons were singing. $Bqv = m(v^2/r)$. $_1H^1 + _0n^1 \rightarrow _1H^2$. And the lines budded, grew other lines. Lines lacing lines. More lines against empty white. Spokes of lines, flights of lines, webs of lines coming in from the vertical and the horizontal. Lines weaving together and exhausting the emptiness, filling it. And the darkness that all the lines created lulled him. It was bulging. It was full of mind.

In the morning, Conrad dressed before she awoke. He showered, and came out of the shower with the scent of her still clinging to him. He tried to cover that with deodorant, with a splash of after-shave lotion on the chest of his sweater. He left their bedroom with the morning still baffled by the curtains.

Upstairs, the dining room of the inn looked west toward the ski slopes. The sun came back off the snow, superheating the room. There were families and groups of two and three surrounding most of the tables. Among other places, there was room for him at the table set deepest in the corner where the two walls of glass met. The ski patrol boy was seated there. Conrad moved instinctively toward that familiarity, and took the chair opposite him.

"Good morning." There was a pyrex coffee carafe over a

candle in the middle of the table. The cloth was checkered red and black, limp from a repetition of washings. Conrad looked at the boy. His nose was red and had peeled slick. The boy seemed confused.

Finally he said a grudging "Hello."

"You have to excuse Julie," Conrad said, falling into the litany of coffeepot and creamer, two level spoons of sugar. "She isn't herself," Conrad said.

The boy didn't answer him; he dug into his cereal bowl and seemed as though trying to give the impression of being exasperated.

"You don't work here the year around, do you?" Conrad said. The boy said, "No."

"You go to college, I suppose," Conrad said. "This is between semesters for you, isn't it?"

"That's right," the boy said.

Conrad changed his fingering on the handle of the coffee cup; he folded his legs under the table and leaned back in the bentwood chair. He listened to the boy chewing his corn flakes, watched the articulation of his clumsy, thick fingers and the uncertain path of his loaded spoon. The sunlight made the dining room very stuffy. Conrad shifted his weight in the chair.

"My wife hasn't been herself for some time now," Conrad said. The boy began to look at him, and then carried on with his eyes over Conrad's shoulder.

"Julie would want me to apologize for both of us," Conrad said. "So I hope you'll—" He broke off there.

The boy went on chewing his cereal. He sipped at a glass of milk. Some of the milk ran over his lower lip, into the cleft of his chin. He dabbed the dripping away with an effete, almost coy flick of the checkered napkin.

Conrad couldn't control himself. "Neither of us paid any attention to it at first," he said. "How could we know that we were—"

The boy stood up, balling his napkin. He pushed his chair aside and went around the table, out of Conrad's sight.

When Julie came upstairs, it was almost noon. Conrad had been trying to read a stale copy of *The New York Times,* but the ink on the newsprint refused to congeal into words. She had the leopard jacket on and was carrying his windbreaker. She wanted him to take her for a ride into the hills. He said he wouldn't mind; but that she should get some exercise. Otherwise, she'd go back to New York as pale as she had left it. She called him a fetishist.

Outside, there was a skin of frost on the windshield like heavy dust. Conrad started the car and left the choke nursing the cold engine while he attacked the frost with a plastic scraper. It came off hard at first, gradually easier as the car's defroster began to throw warm air at the base of the glass inside. She was already within the car, and as he scraped he exposed piece after piece of her to the light like a jigsaw puzzle, until she was full-face, staring at him, blinking.

He discovered her every morning of their lives that way. Either it was as the sleep gradually left his eyes or as he glimpsed her moving between bed and shower and closet and dresser and vanity. The function of her was etched in outline in his mind, and every day he observed her afresh, waiting for her catechism of movements to color all the familiar blank spaces. There was something missing in him until her morning smile fleshed out the skeleton of his recollection of her.

She was smiling. "It's marvelous country, Vermont."

"Yes?" He slammed the door of the car shut after him and locked it.

"I said it's marvelous country."

"Yes," he said, and glanced at her. "Yes, it is. Do you want to do your seat belt up, Julie?"

"Why should I? Just give me one good reason." Then she leaned over and touched him. "Ricky, please don't be a prig today, will you?"

"Well, it doesn't cost you anything," he said. Then he blew a breath into the palms of his gloves and applied it to his face. He didn't want any more unnecessary arguments. "You just can't lie around while we're up here, Julie," he said. "You know we planned this so that you could have some exercise. It will do you a world—"

She was laughing. "Ricky, stop." She shook her hair out. "Drive us up into the hills," she said. "A long way. And don't be so sensible for a while. I want to smell the white and green."

They drove a long way: all afternoon. Several times they passed through towns that were only a few stores and a post office clustering into the crevices where a north-south road crossed one coming from the east. There was always a padding of snow on the roofs of the frame buildings, and every weather-cock they saw was frozen pointing to south. In the end, they found a half-cleared road that broke away toward higher ground. The car climbed it with snorting and flinching, until the country leveled off and the road was entirely under snow. When their way ended against a triple-laced guardrail, they were just under the summit of a treeless, drifted hill.

"Let's go back," she said. "Try another way. I want to go higher."

"If you want to go higher, walk," he said, with some small laughter.

"You're talking exercise again, aren't you?" she said.

"Yes," he said. He twisted the ignition key and the engine died in burbling.

"Well, fine," she said. She opened the door of the car and the evening cold came in upon them. She swung her boots out and Conrad heard them on the parchment crust of the snow. "Aren't you coming?" she said. She pointed upward, toward where the whiteness ended in a blue that was dropping into purple.

There was shade in the valley that held the last brief town they had passed through. A few lights were coming on. The wind behind them was bitter, slapped at the sleeves of their jackets. There was snow on the wind.

Soon, in the last twilight, her hair was sparkling with the moisture and there were dots of white in her eyebrows and occasionally on her lashes. The night edged up about their feet, mingling with their shadows.

Once she looked up at him through the driving of flakes and said, "Everything is falling, Ricky. Ricky, everything is falling earthward." She stuffed her gloves into her pockets and cupped her hands before her to clutch the feel of the snow.